THE FORGOTTEN WORLDS
BOOK 3

THE NECROPOLIS

P.J. HOOVER

CHILDREN'S BRAINS ARE YUMMY BOOKS
AUSTIN, TEXAS

The Necropolis
The Forgotten Worlds
Book 3

Text Copyright © 2010 by P.J. Hoover

Jacket Art © iStockphoto.com

First Edition 2010
ISBN(10): 1-933767-15-4
ISBN (13): 978-1-933767-15-4

Children's Brains are Yummy Books
Austin, Texas
www.cbaybooks.com

Printed in the United States of America.

For information on CPSIA compliance, see
www.cbaybooks.com/cpsia.html

For Lola, who I want to be like when I grow up

TABLE OF CONTENTS

CHAPTER 1

EVERYTHING IN BENJAMIN'S HOUSE TELEPORTS AWAY

Flashing lights inside his brain was not the way Benjamin wanted to start his day—especially when his day was starting at three in the morning. If only he could travel back in time to midnight and sleep for three more hours. He'd hardly even fallen asleep. Most of the time his creepy eyeball implant came in handy. But now, with its alarm going off, he really just wanted to teleport it out of his head.

"Wake up, Benjamin."

"No." Benjamin squeezed his eyes shut and pretended his mom's voice was just a dream. And he turned off the alarm.

"Yes." His mom flipped on the light. "Now. We're behind schedule. Andy's family is gone already."

Okay, that got his attention. His best friend's family was gone? "Gone where?" His freshman year had just started a couple of months ago; Benjamin was supposed to be stuck in Virginia hiding his telekinetic powers for another seven months.

"We're moving." She pulled the covers off him and stuffed them in a bag. "The truck's out front."

Benjamin jumped out of bed and headed for the window. His mom wasn't kidding. Parked out front was a huge moving truck with the words "Lemurian Movers—We make your problems disappear" printed on the side. The back door was open, and two men were putting his mom's china cabinet inside.

"Moving to where?" he asked.

"To Lemuria. We're being called back." She grabbed his pillow and put it in the bag, too. No chance of going back to bed now. "Make sure to pack everything. I need to wake the twins and Becca."

By the time Benjamin finished packing and had carried all his boxes (and the twin's boxes, and Becca's boxes) into the moving truck, he was wiped. And the worst part was everything had just been teleported away from inside the truck. That was the part that stunk about living around humans: you had to act like one. Humans used moving trucks when they moved, and so, as telegens living among humans, they had to use moving trucks when they moved. Otherwise they could have just teleported all the boxes from inside the house. He sank to the grass, waiting for his parents to finish up.

"*Heidi?*" If there was one person who could hear his telepathic call from no matter where, it was Heidi Dylan. Nobody was better at telepathy than her. Except Jack, but he was a Nogical so it wasn't really fair to compare them.

"*Hey, Benjamin.*" As expected, she answered right away.

"*Are you moving, too?*"

"*Yeah,*" she replied telepathically. "*My parents just finished packing.*"

"*Any idea why everyone's going back to Lemuria?*" he asked.

"No," she replied. *"But I talked with Josh just a couple minutes ago and he seemed to think it might have something to do with all the teleporter problems in and out of Lemuria."*

Benjamin's heart skipped a beat when she mentioned Josh. He wasn't sure why, but he was sure he didn't want her to know. Had she been talking with Josh a lot since summer school had let out?

"Oh," he said. *"That's nice."* He knew it sounded stupid, but it was all he trusted himself to say. She could talk to whoever she wanted; he and Heidi were only friends. Why should he care if she and some stupid older kid who wore a black leather jacket in the middle of summer and forgot to shave were talking? It didn't bother him at all.

"I gotta go," she said. *"We're leaving. I guess I'll see you at school."*

"Will you?" Benjamin asked. *"Will we even be going to school?"*

Heidi paused. *"I don't know. Maybe. Probably."*

"Okay," Benjamin said. *"Get in touch once you're settled. If you're not too busy talking to Josh."* But as soon as he said it he regretted it. Actually before he said it he regretted it. Why had he gone and said that? It just sounded so… pathetic.

But the fates were with Benjamin; Heidi must not have noticed. *"Sure. See ya."* And the telepathic connection ended.

His mom teleported first, holding his baby sister Becca in one arm and trying to control both the twins with the other. The twins acted like they'd never known

 3

there was anything special about the velvet tiger picture in the hallway, but when the teleporter didn't activate at first, Derrick gave it away.

"You typed the fifteenth number wrong," Derrick said. "It's a six, not a nine."

For only being seven years-old, they had minds like steel traps—and self-control like fishing nets. Their latest fiasco had involved one bag of flour, their little sister Becca, and two very angry parents. His mom hadn't let them come near the kitchen for a month.

Benjamin's mom shook her head. "We're getting out of here just in time." And they vanished.

After they left it was just Benjamin and his dad. "The doors are locked and the lights are off," his dad said.

"What about the teleporter?" Benjamin asked. "What if the next people who move into our house find it?"

"That's why you'll go before me," his dad replied. "After you teleport, I'll enter the self destruct sequence on the teleporter."

"Self destruct?" Benjamin asked. "Is the house going to blow up or something?"

His dad laughed. "No, nothing quite that spectacular. It renders the teleporter useless, and then the picture implodes."

This would definitely be an improvement to the picture.

Benjamin entered the thirty-two number sequence himself; the twins weren't the only ones who'd committed it to memory. And they were right—the fifteenth number was a six, not a nine. He put his palm on the velvet tiger and flashed away into a pinprick of light. But instead of wherever he was supposed to end up, he wound up some-where altogether different: white walls made of stone; block windows with the sun shining through; and Nathan Nyx, the guy who'd tried to trap Benjamin back in the Trojan War last summer, perched on a bench.

"You two-faced, back-stabbing—" Benjamin began. He tried to lunge toward Nathan, hoping to get his hands around his slimy throat, but found that he couldn't move very well. Actually, he couldn't move at all. It was like in-visible ropes had been tied around his arms and legs.

"Calm down, Benjamin." Nathan stood up and walked toward him.

"What did you do this time?" Benjamin struggled against his bonds. "Where's my family?"

"Ah, and which family would that be?" Nathan asked. "Your sweet little family from Virginia, or your long lost brother, Cory, who seems to be missing without a trace?"

"You know exactly what I'm asking," Benjamin said, yet Nathan's mention of Cory gave Benjamin a glimmer of hope. Benjamin might not know where Cory was, but neither did Nathan.

Nathan laughed. "Don't worry. I didn't disrupt your family's teleportation. It's you I want to talk to."

"We have nothing to talk about," Benjamin said. "You double crossed my dad and lied to us both all summer."

"I never lied to you." Nathan walked around Benjamin, staying just out of his reach. "I told you I was working for our father, and I was."

"You misled—" And then it hit Benjamin. What had Nathan just said? Our father? Was he serious? All of a sud-den, Benjamin's stomach twisted into a knot. Nathan just

 5

couldn't be his other missing sibling—the third of the triplets.

"No, I'm not one of the chosen ones," Nathan held his voice flat. "I'm not one of the triplets. But we do share a father."

Benjamin opened his mouth to speak, but then shut it again. He had no idea what to say.

"I see you're surprised," Nathan said.

"Surprised you're lying—again."

"Ah, but it's not a lie, Benjamin. You see, our father does have a way of getting around," Nathan said. He ran a hand through his greasy hair, pushing it back. "We're half-brothers, though I wouldn't hang too much on that. I'll kill you long before you have the chance to kill me."

"What are you talking about?" Benjamin said. True, if there was anyone he'd love to kill right now, it was Nathan, but to be honest, Benjamin had never really contemplated killing anyone before. At least not seriously.

"As if you don't know," Nathan replied. "I'm sure your friend Iva Marinina told you all about it."

"Iva's told me lots of things," Benjamin said. Inwardly, he cursed. Iva hadn't told him squat. At least nothing about Nathan Nyx.

"Then you know the stupid oracles foresaw one of my half-siblings killing me," Nathan said. "Which is why I need to murder them all first."

"Right," Benjamin said slowly, trying to figure out the correct response to a death threat from a psychotic half-brother. "So how many have you killed so far?"

Nathan twisted his lips into something that resembled a grin. "After I disposed of that worthless oracle, I got two of them pretty fast. But then Caelus found out and put a stop to it." He chuckled. "At least he made me postpone it."

"Who's Caelus?" The name sounded familiar to Benjamin but he couldn't place it. Where was Gary Goodweather when you needed him? Gary was always Benjamin's answer to useless trivia questions.

"Our father, of course," Nathan said. "Don't you know anything?"

"Apparently not." This conversation was over. Benjamin had nothing to talk to Nathan about. He looked around the stone room, but it figured there wasn't a door. And when he tried teleporting, nothing happened. He'd have to levitate himself to the windows and get out.

"Are you going somewhere?" Nathan asked.

"Unless you have some reason for bringing me here," Benjamin said.

"Only to tell you that when Caelus is done with you, you're mine," Nathan said. "I want you to think about that."

The look on Nathan's face had already given Benjamin plenty to think about. Nathan was crazy. Not to mention he made Benjamin's skin crawl.

"I'll make your death slow—just to make sure you fully appreciate my power," Nathan continued. "Then you'll find out what it really means to be one of the chosen ones."

And then Nathan laughed, and Benjamin was teleported out of the stone room.

CHAPTER 2

IVA KEEPS SECRETS

Nathan hadn't lied about Benjamin's family. Time had seemed to freeze, and Benjamin still got to his new house in Lemuria before his dad. It was like nothing had happened. Things were, in fact, normal. The twins were arguing about who could burp louder; Becca was whining incessantly that she needed candy; and his mom was setting up the coffee maker. Using all the common sense he could muster, Benjamin decided it might not be a good time to mention his encounter with Nathan. He could talk about it once things settled down.

But things didn't settle down. The rulers of Lemuria sent out a nationwide announcement that, summer or not, all summer school students should get their butts to school pronto. At least that was how his mom has phrased it. Before he knew what was happening, his parents kissed him goodbye and shoved him onto another teleporter, promising to teleport his stuff right to his dorm room. Either they didn't want to argue with Helios and Selene Deimos or they wanted one less kid to worry about. Not that Benjamin was going to complain. School was fun.

Benjamin squeezed his eyes shut. Had he really just thought that?

He wound up directly under the giant dome in the middle of the school atrium. And just like summer, the place was jammed with students.

"Move. Move."

Benjamin didn't even have to turn to see who was talking. Did he get the same teleporter operator every year? And as if the old man's gargantuan ears weren't enough, he'd grown a second set of arms.

Benjamin opened his mouth to comment, but the old man put up one of the extra arms to silence him. "No talking, Benjamin Holt. We've got kids coming out our ears around here." He pointed to his giant ears as if to make the point more clear.

Which didn't seem to be necessary. There were twice as many kids as normal, in fact, like kids went here year round and the summer school students were coming late to the party. So Benjamin moved off the pad.

"Thanks," Benjamin said.

But apparently talking took too much time. "Yes, yes, have a nice year," the old man said. And he turned back to the teleporter platform.

Once he got his homeroom assignment, Benjamin found his best friend Andy off in one of the tertiary hallways kissing Iva. Great. Was anything ever going to be normal again? He cleared his throat—obviously.

"Benjamin!" Iva untangled herself from Andy to walk over to give him a hug. Her brown hair which was normally straight and long was completely rumpled. But she waved her hands over it and smoothed it down. And she immediately transformed back into the perfect and gorgeous Iva he knew. "We were just talking about you."

Benjamin looked from Iva to Andy and then back to Iva. "I can see that. It looks like it was a pretty interesting conversation."

Andy flushed as red as a fireball but still managed to look smug. "We were catching up."

Benjamin put up his hand. The last thing he wanted to hear about was how much Andy had missed Iva. "Whatever." And then he got to the point. "Iva, why didn't you tell me Nathan murdered an oracle at Delphi?"

Her mouth dropped open before she regained her composure. "I didn't have a chance."

"You didn't think it was something important enough to call me on the telecom?" Now that Benjamin thought about it, wasn't it really important information? Information the person the Emerald Tablet had picked to save the world—namely Benjamin—really ought to know?

"I didn't want to risk having it intercepted." She put her hands on her hips. "I contacted the ruling hall on a private channel, but I—"

"You talked with Helios and Selene, and you didn't think to tell me that either?" Benjamin asked.

"Benjamin," she said, "it's only been a few months since we saw each other. I would've told you over break when we all got together."

"Would you have told me what the oracle prophesied for Nathan?" Benjamin asked. "Would you have thought that was important enough?"

This time Iva didn't even try to hide her surprise. "How do you know—?"

Benjamin cut her off. "Nathan paid me a little visit. Actually I paid him a visit. I guess he thought it was important enough to tell me he planned on killing me."

"Killing you?" Andy asked. "I thought he was working

with your birth father to find you."

"It's his father, too," Benjamin said. "And he only plans to kill me after Caelus is done with me."

"Who's Caelus?" Andy asked. But then he paused. "What do you mean, his father, too?"

It was obvious from Iva's expression that she already knew. She knew everything.

"Iva." He shook his head. "Why didn't you tell me?"

"I couldn't tell you, Benjamin," she replied. "It's against the code of the oracles."

"But it involves one of your best friends being murdered," Benjamin said. "Couldn't some stupid code be broken to protect my life and the lives of my other countless half-brothers and sisters?"

Andy's head went back and forth, from one to the other. "What the heck is going on with you two?"

Benjamin balled his hands into fists to keep his temper from exploding. This was beyond acceptable. "Why don't you let Iva fill you in while you guys catch up? I'm sure she knows more than I do at this point." And just to make it look good, he teleported away rather than walking. It would ruin everything if he tripped on the way out.

Benjamin teleported a couple hallways away. Sitting down on a bench, he took a moment to gather his thoughts. In the space of only a couple hours, he'd moved from Virginia, found out Nathan Nyx was his crazy half-brother who planned to kill him, and learned that Iva had known everything all along. He couldn't believe she hadn't told him. Was she so caught up in Andy that she'd forgotten about Benjamin's burden? As if he wanted to save the world.

"So what's got you down this time?" Jack teleported

 11

onto the bench beside Benjamin. "Telekinesis woes? Love woes?"

Benjamin smiled at the little green Nogical. Man, had he missed Jack. If he hadn't thought he'd crush the six-inch high telegen, Benjamin would've hugged him. But he settled for a high five.

"No, nothing like that." Benjamin laughed, despite himself.

"Okay." Jack teleported to the other side of Benjamin. Benjamin turned as Jack continued. "Let me guess again. Are you lost? Can't find your homeroom? Don't like your room-mates?"

"Wrong again." Benjamin tried not to smile, but couldn't help it—until he remembered everything Nathan had said. "You already know, don't you?"

Jack sat down on the bench. "You're not shielding your mind very well."

"What are you talking about?" Benjamin said. "I have a great mind block in place."

"Sure you do, but you forget—I'm a Nogical," Jack said. "Your pathetic telejamming techniques are useless against my superior cerebral powers." He flicked some invisible dust off his shoulder.

Benjamin took a deep breath. "So what do you think?"

"I think that given the information you just found out," Jack replied, "now's not the time to be picking fights with your friends."

"I didn't pick a fight." Benjamin jumped to his feet. "Iva should have told me what she knew."

"No, she shouldn't have. Iva would never violate her oracle vows. I don't think she could even it she tried." Jack levitated up to perch on Benjamin's shoulder. "Think about it. You lashed out at her because you were upset about Nathan. You know it's true."

Benjamin opened his mouth to protest but paused. He really had nothing he could say to defend himself. Jack was right. Getting in a fight with Iva after five minutes in Lemuria wasn't the best strategy for saving the world.

"Great," Jack said. "So let's go find your homeroom."

But Benjamin didn't even have time to stand up. Something else materialized right in front of him.

"Telepathy."

Benjamin scooted back against the bench. "What?"

"You!" Jack said.

The new Nogical in front of Benjamin smiled. "Yes, me." She looked a lot like Jack, even down to the green skin and sarcastic attitude. But instead of aqua blue hair like Jack's, hers looked like a mass of flames. Their eyes were the same—both yellow, like a sunflower with a spot of black in the middle.

The six-inch tall Nogical girl flipped backwards from a sitting position and landed on Benjamin's thigh. "Betcha don't remember my name."

Benjamin racked his brain. He should remember the Nogical girl's name. She helped him last summer when he'd traveled back in time and needed to hide some golden disk for himself to find in the future. After all, he hadn't been able to touch it, and well, whatever it was, Nogicals could touch it and not be affected.

"Just ignore her," Jack said. "That's what I always do."

She smirked. "See, you don't remember."

Benjamin crossed his arms. "That was like three thousand years ago."

The Nogical laughed. "It was a few months ago. And it's Lulu."

Benjamin nodded like he knew all along. "Of course. Lulu. You guys are friends, right?"

Lulu coughed out a laugh. "Friends. More like he's my annoying little brother who never stops pestering me. 'Travel back in time and help my friend Benjamin,' he says. And then he doesn't even bother to tell me what kind of help you need. Anyway, the answer is telepathy."

"What's the question?" Benjamin said.

Lulu jabbed her little green finger into his chest. "Your shirt. Telepathy."

Benjamin looked down at his blue t-shirt. It was the same one he'd been asleep in only a couple hours ago. In white letters across the front it read, "TELEKINESIS or TELEPATHY?"

Benjamin laughed. "I don't know, telekinesis is pretty cool, too."

"Telekinesis is for wusses," Lulu said.

"You're just no good at it," Jack replied.

"No. I just like knowing how awesome people think I am," Lulu said.

"Annoying you mean," Jack said.

"Whatever. Helios needs you," she told Jack. "And when you talk to him, tell him not to order me around. I'm not a servant, you know." And then Lulu teleported away.

Jack turned back to Benjamin. "See what I have to put up with? Too bad genetic engineering doesn't eliminate big sisters from the gene pool."

And before Benjamin could ask what Helios wanted to see Jack about, Jack teleported away.

 14

CHAPTER 3

ANDY GETS IN A FIGHT

Something that smelled a lot like natural gas emanated from the dining hall. But once Benjamin sat at a table with Andy and Gary, he figured maybe the whole place exploding would have been better. The menu system was hosed and only seemed to be making cabbage soup and oatmeal. And not even oatmeal cookies or anything mediocre like that. Plain oatmeal so thick they could have used it to tack pictures on the wall.

Benjamin scanned the dining hall for the kid in their homeroom who'd managed to fix the menu system—until it broke again at the end of summer—but didn't see him. "Where's Magic Pan?" Benjamin asked.

"No one's seen him yet," Andy answered. "At least that's what my sources tell me."

"Pretty suspicious, huh?" Heidi asked as she and Iva came over to join them.

"What?" Benjamin said.

"Menus are broken. Magic Pan is nowhere to be found." Heidi ticked off the items on her hand. Her blond ringlets bounced around each time she extended a finger.

"So what are you trying to say?" Benjamin asked, yanking his eyes away from her ringlets and back to her face. Boyfriend or no boyfriend, it was really nice to see Heidi again.

"Are you dense?" Heidi said. "How much clearer do I have to be? Magic Pan is responsible for the menu malfunctions."

Benjamin looked at Gary.

Gary nodded. "Heidi's right. I did some checking over the last few months. I was studying how the food processing system functions."

"You were trying to figure out how to fix the menus yourself," Heidi cut in.

Gary spent about half a second looking embarrassed but then reverted into scientific mode. "Okay, fine. I was trying to fix them myself. Given my aptitude with...well, with so many things, it should have been a no-brainer. But what I found was the menu system isn't really broken at all. It's just locked out in a deeply nested, varying algorithm, cryptic loop."

"And no one in all of Lemuria can unlock it?" Andy asked.

"Well, I don't think they really called out the top cryptologists to fix the school menu system," Gary said. "But the fact of the matter is whoever's looked at it can't do anything."

"What about you?" Iva asked.

Gary feigned humility. "I have been working on cracking the code, though at my present rate it may take a few more months to get the random key algorithm just right." He pulled out his thought cache and activated it. "You can see here some of the calculations I've been working on."

Andy shuddered. "Maybe we can look at that some other time?"

"Sounds great." Gary put the thought cache away and

pushed his glasses up on his nose.

"What's up with the glasses?" Benjamin asked.

Gary took them off and looked at them. "Oh, these? I think they make me look smarter."

Andy spit out cabbage soup onto the table. "You think you need glasses to make you look smarter?"

Gary shrugged and put them back on. "You know. It helps when I'm around humans."

"Helps you what?" Heidi asked. "Stand out even more?"

"Iva?"

Benjamin turned and saw Iva smile and Andy frown at the exact same moment. Nick Konstantin, a classmate from last year, walked toward them with a smile the size of a giant squid—and just as slimy. Andy stepped closer to Iva and linked his arm through hers. She unlinked it, using the arm to brush back her long, dark hair. Andy's frown deepened.

"Nick!" Iva walked over and hugged the boy.

Andy flat out scowled.

"I 'ave missed you, my dearest Ivana." Nick kissed the back of her hand.

Iva giggled. "You couldn't have missed me that much, Nick. We just talked a week ago."

"You did?" Andy eyes had bugged open so wide, Benjamin thought they might actually fall out of their sockets.

Nick looked at Andy like he was a pesky fly. "Ah, yes. I spoke with dearest Ivana regarding poem I 'ad written for 'er. Would you like to 'ear it?"

"Um, no," Andy said.

"Then I shall call upon you later, Ivana, when we might

'ave some privacy." And Nick kissed her hand, again. "Until then." He turned and walked away.

Andy started after Nick. Benjamin wasn't sure what Andy was going to say or do, but whatever it was couldn't be good. He reached out with telekinesis and grabbed Andy, who struggled, but then stopped at the sound of a different voice.

"Iva?"

Benjamin turned to look. This time it was Ryan Jordan. Apparently Iva's entire entourage had decided to stop by and say hello. Benjamin figured that's what being drop dead gorgeous would get you: creepy guys declaring their undying love every time you turned around. What was odd was Ryan was alone. Normally he had Jonathan Sheehan in tow.

"Oh, hi, Ryan." Whereas Iva beamed at Nick's attention, Ryan seemed to make her skin crawl.

"Where's Jonathan?" Andy asked, and the telekinetic energy around Andy started increasing. Last summer Ryan's best friend Jonathan had spied on Iva's dreams. Andy had sworn to kick his butt the next time he saw him.

Ryan didn't bother looking at Andy when he answered. He kept his eyes on Iva. "He got kicked out of school."

Heidi scoffed. "Kicked out. Please. He got thrown into juvvie. Or at least the telegen equivalent. Turned out he'd been cheating for the last couple years."

Ryan kind of let out a laugh. "Yeah. Weird, huh? But he made sure I told you he said hi," he said to Iva. "And something about having sweet dreams."

Andy took a step toward him.

"What?" Ryan asked.

Benjamin looked at Ryan. Either Ryan was a really good liar or completely stupid. Benjamin chose to think it was the latter. Ryan probably had no clue Jonathan had been invading Iva's dreams the entire summer. But Andy did, and before Benjamin could tighten his telekinetic restraints, Andy took the final two steps forward and punched Ryan right in the nose. It must've been the adrenaline still pumping from the conversation with Nick, because Andy followed it up with a good three more punches. Ryan fell to the floor.

Benjamin had no idea what to do. Someone in the room did, though he wouldn't have been Benjamin's top choice.

"What is going on over here?" The Panther asked, his voice booming as he walked over.

Okay, their telekinesis teacher would have been last on the list of who Benjamin wanted to break up the fight. Their homeroom teacher Proteus Ajax would have been ideal. The Panther was not. Andy and Ryan levitated off the ground and separated. The Panther held them in the air and began his tirade.

"What in the name of Helios and Selene Deimos is going on here?" The Panther asked. He cracked his knuckles until Benjamin thought they might separate at the joint.

"He started it."

Benjamin looked up at Ryan as he spoke. Talk about pathetic. Ryan hung in mid-air and was covered in blood. Andy, on the other hand, looked like he wasn't done with the fight. His arms threw punches into the air as he struggled against the telekinetic bonds.

"Mr. Grow?" The Panther asked Andy.

Benjamin held his breath. How mad was Andy?

Hopefully not mad enough to tell The Panther that Ryan had to be working for Nathan Nyx last summer.

"He's been stalking us," Andy replied. "I'm just giving him what he deserves."

The Panther turned back to Ryan and eyed him up and down. Benjamin didn't blame The Panther for not believing Andy; Ryan didn't look like he could stalk an anemone.

Andy and Ryan both dropped eight feet to the floor, hovering for just a second before hitting with a solid thud. "If this happens again, you'll be joining your classmate Jonathan in the delinquent center. And I assure you they will not be as kind to you there as I am." And without another word, The Panther left the room.

CHAPTER 4

Benjamin has a Secret Admirer

Benjamin heard the mail tube in the dorm room whoosh. One of them had mail, which almost never happened. Messages came via telepathy or the telecom. And boxes of cookies were teleported.

He hopped down from the upper bunk and consulted his heads up display. Eight o'clock. Just great. Too early to get up and too late to fall back asleep. They were meeting their friend Aurora at the Deimos Diner at ten. And if one word summarized Aurora, it was prompt. Or bizarre. Or free-spirited, though technically that was two words.

Since he was the only one who'd woken up, Benjamin slid open the mail tube, pulled out a package, and pressed his thumb onto the identifier pad on top.

"Identity confirmed. Benjamin Holt," the parcel intoned.

The pad lit up green, and the top popped open. Benjamin upended the box onto the desk in front of him. He felt his heart speed up; someone had sent him a present. And then he noticed the wrapping paper. It was black with three green hearts etched in gold.

"What'd you get?"

Benjamin turned and immediately felt his face grow hot as Andy's eyes settled on the package.

 21

"What's that?" Gary asked from across the dorm room.

"It's nothing." Benjamin tried to cover the present with his arms.

"It's not nothing," Andy said. He walked over and tried to swipe it away. "It looks like you have a secret admirer."

"I do not," Benjamin replied.

"You do, too." Andy finally managed to grab hold of the present. "Let's open it."

"Let's not." Benjamin pulled out the only trick he could think of on demand. He teleported the box right out from under Andy's fingers.

"Bring it back," Andy said. "We have to see what it is."

"No, we don't," Benjamin said. "It's nothing. I'll open it later."

"You know," Gary said, "The probability of it being from a secret admirer is extremely low. Who would it be?"

"Thanks, Gary." Even if Benjamin had been thinking the same thing, no one wanted that kind of thought to be voiced.

"It can't be Julie Macfarlane," Andy said. "She and Ryan are definitely still dating."

"It's not Julie," Benjamin said.

"I know," Andy replied. "That's what I was just saying."

"Maybe Suneeta?" Gary suggested.

Benjamin rolled his eyes and headed toward the shower. This was ridiculous. "It's not from Suneeta," he called back.

"Hey," Andy said, smacking his forehead. "Maybe it's from the girl who's always making googly eyes at you in Telepathy."

"You mean Sherry the Scary?" Gary asked.

Benjamin ignored the comment. No one would want Sherry the Scary as a secret admirer. She was two feet taller than Benjamin and probably could have pounded him into the ground with her pinkie. He cranked the music up on his heads up display and tuned out the rest of the conversation. He figured maybe if he just pretended it hadn't happened, the whole thing would be forgotten.

But Benjamin should have known Andy better than that. They hadn't been at the Deimos Diner longer than thirty seconds before Andy brought it up.

Andy slid into the booth next to Iva. "You guys will never believe who has a secret admirer."

Benjamin tried not to look as Andy leaned over to kiss her. It was getting downright embarrassing to be around the two of them.

"Gary?" Aurora posed. Her hair was egg yolk yellow and done in dreadlocks, and her eyes matched but had glitter sprinkled on them also. Of course, she could get away with that; she lived in Lemuria year round with her dad. She never had to blend in with humans.

Gary's mouth hardly had time to form an expression of disbelief before Aurora said, "I'm just kidding, Gary."

"What?" Benjamin said. "It could be Gary."

"It's not Gary," Aurora said.

"Gee, who does that leave?" Iva put her finger to her mouth as if thinking. "Hmmm, let's see. Benjamin?"

Benjamin's face grew hot. "I don't have a secret admirer. I just got a package this morning, and Andy's making a big deal of it. It's nothing."

"If it's nothing, then why did you teleport it away and hide it?" Andy asked.

 23

"Maybe it's from your mom?" Heidi said. She glanced at Aurora's yellow dreads and changed her own hair the same color but super straight. And then she added some black stripes for good measure.

Benjamin tried to force any thoughts of bumblebees out of his mind. But the more he thought about it, the harder it was not to think about it. Heidi glared at him.

"We can rule out Benjamin's mom," Gary said. "There were hearts all over it."

Benjamin sighed. Why had he ever let Andy and Gary see the package? Why hadn't he teleported it out of the room the second he'd realized it was for him? Benjamin made a mental note to do just that the next time he received any kind of package from a secret admirer. Not that it was from a secret admirer.

"I just got some mail," Benjamin said. "I haven't even opened it yet."

"So open it now," Iva replied.

Benjamin had nothing to hide. There was no secret admirer. So he teleported the package from the hiding spot in his mind to the table in front of him and prayed it was nothing embarrassing.

Andy reached over to take the package, but Iva put her hand on his. "Let Benjamin open it."

Benjamin studied the lumpy package. The three heart pattern was the same symbol on the record from Wondersky City last year. The record Ryan Jordan had made a copy of that had eventually led to Benjamin finding his brother Cory back in the Trojan War. Ryan had probably put someone up to doing this.

"It looks like a tetrahedron," Gary said.

"That's exactly what I was just thinking." Aurora nodded. "And it definitely came from someone here in Lemuria; only telegens can make paper etchings like those hearts."

"I'll open it on one condition," Benjamin said. "No more comments on secret admirers."

Andy opened his mouth to speak, but Benjamin noticed Iva elbow him sharply in the side.

Benjamin worked around the hearts, not ripping them. They just seemed too...pretty...to tear. How stupid did that sound? He tore the rest of the paper off and teleported it to the nearest recycler. Staring at the object in front of him, Benjamin still had no idea what it was.

"A puzzle box." Aurora reached over to pick it up. "But I've never seen any this complicated."

"What's a puzzle box?" Heidi asked. "It just looks like a big wooden blob."

Aurora turned it around and around in her hands. "Look at all the tiny pieces here," she said pointing. "They each have to be moved in a specific sequence to open the box."

"That doesn't sound too hard." Gary reached over to take the puzzle box from Aurora. "There's always a logical solution to any puzzle."

"Gary," Aurora said, "this puzzle box has over one thousand pieces. Do you know how many different combinations there are?"

"Like infinity," Heidi answered before Gary could open his mouth to reply. Apparently, like Benjamin, Heidi didn't want to hear how many different combinations there were for opening the puzzle box either.

"I said by working it out in a logical way," Gary replied. And then he ignored them and started on the puzzle box.

Benjamin realized that now with the puzzle box in front of them, everyone seemed to have forgotten about the whole secret admirer thing. Finally. If the price he had to pay for that was watching Gary solve the puzzle, then it was well worth it. At least that's what he thought for the first hour.

"I thought you said this would be easy," Benjamin said an hour later. If Gary couldn't solve the puzzle, then why didn't he just admit it?

Of course, if Gary couldn't solve the puzzle, they were destined for failure.

Gary sighed and placed the puzzle down on the table. Every single piece which had been slid open locked back into place. Gary rolled his eyes and sighed again. "The basics of the puzzle are fairly simple."

"So what's the problem then?" Iva asked.

Gary mumbled. "Telekinesis."

"What?" Andy asked.

"Telekinesis," Gary said, just a decibel higher this time.

"Did you say telekinesis?" Andy asked.

Gary nodded.

"What does telekinesis have to do with solving the puzzle box?" Heidi asked. And then she must have read his mind. "Oh, I get it. Each piece needs to be held in place with telekinesis while the other ones are moved."

"Right," Gary said. "And I only seem to be able to hold about fifty of the pieces at a time."

"So why didn't you ask for help an hour ago?" Andy asked. "It's not like we want to sit around here all day."

Gary reddened but didn't reply.

"It doesn't matter now," Aurora said. "Between the six of us, we can manage." She slid the puzzle box back over to Gary. "Just tell us when and where to hold."

Even with six telegens holding the pieces in place, it still took them close to two more hours until the thing finally opened.

"Whatcha got there?" Jack teleported onto the table next to the box.

Benjamin stared inside, hardly believing what he saw. "It looks like a whole lot of nothing."

"It's empty," Iva said.

"You guys act like you're surprised," Jack said. "Is there supposed to be something in there?"

"I would've thought so," Benjamin said.

"Maybe your secret admirer just gave you the box as a present," Andy suggested.

"You have a secret admirer?" Jack asked.

And so the conversation had come full circle. Benjamin had avoided it for a couple hours, but now it was back. Between Andy's sarcastic remarks, Benjamin managed to relay the entire story to Jack.

"It really took all of you to open it?" Jack asked.

Gary nodded.

"Why didn't you guys call me?" Jack said. "I could have opened it by myself in a third of the time."

Gary rolled his eyes. "Yeah, right. Easy for you to say now."

"It's true," Jack said.

"What makes you think so?" Benjamin asked.

 27

"Because this type of puzzle box is made in Nogical City," Jack replied. "I've been doing these since I was in diapers."

The image of Jack as a Nogical baby wearing a diaper and drinking from a bottle came to Benjamin's mind. Maybe Lulu could find him a real baby picture.

Gary opened his mouth to speak, but Jack cut him off.

"Which reminds me," Jack said. "Did you guys check the hidden compartment yet?"

And that's where they found the message—a piece of paper rolled into a scroll and sealed with three wax hearts.

"No way," Aurora said. "It's a love note."

Benjamin's face burned, but he took the message. "It's not a love note." Even as he said it, he felt dread in the pit of his stomach. He had to open it now; there wasn't another choice. What if it was some sort of stupid love letter? What if Sherry the Scary really did have a crush on him? He'd never be able to go to Telepathy again.

"I'll open this later," Benjamin said. "It's getting kind of late."

"Now, Benjamin," Iva replied.

He tried again. "But it seems like such a shame to break the wax."

"Now, Benjamin," Iva said again.

Benjamin sighed and resigned himself. He cracked the green wax and slowly unrolled the parchment.

Ghosts tell the tale of times gone by
When guardians watched til the final cry.
Their city fell as the end grew nigh.
And tunnels hid them as they all did die.

 28

"What's that supposed to mean?" Andy asked. "Tunnels? Ghosts? What kind of secret admirer do you have anyway?"

"Yeah, that's just freaky," Heidi said.

Benjamin stood up. This was getting ridiculous. "How many times do I have to tell you guys I don't have a secret admirer? Just stop it already."

"Well who else sent you a heart package with a poem inside?" Andy stood up and got in Benjamin's face. "Nick Konstantin? We've just wasted the entire day trying to open this stupid box for nothing. I don't know about the rest of you, but I've had enough." Andy moved out of the booth and headed for the door.

"Where are you going?" Iva asked.

Andy stopped and turned. "Anywhere but here. Benjamin can figure out his love poem on his own." He continued on to the door and walked outside.

Iva stood up and started following. "Don't worry. I'll talk to Andy. We have plans tonight anyway." And she headed out the door.

Heidi consulted her heads up display and jumped out of the booth. "Oh! I can't believe I let the time get away from me like this. We can talk about this more tomorrow." And she ran for the door.

"Why?" Benjamin asked. "Where are you going?"

Heidi threw up one of her famous mind blocks. "Um, nowhere."

"Nowhere?" he asked. Where was Heidi going? Somewhere with Andy and Iva? But why would Heidi be going out on a Saturday night with Andy and Iva? Wouldn't she feel like a third wheel?

And then it hit Benjamin. Unless she wasn't a third

 29

wheel. He looked over at Gary who sat speechless at the table next to Aurora. And Jack was looking the other way, out the window, whistling.

"Hey, Gary, are you ready to head to the genetic engineering library yet?" Aurora asked.

"You guys are going to the library?" Benjamin said. He couldn't believe this. Did everybody have plans except him?

"You're welcome to come along with us," Gary replied. "We should only be there for a few hours."

Benjamin laughed, even though nothing was the least bit funny. "No, thanks. I have other plans." Okay, that was a big fat lie, but they didn't have to know that; he threw up his own mind block.

"Great," Gary said. "So we can talk about all this some more tomorrow." He motioned to the opened puzzle box and the scroll on the table.

"Right," Benjamin said. "Tomorrow." And then he watched as Gary and Aurora also walked out of the Deimos Diner.

Benjamin turned to Jack. "Has everyone gone crazy except for me?"

"Well, that's one way to look at it," Jack said. He reached out and touched the puzzle box. One at a time, each piece of wood began to slide back into place. Jack reached over and picked up the piece of wrapping paper Benjamin had saved—the piece with the three green hearts engraved on it—and studied it.

"So any ideas what everyone's doing tonight?" Benjamin asked Jack, almost hoping the little Nogical wouldn't answer.

"Duh," Jack said.

"Double date?" Benjamin asked.

 30

"Uh huh," Jack replied.

"Josh?" Benjamin asked.

"Uh huh," Jack said again.

"Oh," Benjamin said.

"You're not surprised," Jack said.

Benjamin sighed. "No, I'm not."

Jack perched on Benjamin's shoulder. "So, do you want to talk about it?"

"Talk about what?" Benjamin said. "I couldn't care less if Heidi wants to go out with that moron."

"I can tell," Jack replied.

"It's true," Benjamin said. "It doesn't bother me at all. Except she's wasting her time when we have important work to do."

"Now I see why Heidi didn't say anything," Jack said. "She knew she'd get just that kind of reaction."

"What reaction?" Benjamin asked. "Heidi can date whoever she wants—even some jerk who wears his coat in the middle of summer."

"It's winter here now," Jack said.

"That's irrelevant," Benjamin replied. "He wears it all summer, too. Face it, the guy's a total loser."

"Heidi doesn't seem to think so," Jack said.

"Anyway," Benjamin replied, "do we have to talk about Heidi and her stupid boyfriend all night?"

"You're the one who brought it up," Jack said. "So what do you want to do instead?"

Benjamin shrugged. "I don't know."

"Good," Jack replied. "Let's go visit Helios."

Benjamin never would have suggested the trip to see Helios. Even though the ruler of Lemuria had saved his life, he just felt like he was imposing. But Jack claimed Helios was expecting them, and seeing as how Benjamin didn't have any better offers, they teleported into the basement of the Ruling Hall. The upside to this was that no one would be able to track them. The downside was it that it was pitch black and stunk like rotten milk when they got there.

"We just go through that door over there," Jack said pointing, "and we'll be near where they used to keep The Emerald Tablet."

"Used to keep?" Benjamin said. "So it's not there anymore?"

"Nope."

"And Hexer?" Benjamin asked.

"Gone with it," Jack replied.

"To where?" Benjamin asked.

Jack shook his head. "Top secret."

"You don't know," Benjamin said, laughing.

"True," Jack replied. "But that's just a technicality."

When Benjamin saw Helios waiting on the other side of the door, it felt like forever and only yesterday since he'd seen the ruler. Time had a way of flying when the world needed saving.

"Jack. Benjamin." Helios smiled and inclined his head at each of them.

Jack attempted to mimic Helios, tilting his tiny head in the same way. "Helios. Traveled back in time lately?"

Helios laughed. "Only a few times. But I can't tell anyone about it." He palmed a pad on the wall, closing the door to the room behind them. "We better go upstairs. Selene will kill me if she misses any of the conversation."

 32

Benjamin couldn't imagine Helios' twin sister killing anyone, especially her co-ruler.

Jack opened his mouth to speak, but Helios put up his hand.

"Yes, she got your Amoeba Juice," Helios said, "pomegranate as requested."

"I thought Selene was away," Benjamin said before he could stop himself.

Helios gave him the eye—the eye that said 'that's really not your business.' So Benjamin opted not to drill him. Jack had other ideas.

Jack teleported around and landed on Helios' shoulder. "You and your secrets. How long is Selene back for?"

Helios smiled. "Just a few days."

Benjamin hardly waited until they got upstairs before he opened his mouth. "I heard you talked to Iva Marinina recently," he said to Helios.

Helios raised an eyebrow. "Actually, I wasn't available."

"I spoke with Iva." Selene sat back with a glass of Amoeba Juice—which Benjamin had politely declined; the purple chunks looked like they could choke a boa constrictor.

Benjamin's heart stopped, just for a second. Why hadn't Iva told him she talked to Selene instead? But, of course, Iva hadn't told him anything.

"So she told you about Nathan?" Benjamin said.

Selene pursed her lips together. "Yes. I'm afraid we acted too late on Nathan. After your return from Delphi last summer, he went back and murdered the oracle who'd foreseen his future. In fact, Iva was very nearly killed herself in the attack."

Benjamin's jaw dropped open. "What?"

Selene nodded.

"She didn't tell me that," Benjamin said.

"Did you give her a chance?" Jack finished the last of his drink and let out a burp the size of a titan. "It seems to me that at the time, you were only concerned with yourself."

"That's not true," Benjamin said, but couldn't help thinking that Jack might be just a little bit right.

"Regardless," Helios said, "Iva is alive. But thanks or no thanks to Nathan, two of his half-siblings are already dead."

"Children of Caelus," Benjamin said.

Helios smiled. "Very resourceful, Benjamin. I see you've found out who your father really is."

Benjamin nodded. "But why didn't you—"

Helios held a hand up in the air in a stopping motion. "Don't ask. You'll just get the same answer."

"The mind block?" Benjamin asked.

Helios nodded. "But what I'm interested in is how you found out about Nathan and Caelus at all."

That's right. Helios and Selene would have no idea Nathan had intercepted Benjamin during teleportation. And apparently, they weren't spying on his thoughts. Quickly, but trying not to leave any of the details out, he relayed the story.

Selene waited for Benjamin to finish even though he could tell she'd had something on her mind.

"You say he diverted you while using a teleportation machine," she said.

Benjamin nodded. "Why? Is that hard to do?"

"Not normally," Selene replied. "But there are some serious teleporter anomalies."

 34

"Like them not working at all," Helios said. "Or people getting trapped inside them. Or erratic destinations. It's why we called all the agents home."

"I heard rumors of telegens getting duplicated," Jack said. "The old Hexer Syndrome."

"That only happened a couple times," Helios replied. "We're working to control the issues."

"And with issues like that, Nathan shouldn't have such perfect control over a teleportation." Selene said it slowly like she was trying to puzzle it out as she spoke.

"Like he has a way around the problems," Benjamin said.

Selene clasped her fingers in front of her chin and nodded.

"Who exactly is Caelus?" Benjamin asked.

"Aside from your biological father?" Helios replied.

"Yeah," Benjamin said. "Besides that minor detail."

Helios levitated the pitcher of Amoeba Juice over and refilled his cup and then leaned over to refill Benjamin's. Somehow it had been drained, and since Benjamin hadn't touched the stuff, it could only have been Jack.

"Where to begin?" Helios began. "Caelus was one of the first false gods. He went by the name of Uranus; he married Gaea. And together they ruled Atlantis."

"Gaea!" Benjamin said. "Please tell me she's not my mother." Gaea was only the most evil telegen woman to ever grace the face of the earth. It was bad enough his biological father was working for the dark side. Two evil parents would be overkill.

The only time he'd come across Gaea was in Xanadu getting the second key of Shambhala. And even though

 35

Ananya, the ruler of Xanadu, had dispelled his thoughts, he swore Gaea was behind his test to get the key.

Helios shook his head. "No, your biological mother is dead. Caelus fathered more children than I believe records would even show. Your mother was just one of the many, many women he deceived, impregnated, and left."

"But why?" Benjamin's stomach twisted into a knot. What kind of man did that?

"Because of a prophecy he heard upon his own visit to Delphi," Helios said. "A prophecy that one day, triplets of his would bring forth the power to rule the world."

"And Gaea didn't care?" Benjamin asked. "I mean care that he was with other women."

Helios laughed. "She cared. Quite a bit in fact. But he always came back to her, and she believed in the oracle's vision. And so she allowed him to indulge his dalliances. But as soon as the oracles in Fortune City foretold your birth, Gaea enlisted Kronos' help to put a stop to Caelus' flings forever."

"Like the Kronos we've met?" Benjamin asked.

"The one and only," Helios replied. "You see, he, too, is one of your half brothers."

"And thus on Nathan's hit list," Benjamin added.

"Nathan has a long list in front of him," Selene said. "But with Caelus putting a temporary stop to the killing, it buys us some time."

"Right," Jack said. "Now we just need you to kill Nathan instead."

Benjamin smiled in reply. "Yeah, I'll work on that. So any ideas where my other brother is?"

"No," Helios said. "But even if I did..." He tapped his

forehead.

"Yeah, I know," Benjamin said. "The mind block. How about Cory? Where is he?"

Helios opened his mouth to reply. Benjamin was sure he'd get the same old answer. "I can't tell you... blah blah blah." But Selene spoke up before Helios had a chance. "Safe. Your brother is safe."

"Safe where?" Benjamin persisted.

Helios held up his hand. "We can't risk his mission by talking about it, Selene. You know that."

Selene nodded. "Yes, I know that. But I think Benjamin has a right to know his twin, though on a mission of the utmost importance, is nonetheless safe."

Benjamin decided to give it one last try. "Can you at least tell me what continent he's on?"

Helios shook his head. "We can't risk talking about it, Benjamin. I'm sure you understand."

Benjamin sighed. He didn't understand. "It's not like I'm going to tell anyone."

Helios silenced Selene before she could respond. "With telepathy as a standard weapon, even promises and secrets cannot be trusted," he said.

By the time all Benjamin's questions had been answered—okay, by the time all his questions had been asked and some of them answered—ten o'clock had rolled around. Benjamin and Jack said goodbye to the Deimos twins and headed back to the school.

Andy still wasn't home. And Gary snored from the other side of the room, so Benjamin decided to go right to bed. He'd have to get serious about finding his other brother tomorrow.

 37

CHAPTER 5

PROTOPLASM IMPRINTS

Andy slept in and didn't look like he was going to wake up anytime soon, so Benjamin and Gary headed out to the city. Benjamin didn't feel like bringing up Heidi or the double date, and Gary was smart enough not to mention it.

Benjamin told Gary he didn't care what they did, but he regretted it the second it was out of his mouth; he was sure they'd end up at the library or something. But by some stroke of luck, Gary suggested a visit to The Silver Touch.

The store owner Morpheus Midas greeted them when the entry bell chimed—which it didn't always do. "Called back to Lemuria for good, I hear."

Benjamin laughed. "I'm not sure about for good, but at least for a while." And then he realized Morpheus probably knew more about it then he did. "So what gives?"

Morpheus looked over his shoulder toward the back of the store before turning back around and answering. "It has to do with the teleporter problems," Morpheus whispered.

"Yeah, so I've heard." And then Benjamin remembered something which had been nagging at his mind since the summer. Something from Benjamin's visit to Lemuria a thousand years in the past. "So what's Walker Pan been up to these days?"

Morpheus reached down and picked up a black knight from the Ammolite chess board. "You know, to tell you the truth, since Gary here beat him and made him lose the chess set, I haven't seen or heard from him."

Benjamin threw up a mind block around the three of them. *"What exactly does a teleportation scrambler do?"*

Morpheus actually dropped the knight, but Benjamin had been expecting this and caught it mid-air with telekinesis.

"How do you know about those?" Morpheus asked. *"They're illegal, not to mention not even manufactured anymore."* He looked back toward his basement again.

"I'm not trying to buy one," Benjamin said. *"And don't worry. I don't care if you have any in the basement."*

"I only have one," Morpheus said quickly. *"And it's tiny—hardly able to stop the teleportation of a marble."*

"So how about a large scale one?" Gary asked, obviously catching on to Benjamin's line of thinking. *"What could it do, and how would someone go about getting one?"*

Morpheus set both of his hands on the chess board, steadying himself. *"A large scale teleportation scrambler would cause world-wide teleportation problems."*

"Exactly like Lemuria is seeing now," Benjamin finished.

"Yes," Morpheus said. *"Exactly like all of the Earth is seeing now."*

Gary shoved his glasses further up on his nose. *"Where does someone get one?"*

Morpheus shook his head. *"Teleportation scramblers of that magnitude haven't been manufactured in Lemuria for a thousand years. Getting one today would be nearly impossible."*

 39

But not getting one in the past just like Benjamin had seen Walker Pan do one thousand years ago. He knew Walker Pan wasn't on the level. It didn't even take an illegal teleportation scrambler to solidify the thought in Benjamin's brain. He'd known it since they first learned he cheated at the Bangkok Chess Open.

"*Bingo,*" Benjamin said silently to only Gary. "*Walker must be behind the teleportation failures.*"

"*I could have told you that last summer,*" Gary said. "*The guy's a snake.*"

But it still made no sense. Why would Walker Pan mess with teleportation systems worldwide? But, come to think of it, why would his son, Magic Pan, mess with the school menu system?

They left the Silver Touch after Gary ogled the chess board just a little bit longer. Benjamin basically had to pull Gary away, and then only after Morpheus had promised Gary a weekly game. Benjamin felt pretty sure Morpheus wanted someone to play with as much as Gary wanted to play, so all in all, it was a win-win situation.

It was only after they'd made it halfway down Mu Way that Heidi finally contacted them.

"*Hey,*" she said.

Benjamin jumped when he heard her voice in his head.

"*Hey what?*" He hoped he sounded cool.

"*Where are you guys?*" she asked. "*I thought we were all gonna do something today.*"

"*We are,*" Benjamin replied. "*It's just that our today already started a couple hours ago.*"

Telepathically she giggled. "*Yeah, I guess Iva and I overslept a little bit.*" And then she must have caught herself.

 40

"Anyway, Andy just got here, so we'll come meet you guys."

"Yeah, whatever," Benjamin said. *"We're meeting Aurora at the Crags."*

It's not like Benjamin was jealous of Josh. And he certainly only thought of Heidi as a friend. But she just acted so stupid whenever Josh was around. And then there was seeing Andy and Iva together constantly. Talk about feeling like a total outcast. And all Gary wanted to do was spend time in some boring science lab. Benjamin decided he'd just have to make a point of excluding them all some in the future.

"That sounds so pathetic," Jack said, teleporting to the top of the Crag where Benjamin sat.

Benjamin jumped up at the intrusion and attempted to step on the Nogical. Jack teleported out of the way.

"Watch where you're stepping," Jack said.

"Keep your mind reading to yourself," Benjamin said. "You're worse than Heidi."

"Work on your telejamming some more," Jack replied. "Then you'd be able to keep me out of your mind. Until then, deal with it." Without waiting for a reply, Jack teleported away, leaving Benjamin alone to watch the waves crash over and over on the shore below.

Benjamin rolled his eyes but sat back down, glancing at Gary and Aurora on the next Crag. Jack was right. It did sound pathetic. Exclude his friends intentionally. What was happening to his brain?

The wind blew through the Crags, making Benjamin appreciate the fact that he could control his body's sensitivity to the winter. Nonetheless, he pulled his sleeves down.

"Maybe you should have brought a coat," Andy said.

Benjamin turned at the new interruption. Andy, Heidi, and Iva had just crested the top of the large eagle's head.

"My coat teleported away in the moving truck. I have no clue where it went." And his mom still hadn't gotten around to sending him half his stuff. She'd claimed she was too busy with the twins and Becca—which actually made a lot of sense given the trouble the twins could get into.

"Hey," Heidi said, walking over toward Benjamin. "Are you hungry?"

Had she heard his stomach growling or just read his mind? "Starving." Benjamin had skipped the cabbage soup and oatmeal this morning.

Heidi smiled at him. "We stopped by the Deimos Diner for donuts." She handed one over to him. "It's your favorite kind."

Man, Heidi really had a nice smile. Not that Benjamin noticed. But there was just something about it that made his insides feel kind of squishy and warm.

He reached out to take the donut, but was so busy thinking about her smile, he dropped it. Heidi moved to catch it, but lost her balance.

"Heidi!" Iva cried.

And then Benjamin wasn't quite sure what happened next. All he knew was that he ended up standing down by the tail of the Crag with Heidi in his arms. She was grabbing hold of him for dear life.

"Are you okay?" he asked, setting her down.

"Yeah," she said. "I think so. Good thing you caught me."

But she was shaking like she was totally not okay. And come to think of it, so was he.

"Stay there," Andy called over the side. "We'll be right down."

By the time Andy and Iva teleported down, Gary and Aurora had joined them, too. And Benjamin had almost gotten his shaking under control.

"Whoa," Aurora said. "That was amazing, Benjamin."

"What?" Benjamin asked.

"What?" Gary said. "Are you kidding, dude? That was about the coolest thing I've ever seen."

"I just caught Heidi," Benjamin replied. Why were they looking at him like he was some superhero? Not that anything was wrong with that.

"Just caught Heidi?" Aurora said. "One second she fell to her death, and another second later, and voilà, you teleported down here and caught her."

"Yeah," Andy said. "I have to admit it. Those were some quick reflexes." And for once Benjamin didn't detect any jealousy from Andy when he said it.

"I teleported?" Benjamin asked. He looked at Heidi who gave him a weak smile in return.

"And it's a good thing too," Heidi said. "Since I can't levitate worth a darn."

He smiled and noticed her hair had turned gray. "You look seriously old."

She pulled a piece around and looked at it. "Yikes!" And it shifted to blond. And Benjamin went back to thinking about her smile.

"Hey, did you guys see this?" Iva brushed off the side of the Crag's tail. "It's some kind of plaque."

"It's a monument to the dead," Aurora said as if that were the most normal thing in the world. Of course she

 43

did grow up in Lemuria. Maybe it was an everyday occurrence.

"The dead?" Andy asked.

"Yeah," Aurora replied. "Remember I told you about it? The battle where every telegen who lived in this city was slaughtered? It was like a gazillion years ago or something."

Okay, Benjamin hoped that didn't happen all the time.

"How?" Heidi leaned over to look at the plaque. "I can't read this."

"It's in Ancient Lemurian," Gary replied, walking over.

"Which you know," Andy added under his breath.

"The plaque talks about the massacre," Gary read. "Hundreds of thousands dead."

Iva shuddered. "I can feel their spirits. It's like they're still crying out for help."

"How did they die?" Benjamin asked.

"Well, first they were forced into the tunnels, and then the entrances were sealed off," Aurora said. "Then, fires were teleported inside, which of course burned the telegens alive."

"Why didn't they just teleport out?" Andy asked.

"Telejammers kept them from doing anything," Aurora said. "The Crag Massacre is known as the bloodiest in Lemurian history. And Lemuria has a pretty long history."

Iva walked away from the Crag, heading toward the cliff walls. She held her arms around herself and continued shivering.

Benjamin started over to her, but then he thought about it. Tunnels. Guardians.

"That's it!" he said.

"What's it?" Andy asked.

"The answer to the riddle," Benjamin replied. "Remember the words:

> *Ghosts tell the tale of times gone by*
> *When guardians watched til the final cry.*
> *Their city fell as the end grew nigh.*
> *And tunnels hid them as they all did die.*"

By this time, Iva had turned back around, and everyone stared at him.

"It's the Crags," Benjamin said. "The answer to the riddle is the Crags."

"Of course," Iva said. "The ghosts are the telegens who died in the massacre."

Andy looked at her and laughed. She cast him her signature ice-cooling glare.

"But ghosts aren't real." Andy held up his hands in defense.

"Of course they are," Gary replied. "It's just a buildup of concentrated protoplasmic energy."

Andy looked at Gary like he'd just told them the sun had teleported out of the sky. The glasses might make Gary look smarter, but they didn't make him any easier to understand.

"Listen," Gary sighed. "If a telegen, or a human for that matter, dies suddenly, all the protoplasm doesn't have enough time to disperse which leaves behind a solid protoplasmic imprint of the person who used to be there. Like a ghostly fingerprint."

Okay, Benjamin had to admit it. At least Gary was

trying to explain this ghost thing in simple terms. Even though it still didn't make a lick of sense.

"I'm willing to bet almost every single one of those telegens left an imprint inside those tunnels." Gary nodded his head toward the tunnel entrances, high up in the cliff walls.

They stared at him, and Benjamin had no idea how to respond, or even if it was time to respond.

Gary threw up his arms. "There are ghosts in those tunnels! How much clearer can I be?"

Andy was just about to open his mouth to reply when Heidi cut him off.

"So what are we waiting for?" she said. "I'll go first."

CHAPTER 6

BENJAMIN VISITS GHOSTS

They levitated to one of the elevated platforms outside of the tunnels. With the cold air whipping around, Benjamin figured anything would be better than standing outside. But still, images of ghosts didn't bring out the most warming of thoughts. Benjamin gave one last glance to the stone guardians on the beach, took a deep breath, and started inside.

"How far in do you think we have to go?" He tried telepathy but got no response.

"How far in do you think we have to go?" he said audibly. It was so dark, he felt compelled to whisper. And even then his voice echoed.

"I'm not sure," Heidi said. "I can already sense spirits, but they aren't interested in us."

"At least not in talking to us," Aurora added.

They walked in silence. Benjamin didn't dare to breathe. It just felt kind of icky to be walking somewhere where you knew lots and lots of people had been slaughtered. He didn't want to breathe in the protoplasm stuff Gary has mentioned. And then he felt something brush at his shoulder.

"What was that?" he asked, wiping at it.

"What was what?" Andy asked.

"Something just touched me," Benjamin replied.

"You're just imagining things," Andy said.

Andy was probably right. This place was eerie; who wouldn't imagine things in here?

They kept walking, but the farther they went, the darker it got. Even with incomparable telegen eyesight, Benjamin couldn't see more than two feet in front of his face. He reached out to touch Aurora who'd been ahead of him, but his hand came up empty. Aurora was gone.

Benjamin stopped walking and whipped around. Heidi bumped into him.

"Why'd you stop?" she asked.

"We're lost," Benjamin replied.

"Lost?"

"Yeah, lost." With the black closing in around him, the word sounded hopeless to Benjamin.

"Iva?" Heidi called out. "Andy?"

No answer.

"Gary?" Benjamin called. "Aurora?"

Still no answer.

"Try telepathy," Benjamin said. Like she wouldn't have thought of that.

"I already did," Heidi replied. "It's useless. This place has so many telejammers, it makes my head ache."

Benjamin let out a small, nervous laugh that sounded a tad on the hysterical side. "Good. I thought it was just me."

"What do we do now?" Heidi asked, and her voice quivered when she spoke. "Should we turn back and try to find where we left the others?"

Benjamin shook his head, though he wasn't sure why he bothered. Heidi couldn't possibly see him in the dark. "No. We should go on. With your empathic abilities, we probably have a better chance than them anyway."

"Okay," Heidi replied. "But hold my hand so we don't get separated."

No arguments there.

They walked on in silence. Benjamin was afraid if he said anything, it would distract her. And being this far in an underground tunnel with only one way out left him feeling edgy.

The wall, which seemed to be made of dirt and stone, curved left. And so they curved left, at least until Heidi stopped. "Do you feel that?" she asked.

Benjamin did. It was like an outpouring of terror coming at him from all directions. "It must be pretty strong for me to pick up on it." He stood still for a minute, listening, and with the darkness and the utter silence, Benjamin thought his heart was going to jump out of his chest. He could feel Heidi's pulse beating as he held her hand and realized she was as nervous as he was.

"They want us to walk forward," he said. "They're calling my name."

"I know," Heidi said. "I can hear it. What do we do?"

Benjamin shrugged, trying to act braver than he felt. "I think we walk forward. Slowly."

They started forward, side by side, still holding hands. Heidi's grip tightened, not that Benjamin minded. It probably masked him doing the same to her. The empathic voices had become audible, creating a song of the dead. They blended together, a chorus of tethered spirits. Crying. Wailing. And saying his name. Benjamin Holt. He felt vaguely aware that it might be odd for ghosts tens of thousands of years old to know his name.

And then a single voice in his mind took the lead, leaving the others to fill the background. *"Come forward, Benjamin Holt."*

They both stopped, and Heidi moved closer to Benjamin. He let go of her hand and put his arm around her.

"Come forward, Benjamin Holt."

The voice in his mind commanded him, and Benjamin felt unable to resist it. Benjamin released his grip on Heidi, and against every bit of common sense he had, he stepped forward.

CHAPTER 7

BENJAMIN CAN'T REMEMBER IF HE HAS AMNESIA

Benjamin woke up to salty air and Jack slapping him across the face. For only being six inches tall, Jack delivered a slap that could have woken the dead.

The dead. There was something about the dead, but Benjamin couldn't quite put his finger on it. Why was he thinking about the dead?

Jack slapped him again.

"That's enough," Iva said. "He's waking up."

"His eyes are still closed," Jack replied.

Benjamin snapped them open, and with telegen-quick reflexes, reached out to slap Jack in return. But Jack's reflexes were faster. The Nogical teleported to the other side of Benjamin's face and held his hand inches away, poised for another slap.

"I'm awake." Benjamin sat up.

"Too bad." Jack put his arm down.

Benjamin looked around. He was outside on top of one of the Crags with his friends gathered around. Heidi sat across from him and looked pretty much like he felt. Crummy. Jack probably hadn't slapped her to wake her up though.

"How did I get up here?" he asked.

"I teleported you," Andy said.

Benjamin felt sure there was a hint of smugness in Andy's voice, and even in his dazed state, it needled him.

"Why'd you do that?" Benjamin asked.

"Because we found you unconscious on the floor of the tunnels." Iva knelt down beside him. "Are you okay?"

Benjamin rubbed his head which he was sure had too much blood pumping inside it. A bump the size of his Geodine seemed to be forming above his ear. "I don't remember anything. I must've hit my head."

"Heidi was out also," Gary said. "And based on your body temperatures, I'm willing to bet you guys were unconscious for a good hour before we got to you."

"An hour? What happened?" Heidi asked.

Andy laughed. "You tell us. We lost you guys in the tunnels."

Heidi shook her head. "I don't remember."

"What's the last thing you do remember?" Iva asked.

Heidi pursed her lips together. "The ghosts. They were everywhere."

"And then there was just the one," Benjamin said.

Heidi nodded. "You're right. But then what happened?"

"I have no idea," Benjamin replied. He searched through his mind, trying to remember, but it came up blank—as if someone had taken a giant mental eraser and wiped the last couple hours out of his brain.

But it wasn't just his memories that got messed up. After the ghost and tunnel incident, nothing was right. Benjamin felt little bits of information slip from his mind, and always at the most inopportune times—like right before The Panther called on him in Telekinesis. Or right after Ryan Jordan insulted him—leaving Benjamin unable to think up any kind of witty retort. The retorts always came an hour later, and by then, the chance to insult Ryan with them was gone.

He could tell Heidi was equally bothered by what had happened. She forgot her thought cache every day and hadn't changed her hair color once. Of course it didn't stop her from talking to Josh in the hallway after class, though Benjamin did his best not to notice.

Okay, who was he fooling? He noticed. All the time. But he noticed the sparks that normally flew off her hair when she was with Josh had vanished.

Something had happened in the tunnels, and Benjamin had to find out what it was. They'd all talked it over, but nothing had turned up. Benjamin had even let Jack peek into his mind to see if the Nogical could figure out what had gone on, but Jack had come out empty. And if a Nogical couldn't read your mind, then things were hopeless.

So given that he had trouble remembering his own name and he felt like a walking zombie, the week sucked. If he could just make it one more day, the weekend would finally arrive—not that it would make any difference.

Benjamin sat in Empathy class on Friday. Sci Omega droned on and on. Why had Benjamin signed up for this class in the first place? Talk about slow. Heidi had sworn up and down how great the class was, but Benjamin just didn't get it. He never should've listened to her, but he had, and here he was, bored stiff.

 53

"...leaving bonding threads between the two parties," Sci said.

What was he talking about? Bonding threads?

"To initiate the joining of minds, it is best to choose a quiet location," Sci went on.

Mind melds. That's what Sci was talking about. Benjamin smiled as he remembered joining minds with Iva last year. Iva was pretty—no, scratch that—Iva was beautiful, but Benjamin never thought of her as anything more than a friend—except when they'd done the mind meld. Then he'd wanted to marry her. Of course the feeling had passed, but still. It had been sweet while it lasted.

Benjamin tried to listen a little bit better. The whole mind meld phenomenon seemed pretty interesting. Maybe, just maybe, if he really learned what he was doing, he could join minds with Heidi some day.

Benjamin groaned inwardly. What was he thinking? Join minds with Heidi?

And then it dawned on him. Maybe by actually joining minds with her, they could figure out what had happened in the tunnels at the Crags. But even as he thought it, he knew he could never suggest it to Heidi. She'd think he was just trying to come up with some excuse. It would sound so pathetic. Still, he focused all his attention on Sci Omega until class ended.

Fate seemed to be on Benjamin's side Saturday morning. No sooner had Benjamin gotten his oatmeal and sat down at the breakfast, Heidi brought up the mind meld thing herself.

"I think we should join minds."

Benjamin looked at her and didn't say anything. In fact he tried not to even breathe. He didn't want to give away the fact that he'd dreamed all last night about doing just that. He looked down at his bowl of gloppy mush but couldn't bring himself to actually eat it.

"Do what?" he asked.

"Join minds," she repeated.

He spooned out a bite of oatmeal and almost brought it to his mouth. Couldn't they at least flavor it? "Oh, you mean like Iva and I did last year?" That sounded pretty casual. Benjamin noticed Iva glanced over at him, but she didn't change the expression on her face.

"Right," Heidi said.

"Will you know how?" Benjamin asked, almost dreading the answer.

And for good reason.

"Oh, yeah," Heidi replied. "I've done it loads of times with Josh. It'll be no problem."

Benjamin opened his mouth and took the bite, forcing himself to swallow. It gave him something else to focus on. "Great," he said. "Sounds like you're a real expert."

Heidi actually blushed.

"I think it's a great idea," Iva said. "Let's finish up eating, and we can get started."

With each step he took, Benjamin's feet felt more and more like boat anchors. Yesterday he'd dreamed of joining minds with Heidi. Now he dreaded it. Numbly, he followed Iva as she led them down the stairs to the telegnosis floor. He hardly even glanced up as they walked into an empty classroom and sat down. All except Heidi that is.

"Maybe Benjamin and I should be alone for this," she said. "The bond seems to be stronger that way."

How much experimenting had she done?

"Good idea," Iva said. "There's a teacher's lounge across the hall. Why don't you guys go in there?"

Benjamin's stomach flip-flopping around like a fish. Alone for the mind meld? He couldn't open his mouth to comment because he was pretty sure if he did, he'd throw up the single bite of cursed oatmeal. So instead he just nodded his head and followed Heidi across the hall to the teacher's lounge. Andy winked at him on the way out; he'd have to remember to punch him the next time he got a chance.

Heidi sat cross-legged on the floor and patted the spot in front of her. "You sit here. If we sit in chairs, we'll be too far apart."

Benjamin nodded his head and managed to squeak out a reply. He couldn't believe how pathetic he was acting. He would've thought with telegen reflexes, skills, and brains he wouldn't be acting like some love-sick puppy dog, but that's exactly how he felt. Why did the mind meld have to be so personal anyway?

Benjamin took a deep breath, partially managing to calm himself, and sat down. He took another deep breath. Okay, things were getting better. He could do this and get through it. No problem.

Heidi smiled at him; if she'd read his mind or sensed his emotions, she wasn't letting on. There was something to be said for friendship. "Just take my hands and close your eyes," she said.

As soon as Benjamin held her hands in his, every bit

of his nervousness dropped away. He could feel Heidi's friendship warming him from the inside. Maybe it was the Alliance bond, or maybe it was her skill in empathy, but she exuded good feelings. He relaxed and waiting for their minds to join.

The mind joining experience with Iva had been brief— a quick trip to gather DNA information. With Heidi, as soon as it began, Benjamin knew it was far more. Yet it wasn't the wonderful experience he'd remembered from before.

Benjamin and Heidi walked together, back in the tunnels, holding hands. And then, Benjamin heard the voice.

"Come forward, Benjamin Holt."

It commanded him, and he stepped forward, letting go of Heidi's hand and putting his arm around her. She moved close to him, and he felt her shivering.

"Come forward, Benjamin Holt."

The voice in his mind commanded him, and Benjamin felt unable to resist it. Benjamin released his grip on Heidi, and against every bit of common sense he had, he stepped forward.

In the background, Benjamin could still hear the other ghosts. They taunted him now, called his name. Called Heidi's name. Told him to run. Told him to jump. But it was one voice which commanded him and no other.

Benjamin remembered why they were here. "We've come to find the answer to the riddle."

"The riddle has just begun," the ghost replied.

At first, Benjamin could see nothing, but an apparition began to materialize in front of them. Hideous and scarred, it hung in the air, its empty eye sockets looking deep into Benjamin's soul.

"The riddle told us to come here," Benjamin said. "It said the ghosts would tell the tale. You know our names; you were expecting us."

"*Yes,*" the ghost replied. "*We have been expecting you. And we have something for you.*"

"Then give it to us so we can leave." Heidi took a step forward.

The ghost leapt forward and seized Heidi by the shoulders, its bony fingers pressing into her skin. She screamed, and Benjamin tried to move forward to save her, but something blocked his way.

"Help me, Benjamin!" Heidi cried.

"I can't move!" Benjamin struggled against the invisible bonds. He looked at the ghost. "Let her go!"

The ghost, still holding Heidi with two hands, pulled a third arm out from below its tattered robe and waggled the bony finger at Benjamin. Benjamin drew back; sure, he'd seen extra arms on telegens before, but never on disembodied ones.

"*I will let Heidi Dylan go and give you what you want if you solve my riddle,*" the ghost said.

"And if I don't?" Benjamin asked, struggling again.

"*Then I'll kill her,*" the ghost replied.

"No," Benjamin said. "You'll let her go now. Then I'll solve your stupid riddle."

The ghost let out a laugh which chilled every drop of blood in Benjamin's veins. "*Perhaps I should kill her first. It doesn't matter to me either way. You will never solve my riddle. Nobody ever has.*"

In the background, the chorus of ghosts began to wail.

Benjamin could see them now, out of the corners of his eyes. This was no bluff. Benjamin knew it as soon as the ghost had said it. Heidi's life depended on Benjamin. This ghost would snuff the life out of Heidi without even blinking an empty eye socket.

Benjamin ceased his struggling. "Fine. But what guarantee do I have that you'll let us go and give us what we need if I solve the riddle?"

"*Guarantee? You want a guarantee?*" The ghost laughed again. "*Do you want to shake on it?*" the ghost asked, putting its third hand out for Benjamin to shake.

Benjamin reached out to grab the hand, but as soon as he touched it, the hand evaporated and the ghost howled with laughed. "*There's your guarantee. Now, let's get on with it.*"

CHAPTER 8

BENJAMIN CREATES CHAOS

Benjamin watched as Heidi shivered. The ghost grasped her shoulders. She looked so small compared to the apparition, so helpless. The ghost had clenched its third hand over her mouth, but her eyes implored Benjamin. He couldn't fail her.

"What's your stupid riddle?" Benjamin demanded. Even through his anger, he knew he didn't have time to waste.

The ghost looked into the air, and the chorus grew in intensity. And then it began.

"Father of shadow, mother of Earth,
Lover of none, to Hell it gave birth,
Emptiness vast,
Forever to last."

The ghost lowered its head and looked at Benjamin. Benjamin met his gaze directly, though he had no idea what the ghost was talking about.

"Your time begins," the ghost said.

"Time!" Benjamin said. "You never mentioned there was a time limit."

"Your time begins," the ghost repeated. *"In one minute, Heidi Dylan will die. Then, you will die."*

Heidi struggled against his arms, and Benjamin's mind flew into thought. One minute. He had to solve it.

 60

Keywords. Benjamin knew solving riddles was all about keywords. What had the riddle said? Earth. Hell. Shadow. Emptiness.

Thinking of Earth immediately brought to mind Gaea, the wife of Benjamin's biological father, Caelus. As soon as Benjamin had told Gary what Nathan had said, Gary had gone right to the library to research everything he could about Gaea and Caelus. Gaea was known throughout history as Earth. Goddess of the Earth.

"*Thirty seconds left*," the ghost said.

"Hurry, Benjamin. It's so cold." Heidi shivered and her lips were blue.

Cold? It was burning up in the tunnel. Was Heidi dying already? Benjamin felt sweat drip down his forehead. Who was the mother of Earth? Gary'd told him. He'd even downloaded some family tree of all the gods and goddesses to Benjamin's heads-up display, but it wasn't working in this stupid cave. Benjamin clenched his fists together and put them to his forehead. Who was Earth's mother?

Almost too late, Benjamin realized he'd forgotten about the rest of the riddle. Keywords. Emptiness. Gave birth to Hell. It was also the mother of Hell. Emptiness. And then Benjamin knew it. He didn't hesitate.

"Chaos," he blurted out.

All at once, the ghost flew into a rage, swooping around the room with Heidi in tow. "*You've cheated! No one can solve my riddle.*"

"I just did, so let Heidi go and give us what we came for," Benjamin demanded. He heard the chorus of ghosts howling in the background. It sounded almost as though they applauded Benjamin.

"I will give you what you came for because I promised to," the ghost said. *"And then I will kill you."*

One step at a time. Benjamin knew he had to take this one step at a time.

"Give it to me now," Benjamin said, and then he saw it. The ghost teleported an image into his mind. The image. That's what they'd come for. It was a picture of some sort with ancient symbols scrawled all over it. He'd take the time to decipher it later. For now, he had to save Heidi.

Taking the only opportunity he knew he'd have, he lunged against the bonds which had restrained him. The ghost hadn't been expecting it, because the bonds snapped, and Benjamin grabbed Heidi, pulling her from the spiny, skeletal fingers. Together, they fell to the floor.

But the ghost wasn't even close to giving up. He flew into the air and hovered above them. *"Your souls are mine, as are all the souls in here. I am the master, and no one can escape from me."*

Coldness enveloped Benjamin as the ghost descended on them. There was nowhere to run. No way to escape. Teleportation was out—the telejammers were too strong. They couldn't run—ghosts were everywhere. But then the other ghosts did something Benjamin never would have expected. They huddled and flew at the large ghost, pulling it away from Benjamin and Heidi. At their touch, it began to burn, to disintegrate right there before Benjamin's eyes.

Benjamin shielded his face to protect himself from the howling ghost and the burning fire. It was dying—again—and its essence rained across the floor. Vapor settled upon Benjamin's face, and all went black.

Benjamin opened his eyes and found himself in the teacher's lounge with Heidi. He didn't move but felt Heidi shaking in his arms. He remembered everything that had happened in the tunnels at the Crags. Every last detail of it.

Heidi pulled away from him. "You saved my life." She started to cry.

And even though words wouldn't form in Benjamin's head, he just sat there holding her. And it was perfect. Without even thinking about it, he leaned forward and kissed her. And she kissed him back. And it was even more perfect. And then he messed it all up by thinking about her loser boyfriend Josh. What would happen now?

Sometimes telepathy sucked. The thought of Josh must've pushed itself to Heidi's mind, because she immediately broke off from the kiss and jumped up from the ground.

"This is wrong."

"No it's not," he said.

"Yes, it is." Heidi shook her head. "We shouldn't be doing this."

But even though she slammed up a huge mind block, he felt confusion seeping through.

"It's Josh, isn't it?" Benjamin asked. Why did Josh have to get between Benjamin and Heidi at a moment like this?

"No," Heidi said. "It has nothing to do with Josh. It's just that you and I are friends and that's all."

Benjamin's mouth fell open. How could Heidi say that? She was lying—to him and to herself. He tried to look at her, but she wouldn't meet his eye.

"Anyway, we got what we needed," she said, "so let's go. The others are waiting."

 63

Benjamin didn't know what to say. If anyone had asked him right now about Heidi, he would've sworn they were more than friends. But apparently, she wouldn't have. All because of an inconvenient boyfriend. His blood began to boil as he thought about it, but he decided not to say anything else. They'd have time to talk more about it later.

Without another word, Benjamin followed Heidi out of the room.

CHAPTER 9

SELENE BREAKS THE RULES

"Did it work?" Iva asked when they came back into the classroom.

Benjamin didn't know how to respond. On one hand, he felt much better. His head wasn't missing any memories, and he no longer felt like an automaton. On the other hand, what had happened with Heidi made his head hurt in a whole new way. The missing memories probably would have been better.

Heidi nodded, but Benjamin noticed she shivered a little, too. "We got more than we bargained for."

Benjamin was pretty sure she was referring to the ghost memories and not their kiss.

Though Heidi still wouldn't look him in the eye, between the two of them, they managed to get out the whole story of what had happened. And it must have been an unspoken agreement, because Benjamin didn't bring up the kiss and neither did Heidi. But at least when Heidi told about Benjamin saving her life, she actually looked at him and smiled. That was encouraging.

"How can we see this picture you got from the ghost?" Andy asked.

"I guess I could draw it," Benjamin said.

"There's a better way," Gary said.

"Good," Andy said. "Because Benjamin sucks at art."

"I'm not that bad," Benjamin said.

"You said the image actually got teleported into your mind by the ghost," Gary said.

Benjamin nodded. "That's what it felt like."

"So you should be able to teleport it out whole," Gary said. "Most probably what happened is that someone teleported something into the ghost's protoplasmic mind, and he, in turn, teleported it into yours."

Gary was right. Aside from the fact that Gary was always right, it made perfect sense. Without giving it another thought, Benjamin grabbed hold of the picture from his mind and teleported it. It materialized on the circular table in front of them. Benjamin reached down for the scroll and unrolled it. He pinned it open on the table so they could all see it.

The image was the same one he'd seen during the mind meld. It almost looked like a map, but the symbols and markings looked like mumbo jumbo. Wordlessly, he looked to Gary and raised an eyebrow.

Gary wrinkled his face and studied the map. "No, I don't recognize these symbols. Aurora might have some ideas. I'll hook up with her later today, and we'll see what we can find out."

Benjamin walked back to his dorm room hoping to sort out the jumble of thoughts running around in his head, but no sooner was he inside, the telecom buzzed. He flipped the telekinetic switch, and the mirror came to life.

"Benji!" The image of Derrick filled the mirror, looking every bit of his seven-year-old self.

"I wanna talk to Benjamin." Douglas ran over and shoved his twin out of the way.

 66

"But I got here first," Derrick said. "That's not fair."

"Mommy says we're from a different world," Douglas said. "Is that true?"

Benjamin looked at his mom in the background who nodded her head. "I guess you could say that," Benjamin replied.

"I haven't seen any aliens yet." Derrick pushed his way back into the picture. "I thought there were aliens on other worlds."

"You're actually the alien," Benjamin said.

Derrick smiled. "Really?"

"Why can't I be the alien?" Douglas said.

Within minutes Benjamin had them both convinced that they were, in fact, extraterrestrials. His baby sister Becca giggled in the background the whole time until she finally ended the telecom call by telekinetically flinging her red telephone rattle at the screen.

But no sooner had the screen gone blank that it started buzzing again. It must just be his mom calling him back. So when Benjamin flipped the switch and saw Selene Deimos' face waiting there, his jaw dropped a good five inches.

But she apparently wasn't up for social pleasantries.

"Can you teleport to the Ruling Chamber?" She glanced over her shoulder as she said it.

Benjamin raised an eyebrow. "Uh, sure. When?"

The smallest of smiles flickered onto her face. "Now. I'll meet you there." And her image vanished.

Benjamin stared at his reflection in the mirror, waiting for her to come back on and tell him the rest of the joke. Or explain where Helios was. Or why he needed to meet her at the Ruling Hall. But the only thing he saw was himself staring back, and after almost a minute of that, he turned around and looked at the empty room. Andy and Gary weren't back yet. Who knew when they would be? So without giving himself any more time to think about his imminent secret meeting with Selene Deimos, he teleported away.

Selene was alone when Benjamin teleported into the ruling chamber. She stood a couple steps down from of one of the twin thrones, and walked over to him as soon as he got there.

"Where's Helios?" Benjamin glanced around in case Helios was hiding in a corner.

Selene shrugged. "I think he went to Japan."

And it was only once she shrugged that Benjamin noticed what was sitting on her shoulder.

"You!"

The girl Nogical jumped over to Selene's other shoulder. "That's right. Lulu, in case you forgot again."

Talk about attitude. "I didn't forget," Benjamin said.

Lulu smirked. "Yeah, sure. And tell Jack I'm not time traveling for him anymore. Next time you need something from the past, get it yourself."

Benjamin scowled. It's not like he'd asked for her help. "I wasn't supposed to touch it."

Lulu smacked her forehead with her hand. "It wouldn't have killed you. Helios is so serious. Talk about sucking the fun out of everything."

"What's a life-force disk do anyway?" Benjamin asked. When he'd traveled into the past last summer, he'd retrieved some kind of golden disk, but Helios had almost gone ballistic, making Benjamin promise not to touch it. Not that he'd had much of a chance. He'd only had the disk for a couple of weeks before he'd had to bargain with it for his life with Achilles.

Selene raised an eyebrow. "You don't know?"

"Helios wouldn't tell me," Benjamin said. "All he said was don't touch it."

Selene turned her head to look at Lulu. "You didn't tell him either?"

Lulu shook her head, making her orange hair fly from side to side. "Are you kidding? Helios threatened to exile me if I did. But somebody should. You know, those things aren't as rare as everyone seems to think."

Selene flicked her hands in a dismissive gesture. "Helios seems to think it's not a good idea."

Lulu teleported up onto a throne and bounced on the cushion. "And Helios doesn't seem to be around right now, does he?"

Selene laughed but didn't volunteer any more information. Benjamin stared at her until she smiled and met his eyes.

"I know what you're thinking," she said.

Benjamin laughed. "That's because you're one of the most powerful telegens on Earth."

"True. But I'm not even reading your mind."

Benjamin crossed his arms. "What am I thinking then?"

"You wonder if Helios and I ever disagree." She smiled. "Right?"

Benjamin tried to keep himself from smiling. "Okay, fine. So do you?"

Selene walked up to the thrones where Lulu sat and

motioned for Benjamin to sit on the already occupied throne.

Benjamin stared at the Nogical who rolled her eyes, sighed, and moved onto the arm rest. He sat down next to Selene.

"You have two twin brothers, don't you?" Selene asked.

Benjamin's mind immediately flew to Cory and his other missing brother, but Selene shook her head. "No, I'm not talking about the triplets. I'm talking about your brothers you grew up with."

Benjamin smiled. "Derrick and Douglas."

Selene nodded. "Do they ever argue?"

Benjamin looked at Selene and then burst out laughing. "Are you kidding? Their middle names should be 'Bicker.'"

Selene put her arm down on the arm rest, and Lulu levitated on top of it. "So why should it be any different for Helios and me?"

Benjamin twisted up his mouth. "Because you two rule Lemuria."

Selene looked at him. "And your point is...?"

Benjamin thought of Derrick and Douglas. The only time they ever agreed was when they played tricks on either him or Becca. "I have no idea what my point is."

Selene put her hand out and a glass of water appeared in front of it. She reached for it, took a long sip, and them set it down. "Are you curious why I called you here?"

Curious didn't really even begin to describe it. "Yeah, kind of," Benjamin said.

Selene took a deep breath. "I thought you might want to talk to Cory."

Benjamin felt his mouth form a perfect O.

"You might catch a bug that way," Lulu said, and made to throw something at his open mouth.

He shut it.

"I'll take that as a yes," Selene said.

Benjamin nodded. "Yes."

"Good," Selene said. And without another word she teleported out of the room.

Benjamin stared at where she'd been. Lulu still levitated there, watching him. He opened his mouth, but she beat him to it. "Tell my baby brother I'm not his little errand girl." And then she teleported away also.

Benjamin only had to wait a second for something to happen. And that something was Cory teleporting into the room.

Benjamin jumped off the throne. "Cory!"

"Hey, little brother." Cory gave Benjamin a hug.

"Little brother." Benjamin laughed. "Technically, I'm your older brother."

Cory looked down at himself and then looked at Benjamin. "It doesn't look that way to me. Although you have grown in the last few months."

Benjamin smiled. Not only had he grown taller, he'd also put on more muscle, and even started to shave. Without thinking about it, he felt his chin and smiled. Finally stubble.

"So you've been alive for longer, but that doesn't change anything," Benjamin said. "I'm still the older one."

"Whatever you say." Cory smiled and sat down on the larger of the two thrones. "So funny enough the guy I'm working with knows you."

"Joey Duncan." Benjamin remembered thinking Joey had been involved when Cory was taken away.

Cory nodded. "Did you know he and Selene Deimos are pretty serious?"

"Serious? Like dating?"

Cory laughed. "Yeah. Like dating. She's been hanging around so much, if it weren't for that Nogical I'd feel like a total third wheel."

Benjamin sat down in the opposite throne, the one Lulu had been bouncing on only minutes before. "You don't mean Lulu, do you?"

"Yeah, Lulu," Cory said. "For as annoying as she can be, she does lighten up things while we wait."

"Wait for what?" Benjamin asked.

Cory shrugged. "It's hard to say. According to Helios, quite a few events need to fall into place before we can make our move."

"What move?" Benjamin asked.

Cory sighed. "I can't tell you."

"Sure you can," Benjamin persisted. "I won't tell anyone. I promise."

"I wish I could, Benjamin. I really do," Cory said. "But the mission we're on is so important, we can't take any risk of it being compromised. I think Helios would flail Selene if he knew she'd arranged this meeting."

"Will everything be okay?" Benjamin asked.

"We're not in immediate danger," Cory said. "Though I have the feeling that in the weeks to come, that may change."

"Just be careful, okay?"

"Yeah, okay, little brother," Cory said, messing up

Benjamin's hair. "So any luck finding our other brother?"

Benjamin shook his head. "No, but I found out more about a half-brother of ours." And then Benjamin told him as much of what had happened as he could—about Nathan and his oracle's foretelling and thereafter murder, and his killing spree.

"Nathan Nyx is trying to kill us?" Cory said.

Benjamin nodded.

"And we're actually related to him?" Cory asked.

Benjamin nodded again. "Through our father. Caelus. But he can't kill us yet. Caelus needs us for something."

"Just because the oracle did her job, he killed her." Cory shook his head. "But that reminds me—"

"What?" Benjamin asked.

"About Delphi," Cory said. "Remember how I told you I'd visited it years ago and had a foretelling, but that I couldn't remember anything?"

Benjamin nodded. Cory had told him about it last summer.

"Well, it unraveled," Cory said.

"Into what?" Benjamin felt his heart start to race. Maybe, just maybe, something Cory had remembered could help in his quest for their missing brother.

"The oracle talked about family," Cory said. "She said someone in our family will betray us. Someone in our immediate family."

"Someone besides Nathan?" Benjamin said.

Cory nodded. "I'd guess so. I don't consider him close. We need to consider the real possibility that our other brother is with Caelus or Gaea right now."

"In Atlantis?" Benjamin asked.

"Yeah, in Atlantis. And you wouldn't believe the state of things here either."

"What!" Benjamin asked. "What did you just say?"

Cory covered his mouth with his hand, but it was too late.

"You're in Atlantis," Benjamin stated.

"Shhhh...." Cory looked around. "Okay, you're right. But you can't tell anyone."

"I won't," Benjamin said. "I told you I won't."

Cory looked straight into his eyes. "I believe you. And I trust you. We can trust each other and we can trust our friends."

Benjamin sighed at the mention of friends.

"What?" Cory asked.

Benjamin sighed again. "I'm struggling a bit on the friendship thing this year."

"I find that hard to believe," Cory said. "Your friends would stick by you through anything."

"Maybe," Benjamin said. "But it seems like I've done nothing but fight with them so far."

"I'm sure it's not as bad as you make it sound," Cory said.

"It is," Benjamin sighed. "Iva and Andy are dating and horrible to be around. And Gary's helpful, but why does he have to be right all the time?"

"And Heidi?" Cory asked. "What about her?"

Benjamin had intentionally left out Heidi. He didn't want to talk about her. Not now. Come to think of it, not ever.

"You're not telling me something," Cory said. "I'm not stupid you know."

"It's just she has this dumb boyfriend and won't talk to me," Benjamin said. And then he let it all out. He told Cory about the mind meld, he told him about the kiss. And aside from being completely embarrassed at having said everything, it actually felt pretty good to get it off his chest.

Once Benjamin finished talking, Cory smiled. "Sounds to me like you and Heidi have a few things left to talk about."

"If she'll ever talk to me again," Benjamin said. "I hate to admit it, but I think I may actually like Heidi more than a friend."

Cory laughed. "You don't say?"

Benjamin felt himself flush. He only hoped it hadn't been so obvious to everyone else.

"So can we see each other again?" Benjamin asked.

Cory shrugged. "It's up to Selene. And Lulu. They're the ones who got me here."

"Perfect." Benjamin's voice dripped with sarcasm. "In case she hasn't told you, Lulu's not a servant."

Cored smiled. "Yeah. She's told me, only about a hundred times."

"But still ask," Benjamin said.

"Yeah, I will." And they said goodbye, and Cory teleported from the room.

CHAPTER 10

A FUN DAY OF CRYPTOGRAPHY

Benjamin woke Saturday morning and sat up in bed. Snores came from Andy in the bunk below him, but Gary's bed was empty. Empty that is except for Jack, who perched on the pillow.

"Good morning, sunshine," Jack said.

"Is it?" Benjamin asked, throwing a pillow toward the Nogical. "I saw your annoying sister last night."

Jack easily diverted the flying pillow. "Lulu? Please tell me you didn't."

Benjamin nodded and managed to get up out of bed. "She didn't tell you?"

Jack smacked his forehead with his hand and levitated over to the mirror, turned on the water, and splashed water on his face. "So did she have lots of nice things to say?"

Benjamin frowned. "She told me to tell you she's not your little errand girl."

Jack let out a laugh. "Yeah, well next time you see her, you tell her if she's got issues with holding down a job not to come running to me."

Benjamin stared at Jack. "You're really not serious, are you?"

Jack grew a smug smile. "Totally. She's had at least five hundred jobs in the last century."

But Benjamin shook his head. "No, I mean you don't seriously expect me to deliver messages back and forth between you two, do you?"

Jack looked about to snap out a sarcastic reply, but didn't get the chance. "So why am I up at the crack of dawn?" Benjamin asked.

Jack levitated back over to Benjamin. "Gary's on the trail of something hot. He's been in the library all night working on decrypting the map you got from the ghosts."

"It is a map?" Benjamin asked, rubbing his eyes.

"Yep," Jack said. "So let's get going. I told Gary I'd have you there in an hour."

It took a good amount of pestering, but between Benjamin and Jack and a bucket of cold water, Andy managed to wake up and get dressed.

"Tell me again why we're going to the library?" Andy asked once they'd teleported to the Ruling Hall. "In fact, why are we always going to libraries? There's like a million other cool places to go in Lemuria. Why is it always the library?"

"To work on the second clue," Benjamin said.

Andy groaned. "But it's Saturday. I had plans with Iva today."

"Iva and Heidi are already at the library," Jack said. "Did I forget to mention that?"

"But we had plans," Andy said.

"So you still do," Jack replied. "Just think of them as being much more fun now."

Gary couldn't have picked a more obscure library.

"Cryptography Library," Andy read as they walked

through the door. It had taken them a good fifteen minutes to find the place, buried deep in dust on one of the upper levels.

Gary looked up from the table where he sat with Iva, Heidi, and Aurora, and motioned them over. The way his eyes shined, he didn't look like he'd just pulled an all-nighter.

"How's it—?" Benjamin began.

"Shhhh…." Heidi said. "Gary's just about got it solved."

"You do?" Benjamin asked.

"Shhhh…." Heidi said again.

Benjamin noticed she looked at him when she shushed him which he took as an encouraging sign. He smiled back and kept his mouth shut.

Andy, of course, sat next to Iva, and kissed her before even looking at anyone else. Benjamin tried to avert his eyes, but the only other thing to look at was weird symbols that crawled all over the walls.

Gary looked up from the scroll. Except this wasn't the same scroll Benjamin had teleported from his mind. This scroll had all sorts of extra letters and symbols drawn all over it.

"What happened to my scroll?" Benjamin reached over to grab it, but Gary moved it away.

"I've been decoding it." Gary pointed in front of him.

"You wrote all over it?" Benjamin heard the annoyance creep into his voice, but he didn't care. Gary shouldn't have written on it. He'd battled ghosts to get it.

"Gary didn't write anything." Aurora turned the scroll around and pointed at a symbol. "Look."

Benjamin recognized it immediately. The three hearts,

 78

etched in gold, just like the wrapping paper on the puzzle box; they hadn't been there the last time he'd seen the map. A shiver ran down his spine.

"What happened?" Benjamin ran his finger over the design.

"It looks like your secret admirer marked this one, too," Andy said.

Benjamin glared at him. It was way too early in the morning to be talking about secret admirers.

"We managed to shift the phase of the molecules on the scroll fractionally, and everything you see here came to life," Gary said.

"You did what?" Andy asked.

But Benjamin wasn't listening. He studied the map, seeing the new symbols which matched the symbols moving all over the walls of the library. "These look familiar."

"They should," Aurora replied. "We have some like them on the walls of the lava tube where I live."

"That's right," Benjamin said. "I knew I'd seen them before."

"I have all the decoding results on a crystal back home." Aurora stood up. "It'll only take me a couple minutes to go get it."

Aurora teleported away and was back in a matter of minutes. But two seconds after she rematerialized, Ryan Jordan also appeared in the door. He smirked at them with his unwelcome presence and walked in.

Why did Ryan always turn up at the wrong time? It was just so…so uncanny. No, not uncanny. Ryan was eavesdropping intentionally, no doubt for Nathan Nyx. Again.

Benjamin walked over to Ryan. "We're using this library."

"I doesn't look that way to me," Ryan said. "But you know, whatever. Don't let me bother you."

"What are you doing here?" Andy walked over to join Benjamin. Benjamin noticed Andy's fists clenched as he spoke.

"*Calm down*," Benjamin said telepathically though he really wouldn't have minded too much if Andy hauled off and punched Ryan again. Heck, he'd have liked to get one or two good punches in himself.

"Good question." Ryan said. "I was just about to ask you the same thing."

Aurora walked over and got right up into Ryan's face. Her dreadlocks seemed to double in size which made her almost tower over Ryan. "What we're doing here is none of your business."

Ryan stayed face-to-face with her, until finally, he took a step back. "Maybe I'll just stay and see for myself."

Nobody spoke, but then Andy let out a deep breath. "Okay, the truth is Benjamin has a secret admirer who's leaving him coded messages, and we're just trying to figure out what they say."

Benjamin could have killed Andy. He felt his face turn so red, he was sure he looked like someone had painted it. And Ryan took it for everything it was worth. He doubled over laughing. Benjamin glared at Andy who didn't seem to notice.

"I bet it's Sherry the Scary," Ryan said between laughs. "I always knew she had the hots for you."

Benjamin gritted his teeth. "Sherry the Scary is not my secret admirer."

"How do you know if you're in here trying to decode

secret messages?" Ryan laughed for another few minutes before managing to regain his composure. "Well, I guess I'll be going then. I don't want to get in the way of true love." He smiled, waved, and teleported away.

"That was a little too close," Andy said.

"But how would Ryan know to come here?" Iva said.

Aurora put her head in her hand. "Yikes, guys. I think it was me. When I teleported back to the lava tube, I felt someone connect to my teleportation signature."

"You felt it?" Andy asked.

"Oh yeah," Aurora said. "As crazy as all these teleportation issues have been, I've been keeping really close tabs. It must've been Ryan."

"Maybe so, but it doesn't matter," Gary said. "We need to get back to work."

And Gary got back to work.

Aurora plugged the storage crystal into one of the readers. "I'll program it to broadcast to our heads-up displays," she said. "That way, we can all see the code."

As good as her word, in a couple seconds Benjamin saw strange symbols and pictures scroll across his screen. But even after watching them, they still looked like a bunch of nonsense.

"It looks like a derivative of Rongorongo, though there are some major differences," Gary said.

"Rongor-what?" Andy said.

"Rongorongo," Gary repeated. "You know. Like they spoke on Easter Island."

Andy laughed. "Is this that Easter Bunny Island again? Nobody believes in the Easter Bunny."

"Maybe they should." Jack appeared on top of

Benjamin's shoulder. "With genetic engineering, anything is possible—even giant bunnies."

"Who deliver eggs into baskets?" Andy asked.

"I thought it was chocolate. And plastic grass." Jack scratched his head. "Why would anyone want plastic grass anyway?"

"Don't you guys see the similarities here?" Gary pointed out a few of the symbols he'd projected onto the table in front of them.

"Oh, sure." Andy pointed to one symbol. "Here's a little man holding a stick. And here's a little man running. And look—this little man is doing a headstand."

"What's up with Easter Island anyway?" Heidi asked. "My Empathy teacher avoids the subject like the plague."

"No wonder," Jack said. "Easter Island is one of those things most telegens don't like to talk about."

"Why?" she asked.

"Because basically it was a huge disaster," Jack replied. "It was an island Lemuria left above the ocean on purpose when they sunk the continent. And they left it inhabited, but wiped the memories of the telegens who stayed there."

"Wiped their memories?" Heidi asked. "Isn't that against the law?"

"Not back then," Jack said. "Almost nothing was against the law back then—during the sinking."

"So what happened?" Benjamin asked. By the looks on his friend's faces, they wanted to know as much as he did. Jack had even caught Andy's attention.

"Well the island was left with these super powerful telegens who had no idea about anything—Lemuria, Atlantis, Earth," Jack said. "So like telegens—and humans for that matter—are so apt to do, these people separated off into different tribes. You can probably guess the rest. The tribes grew. The tribes fought. One tribe knocked over another tribe's Moai. That tribe retaliated. They cut down all the trees. The animals all died, and before anyone knew what had happened, so did all the telegens, leaving nothing but a bunch of upturned statues scattered all over the island."

"It's the statue island," Heidi said. "I knew I recognized it from somewhere. And everyone died?"

She shuddered as she asked it, and immediately Benjamin felt fear in her mind. And he knew why. Heidi, like him, was thinking about the tunnel full of ghosts. The dead telegens. The last thing they needed was an entire island full of more ghosts. Benjamin shook his head and tried to brush away the thought.

"Okay, so the language on this scroll is similar to the language of ancient Easter Island," Benjamin said. "What does that mean to us?"

Jack twisted up his face. "Beats me. I'm just here to give the history lessons."

"What do you think, Gary?" Benjamin asked.

But Gary didn't reply. He put up his hand in a hang-on-a-second motion, and his eyes were glazed over in that heads-up display way, so Benjamin waited. But not very long. Gary whipped the scroll around and began tracing something out with his hand.

"Look at these symbols," he said, pointing.

"Okay," Andy said. "Then what?"

"I just accessed the Easter Island maps, and these symbols here correspond to basically every Moai on the

 83

island," Gary said.

"And a Moai is what?" Andy asked.

Gary rolled his eyes. "Duh. It's a statue."

"Duh," Benjamin echoed. Did Gary know everything?

"But you'll notice there are a few more on this scroll than in the Easter Island database," Gary said. He was talking faster now; the air almost tingled around Gary.

"Right," Andy said. "I was just about to say that."

Which couldn't have been true.

Heidi smiled. "I bet that means they have something to do with solving this riddle."

"Exactly what I was thinking," Gary replied.

"So, what do we do?" Iva asked. "Do we try to find more information on these extra statues?"

Gary nodded his head and opened his mouth to speak, but Benjamin didn't let him reply. They'd wasted enough time. "It means we visit Easter Island," Benjamin said.

Iva turned on him. "We can't leave Lemuria. It's against the rules."

Benjamin knew she'd take some convincing. Andy, on the other hand, looked like he was ready to teleport right then and there. Benjamin motioned with his head toward Iva.

Andy sighed and turned to Iva. "You know, sometimes the rules are meant to be bent just a little."

But Iva shook her head. "I'm not teleporting out of the dome. We could all get stuck out there."

"Oh come on, Iva," Heidi said. Benjamin saw the adventure in Heidi's eyes and knew she was in. Apparently the fear of deadly ghosts had been replaced with the excitement of unsolved mysteries. "We'll just teleport there and come right back. It'll be fun."

"No, Iva's right," Gary said. "We can probably find out what we need from the library."

Andy laughed aloud. "Okay, Gary, you can stay here and look up all the information you want here in the library. But I'm teleporting to this Easter Bunny Island to find out what's really going on with Benjamin's secret admirer."

Benjamin opened his mouth to reply, but shut it again. He figured the best thing he could do right now was let Andy try to convince everyone to visit the island. The sad fact was that they really did need Gary there, unless someone else could automatically pick up ancient Rongorongo, which, given the short amount of time they had, was as likely to happen as Nathan Nyx turning away from the dark side.

CHAPTER 11

MOVING MOAI IS HARD WORK

It took a little bit of convincing to get Iva and Gary to agree to teleport to Easter Island. Okay, it took a ton of convincing. Iva was sure they'd get caught by one of the teachers, and Gary was sure they'd get stuck outside the dome. And even the next morning, Gary was still complaining.

"Do you realize where Easter Island is?" Gary said.

Nobody answered.

He threw up his hands. "It's in the middle of nowhere. That's where."

Andy let out a deep breath. "Gary, we've come up with five backup plans in case we can't get back in." He held up his hand, all five fingers extended.

"I'm just saying," Gary said. "What we're doing is risky."

"Life is about risk, right?" Jack said. "At least that's what I try to tell Lulu."

"Even Aurora cancelled on us," Gary went on, ignoring Jack. "She knows we'll never get back through the dome."

Heidi let out an exaggerated sigh. "She said her dad needed her help with something. Don't be such a chicken."

"Yeah, would you just teleport already?" Benjamin said.

Getting to Easter Island was the simple part. Iva showed off the teleportation skills she'd developed during her year at Delphi. Jack vanished right after her. Andy and Gary teleported next, leaving only Heidi and Benjamin.

"Sure you don't want to try it yourself?" Benjamin asked looking for something to say. He knew Andy must've teleported bugs into his stomach as a joke; there was just no other explanation for the jitters he felt in there.

Heidi shook her head, and Benjamin noticed her hair. Red ringlets that bounced around when she moved. He looked away. He had to stop thinking about her. They had serious business to take care of, and beside, even though she'd been a little bit more friendly, nothing else had changed. She and Josh were still together.

"No way," she said. "I only teleported by myself yesterday for the first time, and that was just across the room."

"Okay," Benjamin said. And then, before he could re-think it, he moved close to her and grabbed her hand. She opened her mouth to say something, but he looked away and teleported them, keeping the image of Easter Island fresh in his mind. Right beside the image of her curly red hair.

As soon as they reached the island, Benjamin released her hand, but didn't move away.

"What is that?" Heidi walked away, toward the rocks.

"El Gigante," Gary said. Even amid all his complaining, he'd picked the teleporter destination himself.

"You aren't kidding." Andy walked over to join Heidi. "That thing is huge. No wonder it's stuck here in the quarry."

"I could have lifted it out," Jack said, settling on El Gigante's head.

"No way," Andy said. "It must weigh a million pounds."

"Three hundred tons to be exact," Gary said. "Which is why no one in their right mind would ever try to lift it."

"I'll try not to be insulted," Jack said. "Unaltered telegens wouldn't have had a chance. Nogicals, on the other hand...."

"Yeah, whatever," Andy said. Obviously the memory of him lifting the stone door to Kronos' chamber last summer was too fresh in his mind. Benjamin had thought at the time that the effort had killed Andy.

"You don't believe me?" Jack asked, and his sunflower eyes sparkled.

"Right. I don't believe you." Andy looked away, surveying the surrounding area.

Behind him, El Gigante lifted off the ground. Not too far—maybe two feet. Jack held it there and cleared his throat.

If Benjamin hadn't known Jack so well, he never would have thought it possible. But he was learning, every day. Being genetically engineered certainly had its benefits.

"Oh, Andy," Jack said. "Look at me."

Andy turned around, and his eyes doubled in size. "No way."

Jack set it back down, and it rolled way more on its side than it was before.

Next to him Gary fidgeted. "I really don't think we should move any statues. It might upset the archaeologists."

Jack just smiled and plunked down on Benjamin's shoulder.

"Let's start by finding these 'extra' Moai on the map," Gary said. "The ones that aren't recorded in any of the

Easter Island surveys."

They followed Gary up to the side of the volcanic crater. Benjamin looked into the fresh water and saw Easter Island reflected back at him.

"Hmmm," Gary said.

"Hmmm, what?" Benjamin asked. The 'Hmmm' had a really bad sound to it.

Gary scratched his head. "Well, based on the longitude and the latitude of our present location, the extra Moai must be at the bottom of this crater."

Iva squinted. "But it's filled with water."

Gary nodded. "Yes. I can see that. But I can also see them down there on the bottom."

"You can?" Iva asked. "Through the water?"

"It's not as deep as it looks," Gary said.

"So we found them." Andy looked at Benjamin. "What now?"

Benjamin shrugged. "I have no idea. Gary?"

But Gary was already heading away from the side of the crater, moving over to a large, flat rock which had been smoothed like a patio.

"Look at this." Gary pointed to the rock.

"More of those Bongo Rongo pictures," Andy said.

Even Gary laughed. "It's Rongorongo." He bent down to run his hand over the symbols carved into the rock.

"Can you read it?" Heidi asked.

She stood right next to Benjamin, and he felt her excitement through the Alliance bond. He shook his head; he had to stop thinking about her. Even with his mind block in place, something was bound to get out.

Gary squinted his eyes. "Of course. Just give me a few

minutes to translate it."

Nobody dared even cough while Gary translated—except for Jack who whistled and jumped and teleported around. Benjamin knew the Nogical was trying to get under Gary's skin—just for fun. But Gary was in the zone, and even Jack's ridiculous antics bounced right off him. And so Jack gave up after a few minutes, settling on Benjamin's shoulder.

Finally, Gary turned around to face them. "I've got it, though it doesn't make any sense."

"Let's hear it," Benjamin said. "We can all figure it out."

"Okay," Gary said. "Here goes:

> *Join us here and hear our wrath.*
> *With it will you know your path.*"

He stopped talking.

"That's it?" Andy asked. "That's all it says." He shook his head in disgust. "What is up with all these short, cryptic riddles? Doesn't Sherry the Scary have anything better to do with her time?"

"Apparently not." Gary sat down on the patio.

"It's not Sherry the Scary," Benjamin put in, though he wasn't sure why he bothered.

"So what does it mean?" Heidi asked. "What do we do?"

"Maybe we have to dive down to the bottom of the crater lake and 'join' the statues there," Iva suggested.

"That water's freezing," Andy said. "No way am I going for a swim."

"But if we're supposed to go in the water, then why is the message way over here?" Benjamin shook his head. "I don't think that's right."

"Of course it's not right," Jack said. "Look around you."

They all looked around. Benjamin saw grass, and rock, and Moai—some standing and some fallen.

"Yeah, so what about it?" Andy said.

"What do you see around you?" Jack asked.

"Not any trees," Gary laughed. "The people wiped them out."

"I see rocks and Moai," Heidi said.

"Right," Jack said. "And what are those Moai doing—or supposed to be doing?"

Benjamin looked out at the Moai, standing like they were guarding the island. It reminded him vaguely of The Crags where the eagle lizards had been sculpted and placed to guard Lemuria. It was the same with the Moai,

"The Moai are meant to stand and guard Easter Island," Benjamin said.

"Exactly," Jack said. "I knew you'd get it out of your thick skull."

"So why are they at the bottom of the lake?" Heidi asked.

"Because nobody's stood them up yet," Benjamin answered before Jack could speak. "We need to get them up here and stand them up on this patio. That's what we need to do."

"My thoughts exactly," Jack said. "And with me doing the bulk of the work, all three will be up here in no time." He turned. "Gary and Heidi can supervise."

Heidi scowled. "What? You don't think I'm good enough to help lift the Moai?"

Jack cocked his head. "That pretty much sums it up."

"I've been working hard at telekinesis," Heidi said. Her red ringlets turned jet black. "In fact, just a month—"

"Listen," Benjamin said. He'd had enough. They needed to get on with solving the clue and get back to Lemuria. "Just save your energy in case we need some telepathy stuff done or something."

She clenched her teeth together and walked over to join Gary. Benjamin, Andy, Iva, and Jack headed to the side of the water.

"We should all do this together," Andy said. But then he must have realized what he said. "Not that I couldn't lift them myself. It's just that we need to save some energy to teleport after this."

"You don't need to make excuses, Andy," Iva said. "I'm sure you could lift all of them."

Was she trying not to smile?

Even with four telegens (one of them genetically engineered) working, lifting the three Moai out of the water and settling them on the patio in just the right spots took two hours. Benjamin fell onto the grass in front of the patio when they finished.

"How in the world did telegens move all the Moai to the edges of the island?" he asked.

Iva sank to the ground beside him and looked around. "They were especially gifted in telekinesis," she said. "I can feel it all around me. The residue of telegen minds is super strong—especially up here on top of the volcano. This may have been a holy place."

"So we've moved the statues," Gary said, "but it hasn't seemed to have made any difference." Benjamin looked over to where Gary squatted at the base of the three giant Moai.

He looked like an ant next to the things, easily squashed.

Andy and Heidi walked over to join him. "And they've covered the original writing," Heidi said.

"Maybe there's writing somewhere on the statues," Andy suggested.

Gary started walking around the Moai. "Nope. No writing," he said, after making a complete circuit.

Benjamin and Iva stood up and headed over. As tired as Benjamin was, he knew the sooner they figured out what the second clue meant, the sooner they'd be done here. And he had to be honest—teleporting back through the dome concerned him. He knew it made no sense, but it just seemed like the longer they were outside the protective shield, the harder it would be to get back in.

Andy, Heidi, and Gary stood on the patio with Jack hovering overhead. But as soon as Benjamin and Iva entered the boundary of the patio and joined their friends, they fell to the ground. Benjamin covered his ears. The statues roared with rage. As they screamed, he realized they weren't screaming at them, but at the long dead islanders. If they could have, the Moai would have shaken with the force of the anger they spewed out.

"Who dared cast us into the depths of the water?"

Benjamin could tell the voices were telepathic, but still kept his ears covered. He turned his head upward, looking at the largest of the Moai.

It was Iva who answered. She'd stood up and moved closer to the Moai. Part of Benjamin wanted to reach out and drag her back, but he didn't. He looked over and noticed Andy, already on his feet, moving closer. Benjamin motioned for Andy not to interrupt.

"The message told us to bring you up from the bottom of the lake and set you here," Iva said. She'd stopped covering her ears, and her voice sounded calm. That made at least one of them.

"*Look around, young telegen,*" the Moai said. "*It is too late. Our island is dead.*"

"That's true," Iva said. "But what difference does it make?"

The Moai roared with rage. "*What difference does it make?*"

Even Iva shrank back under the wrath.

"*If we had been placed earlier, we would have prevented this monstrosity,*" the Moai bellowed. "*Where are the trees? Where are the animals? Where are the people?*"

"Gone," Iva said. "All gone. They didn't realize their own power."

"*Because you did not tell them of their power,*" the Moai said. "*You stranded them on this island and erased their memories. What else were they to do? We were to be their only hope. And now it is too late.*"

Benjamin stood up and moved closer. "Look. We were led to this island and to the three of you, in fact, to find some kind of clue."

"*A treasure hunt!*" The Moai screamed with rage. "*You brought us out to see this catastrophe for a treasure hunt?*"

Apparently, the Moai didn't like that bit of information. But it didn't matter. It was the reason they'd come, and they needed to find out what the second clue meant.

"Right," Benjamin said. "That's pretty much why we raised you from the water. You're supposed to have something for us."

All three Moai laughed. Benjamin covered his ears and tried to block his mind from the mocking sound.

"It's not funny," he shouted. He had to stand up to them. He didn't think they could kill him like the Crags ghost had almost done. Or then again, maybe they could. "Give me what I came for."

"*You demand something of us, little telegen?*" the large Moai said. And it roared with laughter before continuing. "*I know what you speak of. Visit us again in two weeks time, and you'll get what you deserve.*"

"Give it to me now," Benjamin demanded. He'd had enough of this waiting. Enough riddles. Couldn't anyone give him a straight answer? Even a stupid stone statue?

"*Two weeks,*" the Moai said. "*Visit us in two weeks.*"

Benjamin fell to the ground and felt the overwhelming presence of the beings that were the Moai depart. He looked up. The statues remained, but aside from their solid rock forms, there was only emptiness.

Andy rushed over to Iva. "Are you okay?"

"I'm fine." She stood up and brushed herself off.

"Those guys were livid," Heidi said, walking over to Benjamin.

He got to his feet. "That's putting it mildly. What were they?"

"I couldn't read their minds," Heidi said. "I don't think they were telegens or even ghosts for that matter."

"They were filled with pure energy—more powerful than I've ever seen on Earth." Jack levitated over to Benjamin. "That degree of energy shouldn't even be possible."

"Two weeks." Benjamin punched his fist into his hand.

 95

"Did you hear him?"

Heidi nodded. "That's okay. We'll just come back." She looked up and glared at the Moai, but their gaze didn't shift. Not that Benjamin thought they would. Even after what they'd just experienced, he still knew the Moai were made of stone.

They moved down the volcano, away from the Moai, to teleport. Benjamin didn't trust the Moai, and nobody argued with him. Iva teleported first. But no sooner had she disappeared that she reappeared in the same spot.

"What happened?" Andy asked.

She shook her head. "I couldn't get through."

"I knew it." Gary threw up his arms. "I knew we'd have trouble."

"Settle down, Gary," Andy said. "Just because Iva had trouble doesn't mean we're all going to."

Iva glared at Andy, and Benjamin shook his head inwardly. Even after they'd been dating for over a year, Andy still made the stupidest comments.

"I didn't mean anything against your teleportation ability," Andy said, trying to cover up his remark.

"Whatever," Iva said. "Let's see you try."

"Fine," Andy said. And he attempted to teleport himself and Gary. But just like Iva, Andy and Gary returned seconds later.

"Somebody messed with the shield," Andy said even as his face turned five shades of red.

Iva crossed her arms. "That's what I tried to tell you."

Benjamin tried next with Heidi, and Jack even tried, but nobody had any success.

"So what now?" Gary asked. "I knew we shouldn't have

come here."

"Now's not the time for 'should haves', Gary," Benjamin said. "Besides, I think it's pretty obvious that we had to come here." He sighed. "And we have to come back in two weeks."

Gary shook his head. "No, you have to come back. If we ever get back through the shield, I'm not leaving again."

"*Hey!*"

Benjamin heard Aurora's voice in his head, but it was Gary who replied.

"*Aurora!*" Gary said. "*Where are you when we need you?*"

"*Need me?*" she asked. "*What's wrong?*"

"*We're stuck out here,*" Gary said. "*Just like I knew we'd be.*"

"*Would you just stop already on that?*" Andy said. "*I'm sick of hearing how you knew everything.*"

"*It's true,*" Gary said. "*I was against this in the first place.*"

Benjamin had to grab Andy to keep him from going after Gary. Not that Benjamin thought Andy would've really punched Gary or anything. Actually, he wasn't sure what Andy would've done. He just knew he didn't want to find out.

"*Look,*" Benjamin said to Aurora. "*We all tried, but we can't seem to get back through the dome.*"

Aurora laughed. "*Oh, really?*"

"*It's not funny,*" Gary said.

But Aurora kept laughing. "*It's no problem to get back in,*" she said. "*If you know where to teleport.*"

"*Where?*" Benjamin asked.

 97

"Teleport to the lava tube leading to my house," she said."

Aurora was good for her word. Iva went first and didn't return. Jack went next, followed by Andy and Gary, leaving just Benjamin and Heidi.

Benjamin couldn't help but stare at her and Heidi's black ringlets. "Sure you don't want to try yourself?"

She took his hand. "Maybe next time."

Benjamin smiled though inside, his stomach had tied itself in knots. But now wasn't the time to mess up teleportation. He'd better focus. Getting Heidi stranded would probably turn her mood around pretty fast. And so without another word, he pictured the lava tube in his mind and teleported them away.

CHAPTER 12

BENJAMIN GETS
AN ILLEGAL GIFT

Two weeks. It may as well be two months. How could time go by so slowly? Benjamin had gotten so preoccupied checking the time on his heads-up display that he'd finally disabled the clock. And then he had trouble sleeping because all he did was wonder what time it was. And then, as if things weren't weird enough, Magic Pan called him out of the blue and told him to meet him at The Silver Touch—alone. Magic had given zero information, but Benjamin was curious enough not to say no. If anything, maybe he could get the menus working.

Benjamin walked down Mu Way shivering. It was freezing. Sure, he knew it was the simulated environment mimicking the weather above the dome, but seriously, why did they have to make it dip below sixty degrees? He made a mental note to talk to Helios about it the next time he saw him—whenever that might be.

"I though you said the door was locked," Walker Pan said to Morpheus when Benjamin walked through the door to The Silver Touch.

Benjamin stared at Morpheus Midas, Walker, and Magic Pan, all huddled around a counter near the back of the store.

"I told him to meet us here, Dad," Magic said. "Weren't

you listening?"

"It must've slipped my mind," Morpheus said. He waved his hand in front of a control pad, and Benjamin heard the door lock behind him. Great. He was locked inside an oddities shop with the store owner and two fugitives. Okay, not quite. Magic Pan technically was still a student, even if Benjamin did suspect him of sabotaging the entire continent's teleporters.

"Did you come alone like I asked?" Magic said.

"Or did you bring that Gary Goodweather with you?" Walker said with a look that would have chilled liquid nitrogen.

"Are you still upset about being a loser?" Benjamin asked, managing to come out of his frozen shock with just enough wit to deliver the jab. After all, Gary beating the snot out of Walker Pan in chess last summer should be worth something.

"Upset?" Walker said. "Hardly. If I hadn't gone so light on him, I certainly would've won."

"With the Ammolite chess set at risk?" Benjamin laughed. "There was nothing light about your match. Except maybe your abilities."

"Can you talk about something besides chess, Dad?" Magic asked. "It gets so tedious."

"Yeah," Benjamin said. "Like maybe what's going on here."

Magic laughed, and Morpheus stared at him as though he'd lost his mind.

"Like you don't know," Magic said. He turned to his dad. "He's already figured it out."

"He did?" Walker asked.

Could the doubt be any clearer in Walker's mind? Was it really so hard to believe that Benjamin might be smart enough to realize Walker and Magic were not on the level?

"Totally," Magic said.

"What exactly has Benjamin figured out?" Morpheus asked.

"I've figured out that these two are responsible for bringing down all the teleporters on Lemuria and also for the teleporter re-entry problems," Benjamin said.

"You are?" Morpheus' mouth fell open.

Walker gestured with his head as if to say "of course we are".

"But how?" Morpheus asked. "I mean, how could the two of you cause all those problems?"

Walker chuckled. "Child's play, really. We used the teleportation scrambler we got here over the summer, and it worked like a charm."

Morpheus shook his head. "I never sold you a teleportation scrambler."

"No, you didn't," Walker said. "But your ancestor did one thousand years ago."

Before Morpheus could ask another question, Magic turned to Benjamin. "So the reason I called you. I need to give you something." Magic put a small rectangle in Benjamin's hand.

"What is it?" It was only about the size of his thumb; he didn't have the slightest idea what it might do.

"It's a teleportation surger," Magic said. "It should let you get around the current teleportation problems."

Benjamin stared down at it. "Why are you giving this to me?"

"Good question," Morpheus said. "Didn't you just buy that for yourself?"

Magic shook his head. "No, I bought it for Benjamin."

Okay, things were getting strange. Actually, they were plenty strange already and just getting stranger. Why would Magic be giving him this thing?

"Any particular reason?" Benjamin asked.

"You'll be needing it," Walker said. "That's all we can say. Got it, Magic?" He looked to Magic who looked back, and Benjamin knew they were talking with telepathy—well-blocked telepathy. Was Magic getting scolded?

When they finished, Walker moved away from the counter. "Anyway, we'll be going now. As always, Morpheus, it's been a pleasure doing business with you."

"Wait!" Benjamin said.

"There's nothing else to talk about," Walker said.

"There is. Before you go—can you fix the menu system?" Benjamin asked Magic. Even though he was totally confused with whatever was going on, he wasn't stupid.

Magic thought for a moment. "I could change it to liver and onions I suppose."

At the word liver, Benjamin cringed. "No. Seriously, no."

Magic waved his hand. "It's no problem. Consider it done." And without another word, both Walker and Magic teleported away.

CHAPTER 13

MISPLACED MOAI
AND DNA SAMPLES

After Benjamin relayed his exchange with Walker and Magic, nobody—not even Gary—held out any hope of the menu problem ever getting resolved. And with the additional threat of liver, they headed to The Deimos Diner Sunday morning; after two years, nobody even bothered suggesting anywhere else.

"I thought Aurora was going to meet us," Gary said.

"She hasn't shown up yet." Heidi pushed her auburn hair behind her ears. "Wait!" And she put up her hand and closed her eyes.

Benjamin recognized this. Heidi was having a telepathic moment. She didn't have to close her eyes, but Benjamin figured she just did it to let people know not to talk to her.

After a minute, she opened her eyes back up. "Aurora should be here any minute," she said, and sure enough, Aurora sailed through the door not thirty seconds later.

"You're late," Gary said.

"Yeah, for good reason," Aurora replied. "I paid a little visit to Easter Island this morning."

"You did?" Benjamin asked. "Why?"

"I wanted to see these Moai," she replied. "I just couldn't believe that after all these years, new Moai had surfaced. I knew the world would be in an uproar. In fact, I was expecting so much publicity, I teleported a mile away and hiked over so no one would notice me."

"And?" Andy asked.

"And they're gone," Aurora said.

"Gone!" Benjamin jumped to his feet. "That's impossible!"

"Benjamin's right," Andy said. "We lifted them ourselves, and let me tell you—my mind still hurts."

"Well, someone's moved them again then," Aurora replied.

"Not to the bottom of the lake." Andy put his head into his hands. "Please tell me we don't have to lift them again."

Aurora shook her head. "No, not to the bottom of the lake. In fact, not even on the whole island."

"Not even on the island?" Iva asked. "Where did they go?"

"That's what we need to find out," Aurora said.

"And we need to find out soon," Benjamin added. "We only have a week until we need to visit them again." Before two weeks had seemed so long. Now time was compressing around Benjamin.

"A week until what?" Ryan Jordan walked over to the table.

Benjamin snapped his head around to face Ryan. When had that little weasel come into the diner?

"Sounds like you guys are planning something," Ryan said.

"Whatever we're planning isn't your business." Andy stood up and got in Ryan's face.

Ryan laughed. "If it's not my business, you should be more careful where you talk."

"And you should be more careful with your illegal contraband," Jack said, teleporting onto the table. But he wasn't empty-handed. Instead, the tiny Nogical held a black sphere nearly half as big as he was.

Ryan lunged for it. "Hey, give that back!"

But Jack teleported himself and the sphere off the table and onto Benjamin's shoulder.

"You dirty, rotten, little—" Ryan began, attempting to grab the sphere from Jack.

"What is it?" Benjamin asked, taking the sphere Jack offered him. But as soon as he said it, he felt the strange telenergy pulse through him. "It's a telemagnifier."

"And an illegal one at that," Aurora added. "They haven't sold those in Lemuria in thousands of years."

"And it's mine," Ryan said. "So give it back now."

"Why don't you just teleport it back?" Heidi asked and smiled.

Ryan glared at her, but at the same time, took a step back from the table.

"You can't, can you?" Benjamin said and joined Heidi in smiling. "You can't do anything."

"That's not true," Ryan said. "I don't need a stupid telemagnifier for anything. You can keep it."

And then Benjamin heard Ryan's thoughts so clearly, he was sure Ryan hadn't even bothered trying to put up any kind of mind block. *"Nathan is going to kill me. He'll lock me up just like he did Jonathan."*

"Nathan gave you this!" Benjamin said.

Ryan gaped. But then some small part of his brain

must've taken over. "Nathan? What are you talking about?"

"Dude," Andy said. "We all just heard your thoughts. You said Nathan was going to kill you. Seriously, tell him he'd be doing all of us a favor."

Ryan opened his mouth to reply, but shut it again. And then opened it again. "You know, you guys are crazy. Acting like you're so important, running around the world on whatever stupid little quest you're on."

It was Benjamin's turn to be speechless.

"Yeah, I know all about it," Ryan said. "Between piecing things out of your conversations, and following you around, it didn't take a genius."

Which Ryan most certainly was not.

"You don't know anything," Heidi replied. "You can act like you do all you want, but you're as clueless as Julie."

On cue, Julie Macfarlane called over from a table near the door. "Ryan, are you going to stay over there all day or what? Aren't we going to the art museum today, sweetie?"

Ryan glared at the same time he flushed from his head to his toes. He didn't even manage to squeak out another word before he turned and headed back to the table.

"I can't believe it," Benjamin said. "Nathan Nyx hired that moron to spy for him." He held the black sphere out. "How did you get this, Jack?"

Jack shrugged. "It was just some patterns I've been noticing. It happened with Jonathan last summer, too. Every time one of those two did anything even remotely powerful, I felt a strange telenergetic signature coming from them."

"The telemagnifiers," Iva said.

Jack nodded. "I put one and one together, and in

Nogical City, that always equals illegal contraband. So I teleported the telemagnifier out of Ryan's brain as soon as he walked over to the table."

"Does this mean Ryan won't be spying on us anymore?" Heidi asked.

"I think Ryan's biggest problem is going to be explaining to Nathan why he got caught," Jack said.

Which was one less problem to worry about.

Benjamin got up in the middle of the night to go to the bathroom but something teleported him right as he'd walked in the door. And then he was standing on the roof and looking over the entire city of Mu—at least until Lulu appeared right in front of his face.

"Oh, did I get you at a bad time?" she asked.

It took a second for Benjamin to fully wake up. And then another second for him to realize she'd teleported him. "I was about to go to the bathroom."

Lulu knew exactly what he'd been about to do. She pretended to snap her fingers. "Well, I'll just send you back then. Cory can wait for another crack in the shields to teleport through. Maybe in a month or so."

"Wait!" Benjamin said. "I don't have to go that bad."

Lulu smirked. "Yeah, I didn't think so." And she teleported away, and Cory appeared.

"Hey there, little brother," Cory said.

"Don't 'little brother' me," Benjamin said but smiled, and then proceeded to tell Cory about Walker and Magic Pan, and the meeting in The Silver Touch.

"Are they working for us or against us?" Cory asked once Benjamin had finished.

Benjamin shrugged. "Good question. They gave me the teleporter surger to help me get through the dome and back; that much is clear. Whether that's a good thing or a bad thing is anybody's guess."

"Just be careful," Cory looked out at the empty city.

"Aren't I always?" Benjamin shrugged. "How are things in Atlantis anyway?"

"Shhhh!" Cory said. "Don't say the name."

Benjamin chuckled. "Okay, little brother, how are things in the mysterious beyond?"

Cory laughed. "Boring. All I do is play Drop Squash with Lulu."

Benjamin raised an eyebrow. "Drop Squash?"

Cory nodded. "Some weird virtual reality game she stomps me at every single time. It's like having a thousand giant orbs trying to squash you. Nogicals have an unfair advantage. Anyway, the biggest thing going on has been planning for the museum opening."

"Sounds kind of boring," Benjamin said.

"Yeah," Cory said. "It is. The only reason I'm keeping tabs on it is because the rulers are directly involved. They've been spending all their time preparing for it, so as a result, I'm spending all my time watching the exhibits get put in place."

"Why would they take such an interest in a museum?" Benjamin asked. "Especially now? Don't they have more important matters—like world domination—to plan?"

"I would have thought so," Cory said.

"What kind of museum is it?" Benjamin asked. He remembered the museum with the teleporter exhibits he'd visited the first summer he'd come to Lemuria. But Helios and Selene Deimos didn't waste their time there.

"Natural History Museum," Cory said. "But the weird thing about it is that in the last week it's all been restructured to plan around a new exhibit."

"Seriously?" Benjamin asked. "What kind of exhibit?"

"Three huge statues from Easter Island," Cory said.

Benjamin jumped to his feet. "Have you seen them?" They had to be the same statues. They just had to be. The coincidence was too much.

Cory nodded. "Sure. I saw them when they moved them into the city."

"Do they look something like this?" Benjamin asked, and then formed an image in his mind of the three Moai.

"Exactly." Cory tilted his head. "How did you know?"

And so Benjamin filled him in on the second clue, what had happened with the statues, and how they had been commanded to visit the statues again.

"Interesting," Cory said.

"That's putting it mildly," Benjamin said. "So what am I supposed to do?"

Cory smiled. "Sounds like we need to plan a little trip for you. And we may have to get Lulu to help us."

Andy's eyes almost popped out of his head when Benjamin told them what they had to do.

"So let me get this straight," Andy said. "We get to sneak into Atlantis, go undercover at some big event where the rulers of the whole continent are going to be, and covertly speak to the statues?"

Benjamin nodded. "Yep. That pretty much sums it up."

"You're assuming they'll speak again," Gary said.

 109

"Oh, they'll speak," Iva said. "Now that they've been woken up."

"That's gotta be the coolest thing in the whole world," Andy said. "Count me in!"

"Yeah, well count me out," Gary said. "Teleporting to the lion's den is just not a sensible idea. It might not even work."

"Gary," Andy said, "espionage is not sensible."

"It can be if done right," Iva said.

Everyone looked at her and stared.

"What?" she said.

"What kind of response is that?" Benjamin asked.

"A sensible response," Iva replied. "What did you expect?"

"Well, to be completely truthful, I expected you to throw a fit about going," Benjamin said.

"Yeah," Andy agreed. "I was sure you'd side with Gary."

"This is important," Iva said. "So if we're going to do it, we've need to do it right. And the first thing we've need to do is get on the invite list for the museum opening."

Benjamin nodded. "I worked it out with Cory last night. We get Lulu the DNA samples, she'll give them to Selene, and Selene will give them to Cory. And then Cory gets us on the list."

"Wow, that's quite a process," Heidi said.

"You aren't kidding," Benjamin said. "This is going to be huge."

Lulu got back in touch with them two days later. "You're on the list," she said. "All of you. And please don't ask me to do anything else."

"You got me on the list?" Jack said.

Lulu tossed her hair. "No way, bro. It's impossible to get your DNA through the filters."

Jack frowned. "You got yours through. What'd you do? Pester someone to death?"

"Yeah. Exactly," Lulu said.

"...more persistence than ringworm," Jack muttered under his breath.

Lulu glared at him. "What did you say?"

Jack glared back. "Oh, I think you heard me. I seriously can't believe we have the same parents. I'm so perfect, and, well...you're not."

"Perfect," Lulu said. "Not quite the word I would use."

But Benjamin tuned them out. They were going to Atlantis—at least all of them except Jack. This was going to be totally awesome.

CHAPTER 14

INTO THE HOUSE OF THE ENEMY

As coincidence would have it, the teleporter surger came in handy right away. Benjamin teleported back and forth with each of them, using the surger each time. He still hadn't figured out why Magic and Walker had given it to him in the first place, but as long as it helped them get to Atlantis, he didn't really care.

Benjamin wasn't sure what he'd expected of Atlantis—maybe something just like Lemuria. And it wasn't that Atlantis was so different. Everything was just taller. And closer together. And the telegens looked basically the same, though possibly a bit oppressed. No evil monsters roamed the streets. But then, why would there be? Time and again they'd been told how the people of Atlantis weren't the evil ones. The cruel government—the government Benjamin now knew was lead by Gaea and his father Caelus—caused Atlantis' bad reputation. He could only imagine the family reunion when they finally met.

As soon as Benjamin arrived, he felt Nathan's presence—not close by, but somewhere on the continent. And if Benjamin could feel Nathan, then Nathan could feel Benjamin. Had Nathan been watching them this whole time—watching them solve the riddles that had eventually led them here to Atlantis? With Ryan spying, he must've known at least part of what they'd been up to.

"Hey, look," Benjamin said, nodding his head in the direction of a glass window with a holographic sign hanging overhead.

"The Silver Touch," Heidi said. "How can that be?" Without waiting for a response, she walked to the window. And no one seemed to want to stop her since they all followed.

Gary looked up and his mouth fell open. "Look in the window."

Benjamin hadn't reached the window yet, but from the expression on Gary's face, he was sure the treasures of Tutankhamun were on display.

"The chess set," Iva said.

"The Ammolite chess set," Gary echoed. "Here. In Atlantis."

"How can it be in two places at once?" Andy asked.

"It's not the exact same set," Gary said, heading for the door. "But it's close enough that I'd bet my left hand they were made at the same time."

"Bet your left hand," Andy said. "What kind of bet is that? You'd just grow it back."

Gary shrugged as he opened the door. "Maybe. But it would still be an inconvenience while it was gone."

And they went inside.

"Morpheus?" Gary asked.

The man standing by the chess set turned around.

"It is Morpheus," Andy said.

"No, not quite," the Morpheus-look-alike said. "But let me guess: you know my twin brother."

"Twin brother!" Iva said.

"That's right," the man said. "Morpheus Midas is my

twin brother." He reached out and grabbed Gary's already extended hand and shook it. "The name's Mantis. Mantis Midas."

But Benjamin didn't feel ready to shake the man's hand yet. "If you're really Morpheus' twin brother, why are you here in Atlantis when he's in Lemuria?"

"Why are you in both places?" Mantis Midas asked, but then laughed. "No, that's not fair. We don't give away our secrets of the trade, so why should I expect you to give away yours?"

Benjamin didn't answer. No telling what this Mantis Midas person knew.

"Opportunity," Mantis said. "What better business opportunity than to have stores in both major locations? We trade items to sell, and since they've come from somewhere far away, it makes them that much more desirable."

"How do you get back and forth?" Heidi asked.

Mantis turned his head as Benjamin heard an almost inaudible click coming from the back of the store.

"I think you're about to find that out for yourself," Mantis said.

Morpheus stopped when he saw the students. His face looked like he'd walked in through the out door.

"You—? How—?" Morpheus said.

"We liked your store so much, we decided to check out some of the other locations," Heidi said.

"And we came to find out where you get all that illegal stuff you sell," Andy said.

Morpheus cleared his throat. "Most of it's not illegal here in Atlantis." He narrowed his eyes. "What are you doing here anyway? How did you get here?"

"We were about to ask you the same question," Benjamin said. "What's in the back of the store?"

Morpheus stared at them a few seconds more before shrugging, and then he looked at Mantis.

Mantis laughed. "By all means, follow me."

He led the way to the back of the store and then down to the basement. And much like the Lemurian Silver Touch, Mantis's basement, too, was filled with strange moving things in jars and objects that looked like they came from other planets.

"What is all this stuff?" Iva asked.

"I see genetically engineered species aren't confined to Lemuria," Gary said, picking up a jar off the shelf.

"Oh, if anything, it's the exact opposite." Mantis rushed over to Gary and took the jar out of his hands. "Atlantis far surpasses Lemuria when it comes to genetic engineering." He lowered his voice. "There are so many experiments going on, we're actually able to get early samples for next to nothing."

"But these things are living," Iva said. "That's cruel!"

"According to Statute C-64, located in the Genetic Engineering Research Campus itself, early sample experiments are not considered living," Mantis said, looking to Morpheus for confirmation.

Morpheus shrugged and nodded. "That's what the rules say. So that's what we go by."

"Genetic Engineering Research Campus?" Gary and Aurora said it at the same time, and Benjamin was sure he saw matching drool coming out of their mouths.

"Don't get any ideas," Benjamin said. "We don't have time to visit any research campuses. We're here on business."

"What kind of business?" Morpheus asked.

"We're here for a party," Heidi said quickly.

Benjamin relaxed at her answer. He hadn't the faintest idea how to respond, and even though the party excuse was a lame one, at least it was true.

"And which party is that?" Mantis said.

"Oh, just some museum opening," Heidi replied.

Benjamin willed them to stop asking questions, but apparently his powers of telepathic persuasion still needed some refinement.

Mantis gasped and widened his eyes. "Not the museum opening?"

Benjamin shrugged. "It's nothing special. Just some silly art display."

"Nobody around here's been talking about anything else for the last week," Mantis said. "It's impossible to get on the list."

Andy picked some random thing up off a shelf. It didn't move which Benjamin took as a good sign. "Not for us," Andy said.

Benjamin glared at him. This was not the time for bragging. But then he remembered this was Andy; with Andy it was always the time for bragging.

"So what can you tell us about this museum?" Aurora asked. "I mean, what have people been saying?"

"*The rulers themselves are attending,*" Mantis said, switching to telepathy.

Hoping that this conversation might lead to something, Benjamin threw his best mind block up around the group.

"*Is that unusual?*" Iva asked.

Mantis looked at Morpheus and then back at the stu-

 116

dents. "*Very unusual. The rulers don't come out in public at all; but people are saying they've even been an integral part of the planning for this event.*"

And then, if there was such a thing as lowering a telepathic voice, Mantis did. "*I actually came upon a certain item just today which you may be interested in.*"

"*What is it?*" Heidi asked.

Benjamin could feel her excitement. Or maybe it was his excitement. Sometimes with the Alliance bond, it was hard to tell.

"*Think of it as something of a backstage pass,*" Mantis said, pulling a scanner from his pocket and held it up for them to see. "*One simple transfer of the codes in this little baby, and you can get in anywhere.*"

"*But we already have access,*" Andy said. "*We're on the list.*"

"*You may be on the main list,*" Mantis said, "*but I guarantee you aren't on this list yet. This list is only open to a select few. This is your ticket to getting behind the barricades—right up next to the exhibits.*"

Benjamin's mind flew to the Moai. He'd figured they'd be right there for public viewing and that he'd be able to walk right up to them. But maybe that wasn't the case. Maybe they did need this pass to get closer.

"*How did you get this?*" he asked. He didn't want to get his hopes up too high in case it didn't work.

"*We have a contact within the ruling family,*" Mantis said. "*This contact approached us to sell this.*" And then, as if sensing Benjamin's doubts, he continued. "*It's real. And it'll work. Let there be no doubt about that.*" And he scanned it in front of Benjamin's heads-up display.

CHAPTER 15

ENTER STAGE LEFT

They left The Silver Touch with only two hours until the museum opening. The Midas twins suggested a place to stay in the city, so after checking into their rooms, they changed clothes and headed right back out. Well right back out if you took into account it took the girls over an hour to get ready. Not that it wasn't worth it. But still. Benjamin had to pace the room to keep himself from going insane.

Back out in the streets, it would have been impossible to miss the event. Telegens thronged to the museum, and the streets were backed up for miles. By the looks of it, most of the people weren't even on 'the list' to get in, so Benjamin shoved his way through them to the floating red carpet leading to the museum.

He'd managed to restrain himself until now, but just as they passed through the DNA scanning barrier, he put up a mind block around just Heidi and himself.

"You look beautiful." He had to say it—no matter what kind of reaction he risked getting.

Heidi blushed. Even under all her makeup, he could see her face turn red. He'd thought she'd be angry, but there wasn't even a tingle of anger in the Alliance bond. She linked her arm through his, and they walked into the museum together.

The Atlantian Natural History Museum put the

Lemurian version to shame. This wasn't just a museum—it was an entire ecosphere sealed off from the outer city.

Gary stopped, and Benjamin could tell he was scanning his heads-up display.

"My display just got updated with the museum specs," Gary said. "I can't believe this place. The list of library annexes alone is enough to suck up a whole lifetime."

"Which is precisely why you won't be visiting any of them," Benjamin said.

"But the one on telegen evolu—" Gary began.

Benjamin shook his head. "None of them. We aren't here to see libraries."

Gary sighed and turned around. "Well, we should at least split up and scope this place out."

Andy scowled. "I was about to suggest that. Iva and I will head to the second level. Gary—you and Aurora stay here, inside the atrium. And Benjamin, you and Heidi check the public access to the displays."

Benjamin kept his mouth shut. If Andy wanted to pair him and Heidi off, who was he to argue?

And then he felt the presence. "Cory's here." He opened his mind up just enough to send out a telepathic feeler.

"Good," Andy said. "You and Heidi can find him." He consulted his heads-up display. "Meet back here in an hour."

Cory's presence helped take Benjamin's mind off Heidi and remind him why they were here. They hadn't teleported all the way to Atlantis so he could walk around holding her arm. They had work to do. Benjamin had to find the Moai, and, using the access codes they'd just gotten from the Midas twins, get close enough to talk with them. The

Moai had a message for him. They'd refused to give it at Easter Island and made him follow them here. Whatever it was they had to say, Benjamin wasn't going to miss it.

He unlinked arms with Heidi. "I think we should get some food and try to blend in."

She nodded. "Sounds good to me. I saw the dessert table back that way."

"Dessert!" Benjamin said. "I mean real food."

She scowled.

"Okay," he said. "You go get dessert, and I'll get dinner. Meet back here in five minutes."

Benjamin headed over to the buffet table. It consisted of weird squares of meat and wrapped things that might be vegetables, but it smelled like a piece of heaven. He started piling things on his plate.

"You act like you're hungry."

He turned at the sound of the voice, and found, in a red dress, a girl so pretty, she put Iva to shame. Her blond hair was about the same shade as his but way more shiny and long, and when she smiled, feelings of contentment filled him. Her eyes pierced into him to the point where he almost wanted to look away, but he couldn't force his eyes to move.

He managed to laugh. "Yeah, I guess so."

"Is that your girlfriend with you tonight?" the girl asked.

Benjamin glanced over to the dessert table and saw Heidi. And all at once, something strange happened in his mind. He found that he wanted to talk to this girl, and he didn't want Heidi to see him doing it. Before Heidi could sense him watching, he looked back at the girl and shook his head.

"No, not my girlfriend," he said. "Just a friend who's a girl."

"She's pretty," the girl said.

"Um, I guess so," Benjamin said. *But not as pretty as you*, he thought, but he didn't voice it. Still, he found himself mesmerized and couldn't pull his eyes off the girl. "Are you from around here?" He knew it sounded stupid, but he wanted to say something—anything—to keep talking to her.

The girl nodded. "You could say that." And then she looked over at the dessert table. "But I see your friend is finished getting her plate, so I won't keep you."

"Maybe we can talk again?" he asked, hating the fact that she was breaking up the conversation.

"Maybe," the girl said and then turned and walked away.

Benjamin watched her until she blended in with the crowd. And then he kept watching her until even her blond hair and red dress were no longer visible.

"What'cha looking at?" Heidi asked.

Benjamin jumped; he hadn't heard her walk over.

"Oh, nothing," he said, hoping she wasn't reading his mind.

"Seems like a pretty interesting nothing," Heidi said. "Does she have a name?"

Was Heidi jealous? She still had a smile on her face, but it felt too carefully placed.

"I was just talking to someone about what all this different food is." He motioned down to his plate. And then he laughed. "But to tell you the truth, I'm still not sure."

Heidi balanced her plate with one hand and again

interlinked her arm with his. "Why don't we head over there and eat? Then we can finish looking around."

As hungry as Benjamin was, he only picked at his food. He hadn't even asked the girl's name. How stupid was that? And rude. She probably thought he was a total loser. But she'd come up to talk to him in the first place, which was strange in itself. She'd probably just noticed his confusion at the buffet line.

"You know, Josh and I are having a few problems," Heidi said.

Benjamin lifted his head to look at her. Where in the world had that come from?

"Uh, really?" Benjamin had no idea how to respond. Why would Heidi even bring something like that up in the first place?

Heidi nodded her head. "Yeah. He's been acting really possessive lately. Trying to control every little thing that I do." She sighed. "He didn't even want me to come on this trip."

Benjamin thought he caught a glimpse of red fabric through the crowd and looked over, wondering if it was the girl. But then it disappeared.

"Yeah," Heidi continued. "I'm actually thinking of breaking up with him tomorrow when we get back to Lemuria."

"You are?" Benjamin asked. "But what about going on double dates and stuff?"

Heidi rolled her eyes. "I'm not going to keep dating Josh just so I can go on double dates." She punched Benjamin lightly on the shoulder, and Benjamin glanced down as she did it. That seemed a little bit out of place.

"Anyway," she continued. "I can just hang out with you." She lowered her voice, though with the noise in the room, there was no reason to. "You know, I've been doing some thinking about what happened in the teacher's lounge."

That caught Benjamin's attention. "You have?"

She nodded. "Yeah. I mean to be truthful, I've been thinking about it a lot since it happened."

Benjamin just nodded his head slowly, afraid he'd say the wrong thing if he opened his mouth.

Heidi sighed. "I know it wasn't a mistake. We shared something special back in the tunnels at the Crags."

Benjamin caught the red fabric out of the corner of his eye again and turned to look. It was the girl he'd talked to earlier. Her back was to Benjamin and as soon as he saw her, she began moving away. He had to talk to her again. Find out her name, if nothing else.

Without thinking about anything else, Benjamin stood up. "Hey, Heidi, I need to go to the bathroom."

"Right now?" she asked.

She arched an eyebrow, but Benjamin didn't stop to think about it. "Yeah, right now. I'll be right back. Just wait here for me."

He walked away in the direction of the red dress. Benjamin had no idea where the bathroom actually was, but in a place as big as this museum, there was bound to be one in every direction.

As he followed the girl through a maze of corridors, Benjamin thought he lost her. But then, just as he reached a set of doors, he saw her again, at the end of a long hallway. She hadn't looked back, and Benjamin was sure she

 123

didn't know he was following. She pushed a button to open a door, and disappeared into another exhibit hall.

Benjamin reached the door and pushed the same button, but the door didn't open like it had for her. And then he remembered the special codes the Midas brothers had given him. He flashed his eyeball in front of the reader, pushed the button again, and the door slid open.

CHAPTER 16

EXIT STAGE LEFT

His first thought as he went through the opening was that the girl in the red dress had vanished. With the time he'd lost opening the door, she'd have had plenty of time to disappear. And his suspicions were pretty much confirmed; she may as well have teleported away.

His second thought was that he didn't care anymore. There, across a big stretch of grass, stood the three Moai from Easter Island. Benjamin couldn't believe his luck. He'd had no idea how to find them, but luck had led him right to where he needed to go.

As he walked across the grass, he realized he wasn't inside anymore. They'd been placed in an outdoor exhibit, and the stars overhead shone down and reflected off the lake next to the Moai. Signs had been posted all along the grass walkway. *Beware! Danger—Proceed at your own risk. Unstable Exhibit!*

And even though Benjamin felt like he'd almost accomplished his task, he remembered how the Moai had acted before. Would they show the same wrath they had on Easter Island? Maybe that's why the signs had been put up in the first place.

He realized he should probably have someone else with him. Back on Easter Island, Iva's stepping into the square had been the main reason for their coming to life.

And now Benjamin wondered—would they even deliver their message to him alone? Whatever it was.

Ignoring the warning signs, he walked right up to the monolithic monsters. But under their giant forms, Benjamin felt his mind fill with doubt. Was he too close? Should he go back and get his friends? But he didn't want to contact Heidi just yet. She'd be furious that he'd snuck off like this, and he didn't feel like arguing about it right now. He figured first he'd try to get the message himself. He ran his palms over the base of the largest Moai.

"*Benjamin?*"

Benjamin heard the voice in his head. "*Cory! Where are you?*"

"*In the main exhibit hall,*" Cory said. "*Where are you?*"

Benjamin didn't feel like telling Cory just yet either. "*I'm looking at one of the exhibits.*"

"*Is Heidi with you?*" Cory asked.

Benjamin shook his head even though Cory had no way of seeing it. "*No,*" he said. "*I had to go to the bathroom.*" But it was a lie and Cory would know it. Benjamin tried to push the thought out of his head. He ran his hands over the statue's base, until he found some engraved letters. He squatted down to get a better look.

"*Are you alone?*" Cory asked, and even through the telepathic link, Benjamin felt the anger in Cory's question.

"*Well, kind of,*" Benjamin replied.

"*I told you not to go off alone,*" Cory said. "*Don't you re-member what I told you about the oracle? Our other sibling could be working against us.*"

"*Yeah, I remember,*" Benjamin said. "*But it's only for a second. I couldn't bring Heidi to the bathroom with me,*" *could I?"*

"Benjamin," Cory said. *"You didn't have to go to the bathroom."*

Busted. The sibling link between them was way too strong.

"Listen, Cory," Benjamin said. *"Don't tell Heidi, but I was following this girl."*

"What girl?" Cory asked.

Worry flooded from Cory to Benjamin. But looking around, Benjamin knew there was nothing to worry about. *"I don't know. Just some girl in a red dress. I couldn't stop myself. But she's gone now."*

"Listen, Benjamin," Cory said. *"Turn around and leave."*

"It's no big deal," Benjamin said.

"It is a big deal!" If Cory had been speaking, he would have shouted it.

"You're overreacting," Benjamin said, pretending he didn't sense Cory's anger. *"But it doesn't matter. I'm leaving. I'll meet you in the main exhibit room."*

"Good," Cory said, and Benjamin felt his relief. *"We have a lot we need to talk about."*

They severed their telepathic talk, and Benjamin looked up at the Moai again. Nothing about them had changed. No strange telepathic or telegnostic communications. Maybe they'd left their essence back on Easter Island. He figured it was possible. Heck, it seemed like anything was possible these days.

Benjamin turned around and stared walking back toward the door. He'd get Cory, and get his friends, and then they could all head back here together.

And then Benjamin heard the sound. It started as a

low humming—almost inaudible. In fact, for a human, it probably would have been impossible to hear. Benjamin stopped and turned. The largest Moai flashed and the humming stopped. Benjamin walked back over to the three statues, but stayed a few feet back. And then he waited. Waited for what would be next.

He expected an explosive voice, like the Moai had delivered before. But it didn't come. Instead, the humming began again, this time from the middle Moai. Benjamin dared to take a step closer, and the statue flashed and the humming stopped. There must be a point to the humming, but whatever it was, it totally escaped Benjamin.

And then, as he'd suspected it would, the third Moai began to hum. Benjamin walked the few steps over to its base and looked up at it. He stepped closer until he was able to reach out and touch it. And when he did, everything went black.

CHAPTER 17

AS IF THINGS WEREN'T COMPLICATED ENOUGH

It didn't take Benjamin's aching head to let him know he'd screwed up. Big time. If finding himself in an empty room wasn't enough of a clue, the fact that he lay slumped on the floor would have been. Benjamin checked his heads-up display. And then he checked it again. A whole day had gone by! Had he seriously been unconscious for an entire day?

He sat up and surveyed his surroundings. The room had windows; and a door. Aside from that, the only piece of furniture was a paisley arm chair that looked like it had come from some fancy frou-frou museum. And on top of the chair, a tray of food materialized in front on his eyes.

Someone knew he'd woken up.

Benjamin made a mental note that he was being watched. Closely by the looks of it. And then, even though he hated to do it since he now knew he was being watched, Benjamin peed in the toilet in the far corner, because, really, what other choice was there? He could only hold it so long.

He walked over to the tray and without giving it a second though, devoured the food. Why would someone go to all the trouble to keep him here overnight just to poison him on his first bite of food? But even after the tray was empty, Benjamin's stomach still growled.

"Hey, how about some more food in here?" he said. If someone was watching, then someone was listening. And his guess was valid, since in a matter of minutes, the empty tray was replaced by another filled one. Benjamin ate what he could and then sat in the chair. There was nothing else to do, and besides, the floor was harder than bricks.

The hours passed. Benjamin wasn't tired yet, so he tried telepathy with Cory. Nothing. Then Heidi. Still nothing. He kept going through the list, trying to form a telepathic link with anyone he could think of. Even Morpheus Midas. But the room was jammed. He could tell by the way his thoughts kind of bounced back to him, but he still had to try.

Pretty soon, Benjamin gave up on telepathy and fell asleep in the chair.

Benjamin woke to the sun shining through the windows and the door opening.

"You!" he said when he saw her. It was the girl from the party—the girl wearing the long red dress. Except she had on jeans and a t-shirt instead of the dress.

"Hello, Benjamin." She walked over to the chair. "Are you feeling rested?"

Benjamin jumped to his feet. "What's going on here? Where am I?"

"We've invited you to be our guest for a while," the girl said. "My name's Phoebe."

Benjamin's head spun. Guest for a while? "Listen, Phoebe. I have things I need to be doing. I don't want to be anyone's guest right now."

She shrugged, and they both turned at the sound of the door reopening.

"Nathan!" Benjamin said.

Nathan Nyx strode into the room and walked straight to Phoebe. He leaned over to her and gave her a long kiss. In spite of the mass of confusion in his head, Benjamin noticed that the girl, Phoebe, cringed and tried to pull away. But Nathan held her firm.

When the kiss ended, Nathan leaned back, and Phoebe raised her hand to slap his face. But Nathan caught her hand midair and laughed.

"Not happy to see me, sister?" Nathan asked.

Phoebe glared at Nathan in return.

Sister? What in the world was going on here?

"As I was saying, Benjamin," Phoebe said, "you're our guest. You should make yourself comfortable."

As if a chair would make him comfortable. Benjamin glared at her. "You tricked me. You made me follow you to the Moai. And then you kidnapped me."

"I hardly had to do anything," Phoebe said. "Just a little telepathic suggestion. You seemed happy enough to follow me on your own. Not a minute too soon, either. We barely got you out of there before our brother came along."

"Brother?" Benjamin said. And then it dawned on Benjamin. This girl must be another one of his half siblings.

"Yes," Phoebe said. "Our brother—Cory."

"Half-brother," Benjamin said. He didn't want this girl to claim Cory as a brother. She was as bad as Nathan.

But Phoebe shook her head. "No, Benjamin. Brother. Full brother. Haven't you figured it out yet? Can't you feel it inside you?"

And then Benjamin's head started spinning, and his heart started pounding, and sweat broke out on his forehead. He knew what she meant. He could feel it. How had he missed it before? Unless she'd masked it somehow. He wracked his brain, trying to remember what Helios had said. Had he ever actually said all three of the triplets were boys?

"You're my—" Benjamin said.

"Sister," Phoebe said. "I'm your sister. The third of the triplets."

CHAPTER 18

THREE'S A CROWD

They left Benjamin in the room for another four days. Sure, food got teleported in and teleported out, but Benjamin still felt like a caged hyena.

Halfway through the first day, Phoebe came in to check on him. As she walked in the room, she glanced back over her shoulder.

"Looking for someone?" Benjamin asked.

She covered the distance to the chair. "No."

"Sure you are," Benjamin said. "I can feel it. You're looking for your boyfriend—Nathan."

"I don't know what you're talking about," Phoebe said. "And Nathan Nyx is not my boyfriend." She glared at Benjamin as she said it.

"He sure seems to think so," Benjamin said. "I saw him kiss you."

She sighed. "Like a brother would kiss his sister. Actually, a half-brother."

Benjamin shook his head and laughed. "I don't think so. I may not be an expert, but that was no brotherly kiss."

Phoebe shuddered and looked down. She took a deep breath and then looked back up at Benjamin. "How are you enjoying your stay?"

"It sucks," Benjamin said. "If this is how you treat all your guests, it's no wonder everyone hates the ruling family."

"What do you mean everyone hates the ruling family?" Phoebe scowled at him. "The people love us. We rule everything here in Atlantis. And soon, we'll rule the entire world."

"The people are scared to death of you," Benjamin said.

"That's not true," Phoebe said.

"Phoebe," Benjamin said, "have you ever been to Lemuria?"

She shook her head.

"You should visit sometime," Benjamin said. "You'd see what I mean. In Lemuria, the people are free to do what they want, act how they want, and think what they want."

"That's how it is here, too," Phoebe said.

"That's what Caelus and Gaea have probably brainwashed you to think," Benjamin said. "I've been both places, and I'm telling you the truth. Atlantians are oppressed."

"I don't believe you," she said.

But Benjamin could tell she was lying. She was trying to mask her doubt—he could feel it. He'd gotten to her, and that could only be good.

"So how'd you get here in the first place?" Benjamin asked. "Didn't you have a guardian or a family you were placed with?"

"I've been raised here since I was just a baby," Phoebe said. "My guardian and my caretakers all died when I was under a year old."

"They all just up and died?" Benjamin said.

Phoebe nodded. "Yes, it was very tragic, or so I'm told. There was an accident, and before anyone could do anything, all three were dead. That's when our father found me and brought me here to Atlantis to live with him.

I'm forever grateful to him for that. I'm not sure what I would've done if he hadn't come along."

Benjamin's mouth dropped open as she spoke, and when she finished, he couldn't keep it shut. "Don't you think it's a little bit strange that all three died in an accident?"

Phoebe shook her head. "Accidents happen all the time. It's just a part of life."

"Phoebe, you were entrusted to your guardian as soon as you were born," Benjamin said. "He placed you—"

"She," Phoebe interrupted. "My guardian was a she."

"Fine," Benjamin said. "She placed you with a family to be raised until you were old enough to know your destiny."

"I don't know what you're talking about," Phoebe said. "I was stolen away from our father against his will. If anything, my guardian is the one responsible for taking me away from him. It's a good thing she died, or I'd never have been reunited with him."

"Caelus killed your guardian and adoptive parents," Benjamin said. "Can't you see that?"

"You have no idea what you're talking about." Phoebe crossed her arms. "Look, just because you didn't have as nice of an upbringing as I did doesn't mean you should create lies."

"I have a wonderful life," Benjamin said. "My parents love me and always took care of me." He decided to leave out the part about his own guardian, Mr. Burton, really being evil. It was kind of beside the point.

"But you were raised ignorant," Phoebe said. "And then you were lied to. Look around you, Benjamin. You talk about the people of Atlantis being oppressed. Why do you think that is? Because they aren't happy with the rulers? No! It has nothing to do with that. Atlantians have been kept imprisoned for thousands of years now. Kept down by Lemuria. That's why the people seem oppressed. But all that's about the change, and soon the tables will be turned."

Benjamin shook his head. Okay, sure, he'd questioned the validity of the shields in the past himself. And, you know, it really wasn't fair for Atlantians to be kept inside a dome against their will. But it was reality. Without the shields, the earth would have been overrun and enslaved. He knew, deep down, that at some point the shield around Atlantis had to come down. But he wasn't the telegen to decide when. And neither was Phoebe.

"Nothing is going to change," he said with more conviction than he actually felt. "The shields aren't coming down."

Phoebe turned and walked back toward the door. "You're wrong, big brother. Just wait and see. Our dad and Gaea have it all figured out. And trust me—you don't want to be caught on the wrong side when it all comes crashing down."

She came back to visit the second day, but his efforts to engage her in another debate proved futile. Phoebe had a different agenda, though Benjamin wasn't sure what it was.

"Your girlfriend's been looking for you," Phoebe said.

"Heidi?" Finally, a glimmer of hope; his friends hadn't given up on him.

Phoebe put on a sly smile. "So you admit it. She is your girlfriend."

Benjamin shook his head. "No. She's just my friend. She has a boyfriend back in Lemuria." Now why had Benjamin gone and told Phoebe that? It had no relevance to anything.

Phoebe smirked. "It looked like you guys were pretty cozy the other night at the museum. That is at least until you saw me."

Benjamin shot her a look that would have frozen fire. "You tricked me." He felt stupid for having fallen for her. And his own sister! How gross was that?

"Tricked you," Phoebe said. "All I did was come up and talk to you."

Benjamin blew out a breath. He knew she'd put some sort of hex on him or something. "Yeah, whatever." What he really wanted was to learn more about his friends. But he didn't want Phoebe to know how interested he was. "So were they having any luck?"

"Who?" Phoebe said.

"My friends," Benjamin said. "Were they having any luck finding me?"

Phoebe laughed. "Hardly. We've got you tucked away so well, no one will ever find you here. Not that you'll be here for much longer."

Panic rose, but Benjamin tried not to let it show. If they moved him from his current location, his friends might never find him. He'd been holding out hope that from just being in one place for long enough, they'd be able to pick up on some kind of DNA signature or something.

"Oh," Benjamin said. "Where are we going?"

"You'll find out soon enough, big brother," Phoebe said.

"So how's Nathan?" Benjamin asked.

He'd caught her off guard. She flinched but recovered quickly. "Nathan? He's fine. Why?"

"I was just wondering," Benjamin said. "You know—since you two are so close and everything."

"We're half-siblings," Phoebe said. "But we're not close."

"Are you on his list then?" Benjamin asked.

"What list?" Phoebe said.

"His hit list," Benjamin replied.

"I don't have the slightest idea what you're talking about," Phoebe said.

Benjamin smiled inwardly. Now he was the one with the information. "You heard about his visit to Delphi, right?"

Phoebe shook her head. "Nathan never went to Delphi."

Benjamin held his smile inside. "Someone's been keeping you in the dark, little sister. Nathan went to Delphi last year, and the oracle told him one of his half-siblings was going to kill him."

"You're lying," Phoebe said in almost a whisper.

Benjamin shook his head. "No. And I'm only telling you this so you can protect yourself. Nathan killed the oracle and then started killing his half-siblings. That is until Caelus told him to stop."

"Nathan hasn't killed anyone," Phoebe said. "He may not be the nicest guy in the world, but he's no murderer."

"Listen, Phoebe," Benjamin said. "You need to be a little more attentive given the company you keep."

"Stop talking about this," Phoebe said. "I'm done hearing your lies."

 138

"All I'm saying is that Caelus only asked him to stop for a while," Benjamin said. "At some point Nathan's going to start it up again. Just watch your back."

It was on the third day that Benjamin finally managed to form a telepathic link with Heidi. There were any number of reasons why it finally worked: she was just about the strongest telepath in the world; they'd joined minds in the past; he'd done nothing but think about her since he'd been captured. And when he heard her voice in his head, it sounded sweeter than the most beautiful music in the world.

He knew how corny that seemed, but honestly, he'd even come to look forward to Phoebe's visits each day; the room was a quiet, empty place.

"Benjamin."

"Heidi?" Benjamin stopped the pacing he'd been doing around the room.

"Benjamin!" Heidi's telepathic thoughts felt clear as spring water. *"Where are you?"*

"I'm being held prisoner," Benjamin said.

"We can't find you anywhere," Heidi said. *"We've been looking for days."*

"I know," Benjamin said. *"And I don't think they plan to let you find me."*

"Who's holding you?" Heidi asked.

"My sister," Benjamin replied.

"Sister?" Heidi said. *"Not your baby sister?"*

Benjamin shook his head though Heidi didn't see it. *"Heidi, the third of the triplets is a girl. Cory and I have a sister. Her name is Phoebe, and she's been raised by Caelus*

 139

and Gaea her entire life."

Heidi didn't immediately reply, and if Benjamin hadn't felt it, he would've sworn she'd lost the telepathic link.

"Heidi?" he asked.

"I'm still here, Benjamin," Heidi said. *"Just a little surprised. Cory mentioned something about a girl from the museum the other night."*

"It's the same one," Benjamin said. *"She's here with Nathan, but I think they plan to leave soon. With me."*

"To where?" Heidi asked.

"I don't know," Benjamin said. *"Maybe to wherever my father is."*

"Benjamin, we've been so worried about you," Heidi said. *"I've been so worried about you."*

Benjamin smiled when she said it. It was nice to know she cared.

"I've been fine," he said. *"There's nothing to worry about."*

"Benjamin," Heidi said, *"do you remember what I was talking about right before you went off to the bathroom?"*

Benjamin felt a pang of guilt. He hadn't gone to the bathroom. He'd been following Phoebe. *"There's something I want to tell you about that,"* he said.

"I know, Benjamin," she said. *"It doesn't matter. I just wanted to say that what we were talking about—about me and Josh—well, it's over between us. As soon as all this is over and we get back to Lemuria, I'm going to tell him we're through."*

Benjamin turned as he heard the door. *"I gotta go,"* he barely had time to get out before severing the link. He prayed Phoebe hadn't heard any of the telepathic conversation.

 140

But it wasn't Phoebe who walked through the door; it was Nathan. He covered the distance to the paisley chair and upturned it telekinetically, tossing it across the room toward Benjamin. Benjamin just had time to move out of its way before it smashed into the far wall. So much for a comfortable place to sit.

"What kind of lies are you feeding Phoebe?" Nathan said.

"I'm not feeding her any lies." Benjamin met Nathan's gaze, not daring to back down. He knew the best way to deal with the threat of Nathan was not to be afraid, even though his insides felt like jelly.

"She's been asking some interesting questions," Nathan said. "Interesting questions she wouldn't be asking if you hadn't been spreading lies."

"Lies!" Benjamin said. "How can you say anything is a lie?"

"So you admit it," Nathan said. "You have been telling her things. Things you'd be wise not to mention."

"Like about how you plan to kill me and her once all this is done?" Benjamin said.

Nathan laughed. "You? Certainly; you'll be first on the list. But Phoebe? I don't think so. Phoebe I have special plans for."

"What kind of plans?" Benjamin asked. Even though he'd only known Phoebe for a matter of days, and even though she was technically on the wrong side, he felt a kind of bizarre sense of protection for her.

"My plans are my own," Nathan said. "And of course our father's. He's in full agreement." Nathan walked over to Benjamin and placed his face only inches away from

Benjamin's. "Listen carefully, because I'm going to say this one time and one time only. Stay away from Phoebe. Don't talk to her. Don't tell her lies. Don't even so much as look at her. Because I'll kill you if you do."

Benjamin held Nathan's gaze, but his heart and lungs stopped inside him. "I thought you were going to kill me anyway," he said, hoping he didn't squeak the words out.

"Don't screw with me, Benjamin," Nathan said. "Don't screw with me or you'll be sorry."

Benjamin forced himself to laugh. "The way I see it, I have nothing to lose. You'll kill me if I do, and you'll kill me if I don't."

Nathan didn't blink as his face hardened. "You're forgetting about your sweet little family from Virginia."

Benjamin didn't move, even as he felt the panic rise like a giant bubble into his throat.

"Yes, that's right, Benjamin," Nathan said. "If you don't do exactly as I say, I'll not only kill you, but I'll kill your family—little Derrick and Douglas and even sweet little Becca."

And then Benjamin leapt at Nathan, his fingers outstretched for Nathan's eyes. But Nathan teleported away, and Benjamin fell to the floor. Benjamin ran for the door and pounded on it, screaming Nathan's name with rage. But the discussion was over. And Benjamin had lost.

Phoebe didn't visit Benjamin that third day, and Benjamin had to admit he felt relieved. He wanted to talk more to her, but Nathan's threat had left him with a pit in his stomach. Deep down Benjamin knew that no matter what happened Nathan would go after his family. He'd use them as a bartering chip constantly, and the only way Benjamin would ever be able to eliminate the threat would be to kill Nathan.

Imagining how he would kill Nathan filled the rest of the day, and at night, while trying to sleep on the hard-as-bricks floor, Benjamin dreamed about it too. Nathan was psychotic, and nothing would change that. Add blood-thirsty on top of that, and you were left with a danger which had to be removed.

The fourth day, Benjamin knew something was differ-ent. First, Phoebe and Nathan came into the room togeth-er. Benjamin would have thought this was just because of the previous day's conversation with Nathan, but then he noticed they'd changed into matching tan jumpsuits and boots. Nathan threw a jumpsuit and pair of boots at Benjamin.

"Change into this," Nathan ordered.

Benjamin looked at the clothing and then looked back at Nathan. His skin crawled, and he gritted his teeth to-gether to keep from saying something he shouldn't. "No."

"Do it now," Nathan said.

"I'm not changing in front of Phoebe," Benjamin said. "You both leave the room, and I'll change."

Apparently Nathan didn't want to waste time arguing, because he grabbed Phoebe's arm and dragged her out of the room.

Benjamin changed into the outfit. He halfway did it because there was no real reason not to, and halfway did it because his other clothes had started to stink. Just as he fastened the second boot, they walked back in.

"Are we going somewhere?" Benjamin asked. He hoped

now that the time had come, they'd tell him where they planned to take him just in case he was able to form a telepathic link with Heidi.

"Don't ask any questions, Benjamin," Phoebe said. She didn't look at him when she spoke, instead looking at the ground. Benjamin noticed Nathan studied her.

"Phoebe's right." Nathan put his arm around her and pulling her close. She tugged away, but he held her firm. Benjamin saw the revulsion in her eyes as Nathan's hand rubbed her arm. "There aren't any questions you need to ask. Plans have changed, and we need to leave now."

Whatever the reason for the urgency, Benjamin was ready to get out of the room. He shrugged and moved toward them. "Fine. Let's go."

Nathan laughed. "Not so fast. I don't trust you. And because I don't trust you, I'm going to place some constraints around your mind."

"I don't think that's necessary, Nathan," Phoebe said.

"Shut up," Nathan snapped. "Did I ask for your opinion?"

Phoebe bit her lip but said nothing, and for a brief moment, Benjamin felt her emotions as if they were his own. Almost like she were part of the Alliance bond. Fear. Disgust. Anger. Embarrassment.

"What kind of constraints?" Benjamin asked.

"Basically, I'm going to turn you into a zombie," Nathan said. "I'm going to put a shield around your mind so tight, it'll be like you're watching yourself on video. You won't be able to make any decisions. You will only be able to follow my direct orders." He laughed as he let go of Phoebe and walked over to Benjamin. "It's a perfect way to spend the last few hours of your life."

CHAPTER 19

BENJAMIN IS A ZOMBIE

It was every bit as bad as Nathan had described and worse. Benjamin felt his feet lifting, taking one step after another. But he may as well have been a robot. He stopped when Nathan said stop. He sat when Nathan said sit. And he said whatever Nathan told him to say. All in all, it was the most humiliating experience Benjamin could ever remember having. And to top it all off, Phoebe saw every bit of it.

They wound through a series of passages and down some stairs until they came to a life-sized painting of a bunch of people wearing togas. Nathan swiped his eyeball in front of a scanner, and the painting shifted, revealing a teleporter. Nathan ordered Benjamin onto the teleporter, and then he and Phoebe stepped on behind him.

Benjamin was vaguely aware of a feeling of curiosity as to where they were going. But it passed and was replaced with the struggle in his mind to fight against the bonds Nathan had put in place. Even in his zombie state, Benjamin knew he needed to break free. He had to find a way to get in contact with his friends. Or Cory. He hoped Cory had managed to find them, but he hadn't had the chance to ask Heidi when they'd talked.

When the teleportation stopped, Benjamin tried to move around but couldn't. But even without looking

 145

around, Benjamin knew where he was. He'd been in this passageway before. Over a year ago. It was the underground tunnel leading to the city of Shambhala. Leading to the three keys of Shambhala. The keys which had the power to bring down the shields around Atlantis and Lemuria.

Even if Benjamin had wanted to take the keys with him back then, Helios told him it was impossible. Two out of the three triplets were needed to unlock the keys. Well, here were two of the three now. Benjamin and Phoebe. They'd come to the keys so he and Phoebe could use them to disable the shields and raise Atlantis and Lemuria up from the bottom of the ocean.

Benjamin had a mild thought that he should have been panicking at this realization, but in his zombie state, he accepted it.

"Let's go," Nathan said, and Benjamin immediately started following Nathan and Phoebe down the long underground tunnel. At the end, two doors swung open, and they walked into the chamber.

"The children come back to the fold."

Benjamin couldn't even turn his head at the sound of the dominating male voice, but it didn't take a genius to figure out it was Caelus—his birth father.

"Father," Phoebe said. "We've brought him to you as you requested."

Nathan turned Benjamin so he could see the speaker, and Benjamin saw the man give Phoebe a smile that didn't come close to reaching his eyes. Could she not see that?

"Yes, yes," Caelus said. "My son. My very important son."

 146

Nathan's grip on Benjamin's arm tightened like a vise.

"Benjamin Holt," Caelus said. "I've been waiting eons for this moment."

It was only then that Benjamin noticed a woman standing next to Caelus. Through his foggy mind, he figured this must be Gaea—the first of the false gods and the wife of Caelus.

"You realize this is where it all began," Caelus said. "Right here in this very chamber."

Benjamin didn't realize anything of the sort, but even if he'd wanted to convey this to Caelus, Nathan's bonds wouldn't have let him. But apparently, he didn't need any encouragement from Benjamin to keep talking.

"Yes, that's right," Caelus continued. "The three triplets, born in the underground chamber of Shambhala. And it's here that your mother died. She was so weak."

Benjamin felt the first strong emotion he'd felt since the bonds had been placed on him by Nathan. He felt anger.

"It was here that your destiny was formed," Caelus continued. "Here that the keys were bonded to each of you. The Xanadu key was for Phoebe here. The Bangkok key was Cory's. And the final key—the Shambhala key—that was yours, Benjamin. The key that would bring everything together. The key that would seal the other two once they were joined."

"Really, Caelus," the woman who must be Gaea said. "Must we go on with this needless history lesson? The boy will only be killed when we're through with him." She looked at Benjamin, and hatred poured out of her eyes.

"The boy should know how important he is," Caelus

said. "It is why we've gone to all this trouble, isn't it?"

"Then perhaps we should focus on that," Nathan said.

Benjamin saw Gaea smile at Nathan, and it dawned on him that Nathan may actually be her son. He knew Caelus was Nathan's father, but Nathan had never mentioned who his mother was.

"My child is so wise," Gaea cooed at Nathan, confirming Benjamin's suspicions. And then she narrowed her eyes once again. "Let us just focus on what we need to tell this boy before we are through with him. And through with Phoebe." She glared at Phoebe who shrank under her gaze.

"I will tell the story as I see fit," Caelus said.

Through his fog, Benjamin noticed Nathan's displeasure at being silenced, and then he felt a ray of hope. He'd been able to turn his head, just the slightest bit, to get a better sidelong look at Nathan. Almost imperceptibly, he moved it back, hoping no one had noticed.

"Phoebe has known about this day forever," Caelus said. He looked into Benjamin's eyes. "But you were different. We didn't even know where you were until after the Emerald Tablet woke. And when it spoke, we heard it. And we knew the time the oracle foresaw was upon us."

"It was the birth of the triplets that started the entire chain of events," Caelus said. "It began the weakening of the shields. It caused the keys to be hidden around the earth in space and time. It started the new age of the telegens—when telegens would once again rule the world."

Benjamin watched Phoebe as Caelus spoke, and swore he saw pride in her face. How could she be proud of this monster? Caelus was nothing but a power-crazy lunatic.

"We searched for years for you," Caelus said. "And

 148

even after Kennias Burton approached us with his ramblings of your importance, we still didn't believe him. But when he reported back after the Emerald Tablet, we knew. The second child had been found."

"It is actually thanks to you and to my son, Nathan, that Cory was ever found," Caelus said. "He may well have rotted away in the past, though I don't think the keys would have allowed that to happen." Caelus walked to the center pedestal, and it was the first time Benjamin thought to look for the keys.

They sat in the center, raised up from the base, and glowed a faint green even now in their idle state. Had the keys controlled everything? Had the Emerald Tablet?

"But the keys have been kind to us," Caelus said. "Only two of the triplets are required for their strength to be used. Two shall do the task for which they were destined. The sole purpose of the keys is to bring down the shields. And in just a few minutes, you and Phoebe shall do just that."

Benjamin struggled to open his mouth and respond, and his attempt was rewarded.

"You can go to hell," Benjamin said.

Caelus laughed even as Benjamin felt the bonds tighten once more around him.

"Let him speak, Nathan," Caelus said. "Reduce the force of your bonds."

Nathan frowned but did as Caelus instructed, and Benjamin felt his body relax for the first time since the constraints had been put in place.

"Why should I help bring down the shields?" Benjamin asked. It was the question he'd asked himself just about every day since he found out who he really was. Actually, he'd asked himself why he should keep the shields in place. But the motivation was the same. Was the removal of the shields the right thing to do?

Caelus laughed again. "My dear son, you don't have a choice. With the bonds holding you in place, you will simply do as you are instructed. But I'll answer your question anyway." He put his fingers to his chin as he pondered the answer. "The shields should be brought down because their time is over. They should be brought down because for tens of thousands of years they have held millions of telegens in prison. They should be brought down because humans are weak and need control. Look at the state of the world today. Just look at it," Caelus demanded, and he cast in front of Benjamin's eyes a holographic display of the world.

The image zoomed and flashed to show poverty. Starvation. Famine. It shifted and focused on war and all its aftereffects. He saw genocide. Holocaust. Murder. Thievery. Abuse. As the images shifted, Benjamin's stomach turned, and he felt the urge to look away. But he forced himself to watch. He needed to know the truth about the future.

"This is what Earth has become," Caelus said. "This is what humans have resorted to. They need guidance. They are simply not mentally equipped to handle living in this world unguided."

"But what's to say you're the right person to guide them?" Benjamin asked. He couldn't argue with the images he'd been shown. But would anything be different with the Atlantian rulers in place?

"History takes us back twenty thousand years ago, Benjamin," Caelus said.

The holographic images shifted and Benjamin realized he was now viewing Earth's past. Images showed humans living in peace. Carrying food to temples. Worshipping their gods.

"These images are totally biased," Benjamin said. "You've only shown the horrors of today's world, and only peace in the past."

"Is it really any different?" Caelus asked. "Can you honestly tell me the images you saw don't reflect Earth as you know it? Can you?"

Benjamin didn't respond. Everything he'd seen was accurate. But Earth had lots of awesome qualities too. Not every human lived in poverty or fear.

Caelus sighed. "If not for the humans of Earth, than for the telegens of Atlantis. That alone is reason to bring down the shields. The fact that Gaea and I will take control of the earth, Lemuria, and Atlantis is simply a side note. The people of Atlantis must be freed. The Emerald Tablet itself has commanded it."

Benjamin's head spun, and if he'd had the self control to sit, he would have. But as it was, he stood in place and looked at the keys. What did they want him to do? But it seemed the keys would never have the chance to respond.

Gaea stomped her foot down, and the room shook. Even Caelus appeared to shrink under her fury. "Enough time has been wasted! This talk is pointless. Proceed now!" she commanded.

Caelus looked at her but didn't reply. Looking back at Benjamin, he narrowed his eyes. "Yes, the time has come for your destiny to be fulfilled."

Nathan cleared his throat.

"Yes, Nathan?" Caelus asked.

"When we are finished, will you release the bonds you've placed on me?" Nathan asked. "Will you allow me to continue on the path we discussed?"

"Path?" Caelus said. "Ah, yes. Your quest. Your blood quest. Yes, you may continue. In fact you are doing both yourself and me a favor, for it has been foretold that a child of mine shall kill me too. Kill them all," Caelus said. "And you may start with Benjamin Holt."

Nathan smiled and fear shot through Benjamin down to his feet. He knew he'd better come up with something pretty darned quick, or he'd be dead.

"Kill them all except Phoebe, that is," Nathan corrected him. "Remember what we discussed?"

"Ah, yes," Caelus said. "You may do what you want with Phoebe. I couldn't care less. Marry her as you want. Or kill her. It makes no difference to me."

"Father!" Phoebe's face turned ashen.

Caelus laughed. "Father. A name I've had to put up with for thousands of years from all sorts of worthless offspring. All to wait for the birth of the triplets."

"But, Father," Phoebe said, and Benjamin saw tears in her wide eyes. "I thought you loved me. You cared for me after my family was killed."

"I killed your family, silly girl," Caelus said. "If Nathan wants you for his toy, then why should I stop that?"

Phoebe looked like she was caught between clawing his eyes out and running for the door, but from the way she froze, Benjamin knew invisible bonds had been placed around her. They were in the same boat now. Helpless and completely subject to the will of others.

Benjamin didn't know what would happen next. After the shields came down. And they would come down. He knew it as sure as he knew Phoebe was his true blood sister. How was he ever going to explain this one back home?

Against his will, he found himself moving forward—to the pedestal. Phoebe came too, up to the other side, and when he looked at her, their eyes met.

"I'm sorry."

He heard her telepathic thought and saw it in her eyes.

"It's okay," Benjamin replied with telepathy. He smiled. And then he had a brief glimmer of hope. Their telepathy had worked. And if their telepathy had worked, then maybe he'd be able to contact Cory. Maybe the power of the keys would lend itself to Benjamin and aid in the telepathy. He had to try. Even as his hand was raised up to the pedestal, he called out to Cory.

"Cory," he said. *"Can you hear me? Please hear me."*

His hand lowered onto the middle key—the one which had stayed in Shambhala all along. Phoebe's hand rested on the Xanadu key, and once both of their hands were in place, the three keys burst into illumination.

"Benjamin!"

He heard the voice and fought not to smile. It had worked.

"We're in Shambhala. In the cavern. The keys. The shields are coming down. We need help."

And then the thrumming began. And the glowing intensified. And all thoughts of telepathic conversations disappeared. He felt Phoebe's mind in his own. He felt her hurt. Her shame. Her sorrow. At least he'd had over a year to deal with the truth. Her world had turned upside down only minutes ago.

Benjamin tried to peel his eyes off the keys—to see Caelus or Gaea. But he found he couldn't. And in his mind, he thought about the shields. And the Atlantians. And even though part of him fought to stop it, another part fought to bring it on. To lower the shields and raise the continents. The time had come. He felt no such battle in Phoebe's mind. She wanted the shields destroyed. She'd wanted it her entire life. It was what she'd been taught. The part of his mind that fought to keep the shields in place weakened. It couldn't compete against the stronger forces.

The chamber shook around Benjamin, and the earth groaned. Pieces of the ceiling showered down on them, but he couldn't move, and even if he'd been able to, he didn't think he would have. He knew the chamber would not destroy him. The keys protected both him and Phoebe.

The shaking seemed to go on for hours, though Benjamin had no idea how long it really lasted. And when it was finally over, he still felt the tremors. The earth above needed to adjust to her new shape.

Benjamin and Phoebe fell to the floor, all constraining bonds released. Benjamin just had time to glance at Caelus and Gaea as they embraced and teleported away. And then he thought about Nathan.

His mind flew to Phoebe, but he remembered Nathan didn't intend to kill her. He was going to marry her which in Benjamin's opinion was a fate worse than death. Nathan had to die.

That's when Benjamin saw Cory. He'd gotten the message and made it to the chamber. Relief flooded through Benjamin as Cory advanced on Nathan, who apparently had not been expecting his arrival. And then Benjamin saw Joey Duncan. And Heidi.

Nathan turned and froze; Benjamin almost saw Nathan's well-thought-out plans crumbling before his eyes. Doubt clouded over on his face. He surveyed the group, and must've had second thoughts, because before anyone had time to stop him, he grabbed Phoebe around the waist and teleported out of the chamber.

CHAPTER 20

BENJAMIN TAKES A DETOUR

Nobody attempted to go after Nathan and Phoebe. To be fair, Benjamin did at least think about it. But even if he'd decided it was the right thing to do, he felt like he'd have trouble levitating a feather.

"Are you okay?" Cory helped Benjamin sit up.

"Yeah, I'm fine," Benjamin lied. The throbbing in his head matched the sounds of the earth above. "You guys made it here just in time. Nathan was just about to kill me."

"Kill you!" Heidi came closer.

Benjamin noticed she didn't squat down next to him. She actually didn't even get within touching range, which was probably a good thing because Benjamin was so happy to see her, he felt like grabbing her and hugging her—at the very least.

"What about that girl?" Joey said. It was serious Joey talking, not fun, mischievous Joey. "Is she in danger? Should we worry about her?"

Benjamin shook his head. "No. Nathan's planning to marry her, not kill her."

Cory's eyes bore into Benjamin. "Was that who I think it was, little brother?"

Benjamin nodded.

"She's a member of the ruling family," Joey said. "I've seen her in the last few months of surveillance."

 156

Benjamin nodded. "She is a member of the ruling family. And she's also our sister."

"The third of the triplets," Cory finished. "And on the wrong side just like the oracle said."

"And now the shields are down," Heidi said.

Joey crossed his arms over his chest. "The shields couldn't stay up forever. We knew that. Now we just deal with it."

"Which leads us to our whole reason for being in Atlantis in the first place," Cory said.

"Which is what?" Benjamin asked. He still had no clue what Joey and Cory were doing there.

"To take over the government, of course," Joey said.

Heidi raised an eyebrow. "You took over Atlantis? Just you two?"

Joey brushed back his hair behind his ears. "Caelus and Gaea never planned to stay there for long. We only sped up the process. They've been moving stuff out for the last couple months."

Benjamin studied them. "Let me get this straight. If you two took over Atlantis, then who's there right now?"

Joey looked at Benjamin like he'd just fallen out of an alien space ship. "Helios and Selene, of course," he said. "Who do you think masterminded the whole thing?"

"They did?" Benjamin said.

Cory shrugged. "Sure. Do you think the two of us planned to take over an entire continent for ourselves?"

"It would be pretty cool," Joey said. "It could be like our own little amusement park."

They laughed, and Heidi sighed deeply for effect.

"What?" Cory said.

"Aren't you making sort of light of it?" Heidi asked. "I mean isn't government upheaval a pretty big thing?"

"Well, of course," Joey said. "And we've been working and planning for months now."

The ceiling above them shuddered again, which silenced their conversation immediately. It sounded like the entire earth was going to fall down on top of them.

"Maybe we should get out of here," Heidi said when the grumbling sounds took a break.

Benjamin stood up, and even though he figured his legs would collapse under him, they managed to hold him.

"Probably a good idea," Joey said. "Lord Commander Helios did tell us to get back."

Cory laughed. "He's not that bad."

Joey gave a huge eye roll. "Yes, he is. Even Selene agrees."

"He just follows the rules," Cory said.

"Which need to be broken from time to time," Joey said.

"The earth is going to be in utter chaos," Cory said.

"Not surprising since they now have two new continents to deal with," Joey said.

"Two new continents filled with super-humans," Cory added, and then sighed. "We have a lot of work ahead of us."

Maybe the truth hadn't hit Benjamin yet, but he found that he just couldn't believe the shields had really come down. How would he have felt if he'd still been living back in Virginia, never aware of a place called Lemuria? And then, in just a few minutes time, to have history rewritten? Okay, essentially, that is what had happened to him two years ago when he'd found out about Atlantis and Lemuria in the first place. But he'd been one of the superhuman people. Not one of the normal ones.

"You guys go ahead," Benjamin said. "I'll meet you there."

"Why?" Joey said.

"I just want a couple more minutes," Benjamin said. The chamber seemed to be holding him. But then again, he was born here, right?

"I'll stay, too," Heidi said.

Joey shook his head. "Can't do that. King Helios will be ticked. We've already wasted too much time saving you from sure death."

"I'll stay with Benjamin and Heidi," Cory said. He looked around the chamber. "Just tell Helios we wanted to clean up a little."

Joey glanced around. "Helios might actually believe that. The place is trashed."

Did Cory feel the need to stay for a couple minutes, also? Or was he just trying to be nice?

After Joey teleported away, Benjamin got up and attempted to walk across the room.

"I don't think I could have teleported to Atlantis even if I'd wanted to." Benjamin leaned on a column for support. "I might have to walk back."

"I'm sure it won't be long before somebody builds a bridge connecting Atlantis and Europe," Cory said. "They're only a couple miles apart."

Benjamin circled the chamber and then walked to the center. To the pedestal. The three keys of Shambhala sat in the top, still glowing with power. Cory and Heidi walked over to join him.

"So what about these?" Cory said.

Benjamin shrugged. "They did what they were meant to do. They brought down the shields."

"But still, do you feel the power coming off them?" Heidi said.

"We should take them with us," Cory said.

"Won't they be safer here?" Benjamin asked. He wasn't sure he wanted to carry that much power around. They'd brought down the shields. And sure, even though Nathan and Caelus had controlled him while it happened, he knew deep in his heart that if he hadn't at least kind of wanted the shields to come down, they wouldn't have. Whatever they found above, Benjamin was responsible. He'd re-shaped the earth.

"No." Heidi shook her head. "They need to come."

"Heidi's right," Cory said. He reached in and placed his hand on the first key, the one from Bangkok. "This is my key," he said. "It feels…familiar…to me." He tried to pry the key up, but it didn't budge.

"We both need to get the keys out," Benjamin said. "That's what Helios told me last year." He reached in and grabbed both the center key and the second key—the one from Xanadu. Phoebe's key. As smooth as they'd gone in, all three keys slid from the pedestal.

Benjamin stared down at his hands. He took a deep breath. And then another. He could feel their strength. Their power flowed into him, restoring every bit of his energy which had been drained earlier.

He looked over at Cory and felt the power in him, too. But even with Heidi here, the triangle wasn't complete.

 160

The Xanadu key needed its owner—Phoebe. And she needed her key.

Maybe postponing facing reality seemed like a good idea in the short term, but they needed to get back to Atlantis. They all grabbed hands and teleported together.

Except they didn't end up back in Atlantis.

They arrived in a stone room that looked really similar to the one Nathan had teleported Benjamin to on his way to Lemuria.

"Crap!" Benjamin said.

"Your doing?" Cory said.

"Hardly," Benjamin snapped. "This is the same place Nathan brought me."

"But it isn't Nathan this time. I simply borrowed the room from him."

Benjamin scowled even before he turned to see the speaker.

"Kronos," he said. The god of time. It was a young Kronos. Not as young as Benjamin had ever seen him, but keeping track of his age was a full time job. "What is it with you guys stealing people when they teleport?"

"Lord Shaneeswara," Heidi said.

"How nice," Kronos said. "Some Hindu respect." He snapped his fingers and changed her into a traditional Indian sari.

Benjamin glared at Kronos. "Change her clothes back."

"What?" Kronos feigned shock. "You don't like to see your girlfriend dressed up in beautiful clothes?"

"She's not my girlfriend," Benjamin said before he could give it any thought.

Heidi looked at him, and he could see the hurt in her

eyes. But he'd only said the truth. He may want Heidi to be his girlfriend. Okay, he really did want Heidi to be his girlfriend. But technically, she wasn't.

"You're still going out with Josh, aren't you?" he asked, trying to claw his way up out of the hole he'd dug for himself. "Well, aren't you?"

"Technically," Heidi said. "But as soon as I get back to Lemuria, I'm going to break up with him."

"Get back to Lemuria," Kronos said, and chucked to himself. "You think you're getting back to Lemuria?"

"Don't listen to him, little brother," Cory said. "He's just trying to make us doubt ourselves."

"Little brother," Kronos said, laughing all the harder. "How endearing. Now let's see. Who really is the younger one?"

"What do you want, Kronos?" Benjamin asked. "We don't have all day."

"But of course you do," Kronos said. "With time on your side, you have all the days you want. Just like your friends Iva and Andy." Kronos put his finger to his mouth, as if deep in thought. "Now let me see. Didn't they have the pleasure of staying with my grandson Apollo for an entire year? I wouldn't mind a year's company. Think of all the games of Tic-Tac-Toe we could play."

Benjamin gritted his teeth. "We aren't staying here for a year."

"I didn't say I wanted your company, dear Benjamin," Kronos said. "Heidi could stay with me."

Benjamin put his arm around Heidi and pulled her close. "Heidi is not staying here with you for a year."

"Just a second. You said she wasn't your girlfriend,"

Kronos said. "And now, just look at you two lovebirds." He sighed. "Young love. What could be sweeter? But not to worry. I don't want to stay here for a year either. If you haven't heard, the shields are down. I can roam the earth as a free man. Or a free god. It's all just a matter of time." And then he laughed, amused at his own play on words.

"Get to the point, Kronos. Why did you divert us?" Cory asked.

Kronos grew serious. His eyes darkened, and he almost seemed to grow in size. "Because I want to know how you did it? How did you bring down the shields?"

Benjamin's face froze. How had Kronos known? And if Kronos knew Benjamin was responsible for the shields coming down, then everyone would know. Both Atlantians and Lemurians. And humans.

"I'm not sure what you're talking about," Benjamin lied.

"Don't play stupid with me, Benjamin Holt," Kronos said. "I want to know." He rose and moved closer to Benjamin. Benjamin shrank back, pulling Heidi with him. Without thinking, he pushed her behind him.

"Oh, leave him alone, Kronos," a female voice said.

Kronos stopped moving and turned at the sound of the voice. "My dear, sweet Ananya. Did I invite you here today?"

"I don't require an invitation," Ananya said. "And why is it that every time I find you, you're playing tricks on telegens? When will you grow up?"

Kronos laughed, but he did back off. "I hope I never grow up. I've seen myself old." He shuddered. "Now, though, with the gates of Atlantis once again open to me,

I'll quickly be able to resolve that."

"Back to the homeland?" Ananya said. "Back for immortality and the hope of no death?" She laughed. "You know the prophecy."

"Prophecies!" Kronos said. "They're a bunch of hogwash."

"You think so?" Ananya asked. "It seems to me that many of them have come to pass."

Kronos paused, and then sat back on a chair in the center of the room. "You know how Benjamin did it. Tell me, dear Ananya."

Ananya laughed and brushed back her hair. "What is there to tell? It has been foretold since the shields went up that two would bring them down," she said. "It's a perfect example of a prophecy coming true."

Benjamin relaxed, realizing Ananya had basically saved him from Kronos' control. Whatever the relationship between Ananya and Kronos, Ananya always seemed to have the upper hand.

Ananya and Kronos proceeded to start bickering, so Benjamin edged away. He moved off to the side of the chamber, and Cory and Heidi followed. They didn't talk, because even though they weren't part of the conversation, Benjamin still wanted to hear as much of it as he could. Benjamin walked over to the nearby table. He hadn't noticed it before, but in the center of the wooden table sat a green crystal ball as large as a melon. He'd seen the sphere before when he's visited Kronos' temple in Rome. What had Kronos called it? Oh yeah—the Temporal Orb.

"Hey," he said reaching out for it. "I don't think this was here a min—"

 164

"Don't touch it, Benjamin!" Ananya yelled across the chamber, but it was too late. Benjamin felt the Temporal Orb vibrate under his touch, and the world crunched and compressed around them.

CHAPTER 21

A Temple to a Baboon and Other Anomalies

"Perfect," Kronos said. "Perfect."

"You planned this." Ananya's voice wavered. "Didn't you?" She tried to hold her hands calmly at her side, but she looked like she wanted to strike Kronos.

Benjamin lifted his hands off the Temporal Orb as discreetly as he could, hoping that maybe everyone would forget he'd been responsible for whatever had just happened.

"What did you do, Benjamin?" Heidi asked. She moved closer to him as the room settled.

"We've temporally phased," Cory said. "I can tell."

"Brilliant deduction," Kronos said. "And what gave it away? The crunching sounds, or has your heads-up display re-synchronizing?"

Benjamin immediately checked his own heads-up display and gasped. "We're ten years in the future."

"One hundred-and-thirty phases of the moon to be exact," Kronos said. "I never grew totally accustomed to that horrible Gregorian calendar. Dropping days. Adding minutes. Months with different days. How much more confusing could they make things?"

"Why did you bring us to the future?" Cory asked. "I thought you wanted to live free now that the shields were down."

"I do, my dear little Spartan," Kronos said. "But first we need to see what the future will look like. What better way to plan my strategy than to see the state of the world? With that knowledge, I'll be able to plot out my own plan to rule the world."

"Rule the world?" Ananya said. "You want to rule the world?"

"You may have some competition," Benjamin said. "You're forgetting about Caelus and Gaea, aren't you?"

"My mother and father?" Kronos laughed so hard, he grabbed his chair to keep from falling over. "They won't be around. That's one thing I know for sure."

Ananya raised her eyebrow. "Oh, do you now?" she said. "Why don't we just go on out and see what the world has in store for us?"

Kronos regained his composure and stood up, wiping tears from the corners of his eyes. "I couldn't have made a better suggestion myself." He headed for one of the stone walls, and with a flick of his hand, it vanished.

Sand caked under Benjamin's feet, and heat drove across the desert in waves. And in the distance, Benjamin saw the pyramids—as in the Great Pyramid. They were in Egypt. He'd been here last summer, but everything had been crumbling to bits.

Ten years in the future, everything was not crumbling to bits. Every single temple Benjamin saw radiated in the sun. They were painted in gaudy colors and had gold and marble accents. They probably looked better than they had three thousand years ago.

Kronos smiled. "Well, things are off to a nice start."

And then he looked across the network of stone and rage crossed his face. "Why is the Temple of Hapi bigger than mine?" he bellowed. "He's a baboon! And Isis!" Look at her temple. She's a worthless goddess. And what—tell me—what is that horrible monstrosity in the center of everything?"

Benjamin wished Gary were here. He had no idea what Kronos was griping about. Hapi? There was a temple to a baboon?

"It's on the site of the old necropolis," Ananya said. "They've rebuilt it."

"Everything completely overshadows my temple," Kronos said. "Even the temple of Isis." He considered this. "But that may not be a bad thing."

Ananya ignored him and looked back to the necropolis.

"We should head down there," Cory said. "But we're going to stand out."

Kronos didn't even turn. His face held its enraged expression even as he flicked his wrist, and their clothing all changed.

"How do you do that?" Heidi asked, looking down at her clothes.

"Millennia of practice," Kronos said. "And just for the record, I go by Thoth around these parts. Egyptian God of Time. Now let's go."

Cory led the way, and Kronos didn't argue. He was probably too mad to think about anything but the size of his temple just now.

"Stick together," Ananya said. "This place has a hideous feel."

Heidi nodded. "I feel it too, ever since Kronos opened the chamber."

"Thoth," Kronos said.

Heidi ignored him. "I recognize a presence."

"Gaea?" Benjamin asked.

Heidi nodded. "She's nearby, and I'm willing to bet Caelus is too."

Benjamin's mind flew to Phoebe.

"She may be here," Heidi said, responding to his unanswered question. "You have to be prepared for it."

"We all need to be prepared for anything," Cory said. "Phoebe. Nathan. Anything."

Benjamin stayed quiet, and threw up a mind block around all of them. Except Kronos. Benjamin figured Kronos could manage on his own.

As they walked across the sand, people shuffled by with their heads down, moving along as if they didn't want to risk any chance of being noticed.

Maybe Cory didn't pick up on this, because he kept trying to ask questions.

"Can you tell me what's in that building?" Cory asked a man he managed to stop.

The man barely lifted his head as he turned to look to the atrocity where Cory pointed. And then he looked back down and ran before Cory had a chance to say anything else.

The next person Cory stopped gave about the same response, except he shoved Cory off him before he went.

Cory grabbed the arm of the third person. "What is in that building?" he demanded of the man.

The man shook like a leaf, but Cory didn't release his

grip.

"Please, let me go," the man said. "I haven't done anything wrong. I swear it in the names of Caelus and Gaea, may they live forever and rule so generously." He made a strange motion with his hand and his forehead.

"We're not going to hurt you," Cory said. "We just want a few answers."

"I know nothing," the man said. "And if you have any brains in your head, you'll know nothing also. And be happy about it."

"Are Caelus and Gaea in that building?" Benjamin asked.

The man looked at the building and then studied his shoes. "They are the wisest and the kindest rulers man ever desired," he said. "May they live forever."

"You already said that," Benjamin said.

"Let him go," Ananya said, and Cory did.

The man ran off in the opposite direction he'd been heading only minutes before.

"These people are scared to death," Ananya said.

Kronos walked up to join them. "They've managed to at least keep a tight fist around here," he said. "Mind you, that's no excuse for the size of my temple, but it is encouraging."

"Encouraging!" Heidi said. "How can you say that? Did you feel that man's emotions?"

Kronos shrugged. "Felt pretty good to me."

"You're a monster," Heidi said. "You deserve whatever fate has in store for you. I hope you are cut to little bits and buried in the earth."

They reached the outer wall of the necropolis. Benjamin stared at it and his face fell.

"There's no way we're getting through there," he said. "It's huge and thick and impossible to climb. And I don't think we can dare risk teleporting to the other side."

"Maybe you don't," Kronos said, and vanished.

Ananya frowned. "We're better off without him."

"So what do we do?" Heidi asked.

"Well, I don't mean to contradict you, little brother," Cory said, "but I don't think it's impossible."

Benjamin noticed Cory studying the wall.

"You forget I fought in the Spartan army for fifteen years," Cory said. "Breaking though defenses used to be my specialty."

"So what are you thinking, little brother?" Benjamin asked. Truthfully, he didn't mind Cory calling him little brother, though he had no intention of telling Cory that.

"It's all about having a strategy," Cory said.

Cory found a hiding spot next to the Sphinx. They sat watching people come in and out of the necropolis for an hour. It seemed Caelus and Gaea commanded quite a bit of ceremony. Guards marched around the gates. Sentries held positions on the top of the wall. The longer Benjamin watched, the more he doubted Cory would be able to find them a way in.

"Okay, I got it," Cory said.

"You do?" Benjamin asked.

"Did you doubt me?" Cory said.

Benjamin raised an eyebrow. "You haven't told us your plan yet."

Cory leaned close and strengthened the mind block around the four of them. "Here's what I'm thinking."

"No way," Heidi said before he'd gone any farther.

"It's the only way," Cory said. "You've been watching, too."

"I'm not going to do it," Heidi said. "And that's final." She turned. "Right, Ananya."

Ananya sighed. "Cory may have a point. And we do need to get inside."

"Would someone mind filling me in on the plan?" Benjamin said. "You know, all of us aren't as good at telepathy as Heidi."

"You would be if you ever practiced," Heidi said.

"I do practice," Benjamin replied. But inside, he knew Heidi was right. He made a mental note to practice telepathy more if he returned alive. "Regardless, I still need to know the plan."

"It's not the plan," Heidi said. "I'm not doing it."

"Doing what?" Benjamin asked.

"Dressing up as a priestess," Heidi said. She nodded to Cory. "He wants Ananya and me to dress up like priestesses of Isis."

"The only women who've been admitted to the Necropolis in the last hour are priestesses of Isis," Cory said.

Heidi sighed. "Okay, let's hear the whole plan."

"Great," Cory said. "First, we'll sneak over to the Temple of Isis and find some clothes for Heidi and Ananya to wear. Next, we knock out a couple guards and change into their clothes. Once we've done that, the rest should be easy. We just walk up to the gates of the Necropolis and get permission to enter."

"And what happens once we're inside?" Heidi asked. "Why are all those priestesses going in there anyway?"

Ananya put her hand on Heidi's arm. "We won't be staying long enough to find out. And anyway, we'll have Benjamin and Cory to protect us."

They looked over at Benjamin and Cory, and Benjamin gave his best the-crap's-not-scared-out-of-me smile. He didn't think either Heidi or Ananya was fooled, but the determined look on Cory's face reassured even him. And so they walked over to the Temple of Isis.

Five guards stood at the front door, so they headed around back.

"It's about time you got here." Lulu hovered mid-air at the back of the temple and scowled.

"What are you doing here?" Benjamin asked. Did Lulu turn up everywhere?

Lulu shrugged. "Came to play a few games of Drop Squash with Cory. Ready?"

Cory narrowed his eyes. "I'm not really sure now's the time."

Lulu snapped her fingers. "And speaking of time, how about we get this little time traveling adventure moving into full gear."

"You're here to help us?" Benjamin asked.

Lulu put up her hand. "Don't ask. Just suffice it to say I'm way better than Jack at time traveling. And he owes me big time this time. Have you seen this place? It sucks."

"What do we need help with?" Cory said. "We have it under control."

Lulu put her hands on her little hips. "Do you, now? So then tell me, once you get inside the temple and deal with the guards and do all the other little stuff you've planned out, how are you going to mask your DNA?"

"What do you mean: mask our DNA?" Benjamin said.

Lulu looked at him like he was an idiot. "You know, aside from time, other things change in the future. Technology gets better. And if you take one step inside that god-awful necropolis without masking your DNA, you're totally hosed. Like caught in two seconds hosed."

"Seriously?" Benjamin said.

Lulu smirked. "Yeah, seriously, Einstein." She held out her hand and something teleported into it. "This here is a DNA de-phaser. A couple tweaks from this, and you'll be good to go."

Benjamin looked at Heidi who nodded.

"Okay, fine," he said. "So you de-phase our DNA. What do we need to do?"

He'd hardly gotten the words out when Lulu disappeared and reappeared next to his ear. And then he felt something shoving inside it. He jerked his head away.

"Stop moving," she hollered. At least it felt like she hollered. She was right next to his ear.

"What are you doing?"

"I told you," She said and shoved the de-phaser in his ear again. But this time Benjamin tried to hold still, and in a few seconds it was over. She levitated over until she was right in front of his face staring at him.

"What?" he said.

"What do you think?" Lulu said.

He rubbed his ear. "That hurt."

She lifted her lip in a snarl.

Benjamin sighed. "Fine. Thank you."

Lulu crossed her arms. "You're welcome. So who's next?"

 174

Once they were all de-phased, Lulu showed them the best door to sneak into the temple of Isis. "It's how all the priestesses sneak in and out after hours. Naughty priestesses."

"How did you know to come here anyway?" Benjamin asked.

Lulu flipped around and stopped in front of his face. "You asked Jack to ask me to meet you here. Once again, everyone assumes I run errands for a living."

"In the past?" Benjamin said. He wanted to make sure he got it right.

"Duh," Lulu said. "Anyway, there are two guards around the corner."

"I'll sneak up and hit them over the head," Cory said.

"Why don't we just do this?" Heidi asked, and a second later the two guards collapsed to the floor.

"Good thinking," Ananya said, smiling at Heidi.

"What did you do?" Cory asked. If Benjamin hadn't known they were in a hurry, he would have sworn Cory was disappointed.

"I knocked them out with telepathy," Heidi said. "Once I considered knocking out Ryan Jordan one time just to see if it would work."

They dragged the unconscious guards into a small room, and within minutes, Benjamin and Cory had exchanged clothes with the men. Benjamin's uniform looked huge on him. Why hadn't he spent a little more time working out?

Cory motioned with his head. "How long will they be asleep?"

Heidi looked at them, and they started breathing

deeper. "I just added an extra level for them to break out of, so I'd say we have a good two hours before they even think about getting up."

"Great," Cory said. "That should give us enough time to get in the Necropolis and see what's going on."

"So you really do have rocks in your head?" Lulu said.

"What do you mean?" Cory asked.

"The Necropolis," Lulu said. "You're really gonna go through with it?"

"Of course," Cory said. "We have to."

"Just for the record, did you happen to notice how few people actually come out?" Lulu said.

Cory thought for a moment. "Less than the number that went in, but I figured they worked inside."

"Think again, rock-head," Lulu said. "Why do you think it's called the Necropolis? Because it's a great place to work? I'm outta here." And she teleported or time traveled or whatever away.

"Necropolis means 'City of the Dead,'" Ananya said. "They're sacrificing people in there."

"They're what?" Benjamin said.

"Shhhh!" Ananya said. "Sacrificing people."

"And you didn't think to mention this before?" Benjamin asked.

"We needed to get inside," Ananya said. "I didn't see how the information was relevant. Anyway, Heidi knew."

Benjamin whirled on Heidi. "You knew about this?"

"Why do you think I didn't want to dress up as a priestess?" Heidi said.

Benjamin shook his head. "This changes everything. Heidi and Ananya can stay here while Cory and I go inside."

"I'm not staying here," Heidi said.

"Yes, you are," Benjamin replied.

"No, I'm not," Heidi said. "I have just as much right to go in there as you do."

"Stop arguing," Cory said. "The fact of the matter is that we need Heidi and Ananya to even get inside. Otherwise, we won't have any reason to go in."

Benjamin didn't say anything. Even though Cory may be right, it still irked him that now he'd have to spend all his energy protecting Heidi.

"You know," she said to him with a smile. "I'm not that helpless."

He didn't reply. He figured that if he didn't have anything nice to say, then he shouldn't say anything at all.

CHAPTER 22

THINGS CAN
ALWAYS GET WORSE

The DNA de-phaser worked like a charm. They walked right out of the temple of Isis through the front door. The sensors clicked green, and the guards didn't suspect a thing; they even smiled at Benjamin and Cory. And getting into the Necropolis worked as well as Cory had suggested. Benjamin held Heidi's arm as if he were guiding her, and Cory did the same for Ananya. The priestesses they'd seen had been under the control of their guards. When they passed the guards at the main gate, they leered at Heidi and Ananya. Benjamin felt Heidi shudder under his grip.

"What's wrong?" he asked.

"Those men," she said. "They're horrible."

"That's probably part of the job description," Benjamin said, hoping to lighten her mood. It didn't work.

As soon as they were out of sight of the guards, Cory and Benjamin led them into a side room and Cory slid the door shut. And then Heidi started to cry.

Benjamin slid his arm around her. "It's okay, Heidi. Everything's going to be fine."

"It's this place," she said. "Can't you feel it? I feel it deep in my mind. I can't even begin to describe the horrors that go on here. The only reason for this entire place is to build fear. Fear of the Necropolis builds fear of the rulers and

 178

increases their control." She looked back in the direction they'd come from. "Those men bring the women to sacrifice them in front of the rulers."

"We are not going to let anything happen to you," Cory said with a certainty in his voice that matched how Benjamin felt.

"I know," Heidi said, wiping her tears. "But I just can't help myself. Do you know how many dead, tortured souls I can sense?"

"Block them out, Heidi," Ananya said. "Or they will drive you mad. You must turn off your mind to all emotions around you."

Cory cleared his throat. "And I don't mean to hurry you, but can you do it soon? We should get moving. Lulu said the de-phasing wouldn't last forever."

Heidi regained her composure, and they set out along a back hallway. There was no reason to sneak around; they did have a valid reason for being in the Necropolis. And if someone found them somewhere they shouldn't be, Benjamin figured they could just lie and say they got lost.

Heidi picked the location of a hidden room that overlooked the ruling chamber from a guard's mind. From it, they could see everything, but it still hid them from view.

Benjamin moved over to the wall and peered through slats between the stones. "I see Caelus," he said. "And Gaea." And then his heart started pounding.

"What's wrong, little brother?" Cory said.

But Benjamin couldn't reply. He tried but found his mouth wouldn't work.

"Benjamin," Ananya said.

He sank to the ground and put his back to the wall.

  179

Cory rushed over to the wall and looked through a different crack. "Nathan!" he said.

"And Phoebe," Benjamin managed to say. "She's older, but it's definitely her."

Benjamin turned back to the wall, and they all pressed their eyes to the slats, watching the room below.

The rulers sat facing them, and Benjamin could see Phoebe's face perfectly. She'd been beautiful, but now she only looked defeated. Her eyes sank low into their sockets, and her blond hair, once stunning and silky, hung like limp yarn. The dress she wore was exquisite, and her jewelry alone would have fed a starving continent for years. She sat next to Nathan, but he took no notice of her. Instead, he had his attention focused on the speakers in the room.

"But why must it always be bad news?" Caelus slammed his fist down on the side of his throne. "I do not want any more bad news. If I get any more bad news out of New Delphi, I will personally have every oracle brought here and sacrificed."

"But my Lord Caelus, she is my finest oracle," the speaker said. "We must take her foretelling and plan our future based on it."

Benjamin recognized the speaker after the first word. The golden god they'd met last summer. Apollo. He didn't seem to glow quite so much now.

"That oracle has been trouble since she was first placed in New Delphi," Nathan said. "She should have been executed ten years ago."

"The oracle is merely incorrect," Kronos said. But it was a different Kronos, not the one they'd traveled here with. Who knew where he even was? "There will be death

 180

and destruction by the thousands, but it will not fall on us."

"I'm happy to see someone looks for the positive angle," Caelus said. He glared back at Apollo. "I want the oracle brought before me. I would have her dare to speak her prophecies to my face."

"The oracles must not leave New Delphi," Apollo said. "They draw their power from the Omphalos and the surrounding rocks."

"Then you yourself admit they are worthless," Caelus said.

"Father," Nathan said. "Why don't I accompany Apollo back to New Delphi and execute this oracle myself? I would be more than happy to be away from my wife for such an important task."

Caelus looked at Phoebe and laughed. "Your wife. Worthless girl."

Phoebe cast her eyes downward, and Benjamin immediately felt her shame deep in his chest. Next to him, Cory tensed. Before giving any thought to it, he dared to send out a little comfort to her. He wanted to help this Phoebe, but they were ten years in the future, and Benjamin had no intention of staying. He had to return. But as soon as he sent the feelings to her, something inside him shifted. Like a mind block slipping away. He ignored it and sent a little bit more.

Phoebe's eyes widened, and she lifted her head. But then she must have realized what she was doing because she again cast her eyes down. But as Caelus, Nathan, Apollo, and Kronos continued to speak, Phoebe ever so slowly raised her head until she could just see to the cracks in the wall. Her eyes met Benjamin's and pleaded to him.

 181

Leave now, they said. *Leave while you still can.*

Benjamin saw it in her eyes; Phoebe had given up on life. He felt the anguish she'd experienced on a daily basis for the last ten years. She was a shell of the person she'd once been.

"I will not submit," Apollo said. "Iva will stay in New Delphi until the day she dies."

Iva! Benjamin's head snapped away from Phoebe and back to the speakers. Of course it was Iva. The best oracle in the world. Who else would it have been?

"Then you leave me no choice," Caelus said. He turned his head. "Nathan, you have my permission to go to New Delphi and execute this oracle unless she decides to change her prophecy."

Nathan smiled like he'd been waiting for this permission his whole life. "It will be my pleasure."

"We need to get to New Delphi!" Benjamin said. "They're going to kill Iva." He jumped to his feet and started for the door.

"Wait, little brother," Cory said. "We can't run off with our pants down. We need a plan."

"We don't have time for a plan," Benjamin said. "We need to go now."

Heidi got up and stood next to Benjamin. "He's right. We need to go now. There's no time to waste. Nathan intends to kill Iva whether she changes her prophecy or not."

Ananya shook her head. "I can sense Apollo is against Caelus. It may come down to a battle between Apollo and Nathan. He won't give up Iva without a fight."

"But where's New Delphi?" Heidi asked.

"Lulu would probably know," Benjamin said. "Too

bad she—"

The door opened, and three guards walked in.

"These must be the ones," the first guard said, and grabbed Benjamin before he had a chance to react.

The second guard grabbed Heidi and Ananya. "And these must be our priestesses," the guard said. "We've been waiting for you down the hall."

Benjamin struggled, but the guard held him fast. He scanned his mind around the room and found whatever de-phasing had been done to their DNA was gone. Had he messed it up when he'd sent his thoughts to Phoebe?

"Take your hands off them," Cory said, rushing the third and final guard, sending him crashing into the wall. The guard's neck cracked in a sickening way Benjamin felt pretty sure meant he'd broken it. Good thing at least one of them had battle experience.

Benjamin heard the alarm sounding even as five more guards rushed up. So much for maintaining a low profile. The last thing he remembered before slumping to the ground was seeing Heidi and Ananya. Heidi looked pretty much like a cornered bug about to be smashed, but Ananya remained calm. Calm in a way that didn't seem to fit in with their current predicament. Benjamin could only hope that was a good thing.

CHAPTER 23

BENJAMIN THINKS
ABOUT HIS DEATH

Benjamin woke up and saw Cory pacing. It only took a moment for Benjamin's eyes to adjust to the dark. It took a couple more seconds for his nose to adjust to the stench. Why did dark places always have to smell so bad?

"Where are we?" he asked, sitting up.

"Some kind of cell," Cory said. "I've tried telekinesis, and teleportation, but nothing's worked."

"How long have we been here?" Benjamin asked. Panic flooded through him as he remembered the conversation from the Necropolis ruling hall. They needed to get to New Delphi. Iva would die if they didn't.

"I woke up about an hour ago," Cory said. "My heads-up display seems to be jammed."

"Mine, too," Benjamin said, trying to adjust the device with no luck.

"Where are Heidi and Ananya?" Benjamin asked.

Cory shook his head. "I haven't had any contact with them."

Benjamin's chest tightened. "They'll get killed."

"They'll be okay," Cory said. "Ananya is resourceful. She may have a plan."

"So what do we do?" Benjamin asked. "Just sit here and wait?"

"I was hoping you'd have a couple ideas once you woke up," Cory said. "I can't even find a door to this cell."

Cory was right; there was no door. Only four smooth walls. They'd probably been teleported inside.

Benjamin reached out with his mind and looked for Heidi and Ananya. Nothing. He couldn't even sense if they were still alive.

"I've been trying the same thing every five minutes since we got here," Cory said. "They've got this cell tele-jammed pretty good."

"Have you tried anyone else?" Benjamin asked.

Cory shrugged. "Like who?"

"Like Phoebe," Benjamin said.

Cory gave him a pitying look. "Benjamin, you saw her. She's beyond help. She's been tortured and beaten down for ten years. Her mind is probably so closed up, nothing could reach it."

"I reached her earlier," Benjamin said. "Back in the throne room. I sent her some thoughts. And she got them. It's why she looked up at us in the first place."

"She never looked up," Cory said.

"She did," Benjamin replied. "She did it so nobody else would notice, but she did. She looked right at us."

Hope sprang into Cory's eyes. "Do you think you could reach her now?"

"I'm sure going to try," Benjamin said. He sat back down on the bench and closed his eyes. Phoebe had to be out there somewhere, and maybe, just maybe, the triplet link would be enough to break through the telejamming signals around the cell.

He made sure to send out thoughts only for her. He

didn't want the whole Necropolis alerted to his efforts. "*Phoebe,*" he said.

Nothing.

"*Phoebe.*"

Still nothing. Maybe Cory was right. Maybe there was no point. Phoebe probably didn't have any idea they'd even been captured. But he decided to try every five minutes, if for no other reason than to give him something to do.

Five minutes later gave the same response. Ten minutes also. After a half hour, a tray of food that looked like it had been stepped on was teleported into the room. Still, they sat down and devoured it.

"Split the last slice of bread with you?" Cory asked, picking up the knife to cut it.

Benjamin nodded as he thought about the irony of giving prisoners a knife. In a world of telekinesis and teleportation, knives weren't much of a threat. He was about to tell Cory the whole irony of the situation when his eye caught on a green piece of paper which had been tucked under the knife. He literally felt his heart speed up when he saw the three golden hearts etched on the paper. The same symbol which had been on the clues leading him on this whole adventure in the first place.

"Look," he said, reaching over to pick up the piece of paper.

"What is it?" Cory asked.

Benjamin explained about the three hearts symbol as he unwrapped the paper. The writing was microscopic, but Benjamin managed to read it anyway.

His breath caught. "She heard us."

"What does it say?" Cory asked.

"'As soon as the tray disappears, teleport directly below your cell. We will meet you there,'" Benjamin read. "This must be from Phoebe. She's must've been the one who left me all the messages in the first place. She heard us!"

"But who's 'we'?" Cory asked. "Phoebe and who?"

Benjamin shook his head. "I don't know."

"Then we shouldn't do it," Cory said. "I may be a trap. This could be a plan of Nathan's doing."

"It doesn't matter," Benjamin said. "We need to take our chances. It's this or nothing. And I'd rather face Nathan out there then be stuck in here like I'm part of a zoo."

Cory paused, thinking over the situation. Finally, he sighed. "Fine. We'll do it. But we stick together and we need to be prepared for anything." He reached back down and picked up the knife, tucking it into his belt. "And no more telepathy. We can't risk it."

Benjamin nodded, looking down on the tray for a weapon of his own. Aside from the empty plate, there was nothing. And then the tray disappeared.

With like minds, Benjamin and Cory grabbed hands and teleported down under the cell, and it worked. The telejamming signal must have been lifted for just long enough to get the tray out. And Cory and Benjamin.

They arrived in a hallway, and a hooded figure moved toward them. Cory pulled the knife, ready for anything, but Benjamin felt the familiar presence.

"No, Cory," he said. "It's her."

Cory stopped but didn't put down the knife. Phoebe pulled back the hood on her cloak, and without even giving it a second thought, Benjamin rushed over and hugged

 187

her. He'd only met her a handful of times, but this was his sister. And Cory's too, because Cory finally put the knife down and joined in the hug.

As they embraced, Benjamin felt the triplet bond running through each and every part of his body. It strengthened him and restored his energy. And in his pocket, he felt the two keys he carried—the Shambhala key and the Xanadu key. They grew hot and began to pulsate.

"What is it?" Phoebe asked as he pulled away and reached into his pocket for the keys.

"The keys of Shambhala," Benjamin said, holding them out.

Cory joined his with Benjamin's, and together, they watched the glowing gems.

"You still have them?" Phoebe asked as her eyes grew wide.

Benjamin nodded. "I took them after the shields came down. You left them there."

Phoebe cast her eyes down. "I can't begin to tell you how ashamed I am."

Benjamin put the keys away and grabbed her hands. "It doesn't matter now, Phoebe. It's over and done." As he looked at her, he noticed how much better she already looked. Her eyes no longer sunk in her face, and compared to the woman he'd seen hours before in the ruling hall, this Phoebe looked like she might have some fight left in her.

Benjamin and Cory turned as someone else in the hallway cleared his throat.

"I don't mean to be rushing this wonderful reunion here, but we really must be getting on with our plan."

Benjamin recognized the speaker's voice even before

he saw the man's golden hair. "Apollo," he said.

"The one and only." Apollo stepped out of the shadows. "And now, as I was saying, I must insist we get going."

"We need to get to Heidi and Ananya," Cory said.

"Yes, that is the plan," Apollo said.

"Are they okay?" Benjamin asked. "Have they been hurt?"

Apollo shook his head. "They are being saved and kept special. Caelus, Gaea, and Nathan themselves plan to publicly torture and execute all four of you tomorrow at noon."

"Wonderful," Benjamin said. "Sounds like a show I'll be sorry to miss."

"Well you won't miss it unless we get moving," Apollo said.

"What's your part in this?" Benjamin asked. He'd met Apollo before, but couldn't figure out exactly whose side the false god was really on.

Apollo laughed as he led the way down the hallway. "Let's just say I have a vested interest in the matter. Not to mention how many favors I actually do owe my darling Ananya."

"Iva!" Benjamin said. "You don't want Nathan to kill Iva."

"Of course I don't," Apollo said. "Have you any idea how powerful of an oracle she really is?"

Benjamin opened his mouth to reply but didn't get the chance.

"No, you don't," Apollo said. "So let me tell you. The world has never—and I repeat never—seen an oracle like Iva Marinina. Ever. She is worth more than all the oracles I have ever had put together."

Benjamin knew Iva was good at telegnosis and all, but the best in the world? Ever? Even he found that hard to believe. "If she's that good, then I'm surprised you let her go after that year in Delphi."

"I never intended to let her return," Apollo said. "But again, we come back to Ananya. She showed up at just the wrong time to remind me of my promise." He sighed. "But now I have Iva permanently, and I'm not about to let that emperor-wanna-be Nathan Nyx take her away from me." He turned to Phoebe. "No offense to your dear husband."

Phoebe shuddered. "You'd be doing the world a favor if you would actually just kill Nathan when he makes it to New Delphi," she said. "Because he will make it to New Delphi. He always does what he threatens. Believe me, I know."

Benjamin put his arm on Phoebe's and noticed Cory, on the other side of her, did the same. They'd returned the keys to their pockets, but again Benjamin felt their warmth.

"Phoebe," he said. "You could leave with us."

Phoebe shook her head. "No, I can't. My place is here. The time for me to leave is gone."

Benjamin didn't know how to respond. He wasn't ready to give up on her yet.

"This is it," Apollo said, stopping at a thick door.

"Heidi and Ananya?" Cory asked.

Apollo nodded.

"So how do we get them out?" Cory asked.

"Leave that to me," Phoebe said, stepping ahead. She placed her palm on a pad by the door, and it slid open.

Ananya and Heidi jumped up from the bench they sat

on and rushed to the door. Benjamin grabbed Heidi and kissed her before he even knew what he was doing. And he kept on kissing her even after he thought about it. And the best thing about it was that Heidi kissed him back. And it felt good. It took Cory clearing his throat to remind Benjamin that maybe the time for kissing had come to an end. If there even was a time for kissing to come to an end.

"Are you okay?" he asked, once they'd separated.

Heidi smiled. "Yeah, we're fine."

Benjamin looked over to Ananya who stood next to Apollo. Awfully close to Apollo by the looks of things. Had Benjamin missed something?

Phoebe smiled and stepped back, and even before she said anything, Benjamin knew this was goodbye. She reached into her robe and pulled out a small disk.

"Here, take this," she said, pressing it into his palm and closing his fingers over it.

Benjamin's breath caught and he dropped the disk. It landed with a metallic sound and rolled a couple feet away. "I can't touch it," he said.

Phoebe nodded. "Yeah, you can. Just not for a long time." She reached down and picked it back up, handing it back to Benjamin.

He looked down at it in his hand and then stuffed it in his pocket like it might contaminate him. "Why?"

"There's no time to explain," she said. "Just take it and keep it with you."

He looked at her again. "Please come with us."

Phoebe shook her head. "No, that would only make things worse. If I stay here, I can hold off Nathan for a while. Maybe divert his attention. I'm hoping they won't

 191

find out about your escape for at least a few hours."

Benjamin's stomach tightened. What would happen then once Nathan found out they'd escaped? "He might kill you," he said to Phoebe.

Phoebe bit her lip. "I know. But I'm willing to take that chance. Every day for the last ten years I would have welcomed death. If my time has come now, then it would best be served helping you escape."

Benjamin looked at her, and beneath the sadness he felt immense pride. This was his sister. He looked over at Cory, and soundlessly, they all three embraced again.

"Thank you for everything, little sister," Cory said. "You will be remembered forever in our hearts."

"Please just be careful," she said, pulling away from the embrace. "And forgive me for all I have done." Before Benjamin or Cory could say another word, Phoebe turned and walked away, down the long, dark hallway.

"*There is nothing to forgive,*" Benjamin said, hoping she heard him in her mind.

Benjamin felt Iva's presence as soon as they arrived in New Delphi—wherever New Delphi was. With his heads-up display on the fritz, he had no clue.

"Iva's up the hill," Heidi said. She began running, not waiting for any sort of confirmation.

But Heidi was right. Benjamin felt it too. They rushed up the hill, pushed past anyone who happened to get in their way.

Iva was inside a temple. Alone. She turned as soon as they walked in the door.

"Heidi!" Iva rushed over to her. They hugged and both

began to cry. Unlike Phoebe, Iva didn't look like she'd aged a day.

Ananya turned to Apollo and raised her eyebrow.

Apollo shrugged. "I'll give you five minutes, but not a second longer," he said before turning to leave the room.

"Iva," Heidi said once Apollo had gone. "You're in danger here. You need to leave."

Iva shook her head. "But how can you be here? How can any of you be here?"

"We just came from the Necropolis," Benjamin said. "Nathan is coming to kill you."

"I don't understand," Iva said. "You're dead. How can you be here?"

"We came from the past," Cory said. "Due to a trick of Kronos', we traveled forward ten years in time."

"When did we die?" Benjamin asked. He figured if there was only time to ask one question, this would be the one. His other option was asking whether he saved the world, but given the current circumstances, he'd figured out the answer to that.

"At the start of the purges," Iva said. "They executed you as an example of what was to come." She reached out to touch Benjamin's face, running her hands along his cheeks and forehead.

"When, Iva?" Benjamin asked. He didn't push her hands away, though he wished she'd just answer the question. "When did the purges start?"

Iva shook her head, pulling her hands away. "It was a long time ago. Not too long after the shields came down. Once Caelus and Gaea came back to Atlantis they tortured and killed you in a public execution."

"What about Andy and Gary?" Benjamin asked.

Iva bit her lip, and a single tear slid down her face. "Andy, too."

"And Gary?" he asked.

She shook her head. "No, they didn't kill Gary. Like me. They determined we were too useful to be executed. But I live every day knowing that it could be my last. My time may come."

"Iva," Benjamin said. "What went wrong? What could we have done differently?"

"I don't know, Benjamin," Iva said. "The shields came down and Caelus and Gaea escaped and went into hiding."

"In Xanadu," Ananya said.

Benjamin spun on her. How had she known that? But she held up her hand.

Iva nodded. "In Xanadu. But we found out too late, and even then, they'd gained too much power. Helios couldn't save everyone."

"We need more to go on, Iva," Benjamin said. "Tell us how we can change things. How can we make this reality never happen?"

Iva looked Benjamin straight in the eye. "By killing Caelus and Gaea. If they gain control over the humans, then they gain control over everything. Go to Xanadu and kill them. No race should be enslaved. It only leads to this."

Benjamin saw the intensity in her eyes. Iva hadn't given up on him which was some consolation. There had to be a way to defeat Caelus and Gaea before the world came to this. He couldn't let Iva live with these memories. He couldn't let Phoebe live her life wishing she were dead. Nathan must die. And Caelus must die. And Gaea must die.

And then Benjamin remembered the disk Phoebe had given him. He stood up and pulled it from his pocket. "Do you have any idea why Phoebe gave me this?" he asked.

Iva took it and studied it for a while before shaking her head. "No, I don't even know what it is."

"I'll tell you what it is," Apollo said, walking into the temple. "It's Phoebe's death sentence. Personally, I can't even imagine how she got it in the first place."

"Her death sentence?" Cory took the disk from Iva.

Apollo nodded. "If they don't kill her when they find out she helped you escape, they'll surely kill her once they discover she stole that."

"Why?" Cory asked. "What's so special about it?"

"Let's just say Caelus is quite fond of it," Apollo said. "It never leaves the chain around his neck."

"Are you kidding?" Heidi asked. "Won't he miss it?"

"That's putting it mildly," Apollo said. "Like I said, I have no idea how she got it."

"Maybe he won't know Phoebe took it," Benjamin said, taking the disk from Cory's outstretched hand. "Maybe he'll think Nathan took it."

Apollo put his hand to his chin. "Hmmm. That's not a bad thought. And just the kind of rumor I wouldn't mind starting if it would get rid of Nathan."

It didn't take a genius to figure out that Apollo and Nathan were not the best of friends. Was it all because of Iva? And then Benjamin remembered the first oracle Nathan had killed.

"It's because he murdered one of your oracles," Benjamin said. "That's why you can't stand him. Right?"

Apollo laughed. "That's only one grain of sand in the

desert," he said. "But I don't think we should spend the minute we have left discussing the deep rooted hatred between Nathan Nyx and myself."

Benjamin sensed a weakening in the shield surrounding them and felt a familiar if unwelcome presence.

"Looks like I may have been generous in my time estimate," Apollo said. "Nathan has decided to pay us a visit."

"We need to hide Iva," Benjamin said, grabbing her before she could protest.

"My thoughts exactly," Apollo said. "Though I believe it's time for the rest of you to be going. This battle won't be the end of either Nathan or Iva."

"And what about you?" Ananya asked, even as Apollo hurried them toward the center altar. Benjamin was sure he detected genuine concern in her voice. He really must have missed something.

Apollo put his arm around Ananya and smiled. "No, not the end of me either."

He only looked at the altar, and the massive stone slab drew back, revealing a staircase leading down. "Now, hurry," he said. "All of you. Head down until you've passed the third landing. To the Omphalos. Iva knows where to go from there, but that's where the rest of you should leave."

Cory led the way, and Benjamin hurried after Iva and Heidi, turning one last time to see Ananya squeeze Apollo's hand before entering the altar herself. Apollo turned and headed out of the temple, and the slab slid back into place.

They reached the third landing and stopped. If Benjamin knew Nathan was here, then Nathan knew Benjamin was here. And Iva, too, no doubt.

"Come back with us, Iva," Benjamin said. "You'd be

free of this place."

"No." Iva smiled. "My place is here. In this horrible world, New Delphi has actually provided me with a sense of comfort."

Benjamin felt her sorrow through the Alliance bond as if it were his own.

"What can I do, Iva?" he asked. "Please just tell me what to do." He'd do anything to save Iva from that much sorrow. And to save Phoebe from her fate. If he only knew what.

Iva's smile vanished. "I don't know. I don't even know what you did wrong—if you even did anything wrong. But do something. Anything. Do what you normally wouldn't do; maybe that's it. Make a difference and change the world. If anyone can do it, it's you, Benjamin. I've seen different futures. I know it's possible. It's why Caelus and Gaea want me dead." Her eyes glanced back up the stairs. "Go now. Don't waste any more time."

Heidi grabbed for Iva and hugged her, crying all the while. Ananya gently pulled Heidi from Iva, letting Iva slip away into the dark.

Heidi sobbed as Benjamin put his arm around her. He knew there was nothing he could say to comfort her, so he didn't even try. He only held her close and let her cry.

The Omphalos—the Navel of the World—sprang to life on the ground in front of them. They walked over and surrounded it.

"In case anyone had any different ideas," Ananya said, "we are not waiting for Kronos."

"No arguments here," Benjamin said, still holding Heidi. He let go of her and placed his hands on the

Omphalos, and the world crunched and changed around them.

They ended up in the middle of a desert. Not the best place to come back to. And seeing as how their heads-up displays still weren't working, they had zero clue where they were. Benjamin reached out with his thoughts and scanned for Phoebe, part of him hoping he'd find a sign of her and part of him hoping he wouldn't. The latter part won.

"I looked for her, too," Cory said. "Nothing."

"So what do we do?" Heidi asked.

Ananya stood up. "I know what I must do."

Benjamin wondered if she was going to stay and help them. But Heidi must've read her thoughts.

"You're leaving," Heidi said.

Ananya nodded. "My place is in Xanadu. Now that I know what the future may hold, my only choice is to head there and see what I can do."

"I can't go with you yet," Benjamin said. He knew he wasn't ready to confront Caelus and Gaea. And if he'd learned one thing from his visit to the future, it was that he couldn't afford to make mistakes. Too many lives depended on him.

Ananya smiled. "I know. Only you will know when it is time. But until then, this is goodbye." She embraced Cory and Benjamin first, before turning to Heidi. Minutes passed while the two of them held a private telepathic conversation, but Benjamin didn't dare interrupt. He sat silently until he knew the conversation was over. And then she teleported away.

Benjamin stared at the spot where she'd been with his mouth open.

"You'll swallow sand that way," Jack said.

Benjamin shut his mouth and turned to the Nogical. "Where have you been?"

"Where have you been?" Jack asked.

"We saw Lulu," Benjamin said. "Forward in time."

Jack shook his head. "Yeah, I know. You'd have thought I'd asked her to write a dissertation. Who knew one Nogical could complain so much?"

"She already told you?" Benjamin asked.

"Does that surprise you?" Jack said. "She specifically stopped back in this time to file her grievances."

Knowing Lulu, it didn't surprise Benjamin.

"So where to now?" Heidi asked.

"I need to head back to Atlantis," Cory said. "And we should stick together from now on, Benjamin."

Benjamin nodded. "You won't get any argument from me." He turned to Heidi. "Can you sense Gary, Andy, and Iva?"

She scanned the earth as he'd seen her do many times before, and then she nodded. "They're in Atlantis with Aurora."

"And Helios and Selene, too," Jack said. "Not to mention Lulu—unfortunately."

"She's not all that bad," Heidi said.

Jack frowned. "Yeah, she is."

Well, that settled that. "Atlantis it is," Benjamin said. He pulled the teleportation surger from his pocket. "I guess we won't be needing this with the shields down."

"Don't throw it away just yet, little brother," Cory said.

 199

"A device like that could come in handy."

So Benjamin stuffed it back in his pocket along with the two keys of Shambhala, and they teleported back to Atlantis.

CHAPTER 24

NATURAL DISASTERS AND GILGAMESH

Once they teleported to Atlantis, the first thing that occurred to Benjamin was that the sun overhead was the actual real sun not a simulated sun inside a dome under the ocean. Atlantis, and Lemuria for that matter, no longer sat at the bottom of the ocean.

Was it weird for the humans? Had they even realized anything was different?

"We should go to the ruling hall," Cory said. "We're bound to get some sort of update on the state of the world."

Benjamin didn't remember the ruling hall in Atlantis, though he felt pretty sure that's where he'd spent the bulk of his captivity stuffed in the room with the chair. The door to the throne room was ajar when they reached it, and so they walked right in.

Benjamin almost laughed when he saw Joey Duncan sitting in one of the thrones on the raised dais.

"Are you the new king of Atlantis?" Benjamin asked.

Joey smiled and bowed, even while he stayed sitting. "That's right," he said. "I think it does me justice. And where in the name of the false gods have you been?"

"Just getting back," Benjamin said.

Joey gave him a looked like he'd forgot to teleport half his brain. "Apparently."

Cory walked over and punched Joey in greeting. "Are you getting any work done or just goofing off?"

"I've been swamped," Joey said. "Without you here, there's three times as much stuff to do. Lord Helios keeps giving me new commands. And then Selene keeps jumping in adding her opinion on everything. And don't even get me started on that Nogical."

Selene walked into the room. "I heard that. And I'm not sure it shows the proper respect." She smiled at Benjamin. "It's about time you showed up."

Benjamin started to ask what she meant, but someone interrupted him before he got started.

"I heard it, too."

Benjamin hadn't even noticed Lulu sitting on Selene's shoulder. She teleported away and ended up inches from Benjamin's shoulder, right in Jack's face. "Miss me, Jack?

Jack pointed his finger at her, and her hair disappeared.

Her hands flew to her head, and she twisted up her face in a scowl so deep Benjamin figured it would become a permanent fixture. "Don't touch the hair." She grew it back bright orange. "One more time and I'll teleport your head into the nearest sewer."

Benjamin tried to divert the conversation. "So I guess you know the shields went down."

Selene raised an eyebrow, and Joey looked at Benjamin like he'd just told him the ocean was made of water.

"What?" Benjamin said.

"That was like two weeks ago," Joey said.

"Two weeks! You've got to be kidding me," Benjamin said. Okay, getting his heads-up display fixed was a top priority.

Joey and Selene both shook their heads.

"Nope, not kidding," Joey said.

Benjamin let the reality of the situation sink in. They'd been gone for two weeks. Caelus and Gaea had been out free in the world for two weeks. Nathan had been with Phoebe for two weeks. Cory looked at Benjamin, and Benjamin saw his own concern mirrored there. Two weeks had been way too long.

"So seriously, what gives?" Joey said. "Did you forget you were supposed to follow me right back?"

Cory shook his head. "Curse Kronos and his tricks."

"Kronos?" Helios said, walking through the far door into the throne room.

Joey jumped up from the thrones and headed down the steps. If Benjamin hadn't been so concerned at the loss of time, he would have laughed.

"Kronos," Cory repeated.

"What does he have to do with this?" Helios walked over and sat down on the steps.

"He fooled us into temporally phasing," Cory said.

"Ten years in the future," Heidi added.

Any humor which had been present in the room evaporated. Joey sat down a couple steps from Helios, and Selene joined him.

"What was the future like?" Joey asked.

Benjamin didn't know how to respond. He shook his head and tears sprang to the corners of his eyes. He managed to hold them back and looked to Cory, hoping his brother would take the lead on this answer.

Cory sighed. "I'm afraid we have only bad news to report, Helios. The world is in trouble. Serious trouble. And if we can't figure out a way to stop it, then I'm afraid we will all be doomed."

They spent the better part of the next hour filling Helios, Joey, Selene, and the Nogicals in on all that had happened in the future. Benjamin and Heidi kept interrupting Cory, adding bits and pieces as he missed stuff.

"You guys are a downer," Lulu said. "I seriously went there to help you?"

Benjamin looked at Jack. "Well, normally I'd have asked Jack. But seeing as how we already saw you there, the natural conclusion—"

Lulu put up her small hand. "Spare me your natural conclusions."

"The future does not sound promising," Helios said. "But it also does not sound hopeless. After all, we do have Atlantis. And Lemuria."

"Yeah, and they have the rest of the world," Joey said.

"Have they done anything yet?" Heidi asked. "I mean, what's happening with the world out there?"

"Yeah," Benjamin said. "Do the humans know anything's changed?"

"Aside from the two giant continents that popped out of the ocean?" Lulu said. "The Lemurian emergency response teams have actually managed to keep the cataclysms to a minimum."

Joey let out a hollow laugh. "If by a minimum you mean ten earthquakes, six tsunamis, and four volcanic eruptions—all from extinct volcanoes."

Benjamin's mouth dropped open. "You're kidding, right?"

Lulu shook her little head. "Not kidding."

"And you call that a minimum?" Benjamin asked.

A dark cloud moved onto Joey's face; Benjamin never would have believed Joey could be so serious. "Think about it, Benjamin. Two continents bigger than Africa have just surfaced—one in the Atlantic Ocean and one in the Pacific Ocean. The sheer force of those continents catapulting to the surface could have literally destroyed all life on earth. What did you learn about when the continents were sunk in the first place?"

Benjamin shrugged. "I don't know," he said. "They were pushed down to the bottom of the ocean."

"Right," Joey said. "And every culture on Earth has a story to tell about it."

Benjamin shook his head. "No they don't. They didn't even know about Atlantis and Lemuria."

"Wrong," Joey said. "Think Noah and the Ark. Think Gilgamesh and his flood. Those stories recount innumerable human deaths. Populations had to be rebuilt from the ground up."

"And that was all due to the sinking of Lemuria and Atlantis?" Heidi asked.

Joey nodded. "It's not something we actually broadcast, and believe it or not, even back then, human death was kept to a minimum." He sighed. "All I'm trying to say is that anything of this proportion will have consequences. People will die. Humans and telegens alike."

"Then why did Lemuria sink the continents in the first place?" Benjamin asked, directing the question to Helios.

"I suppose the rulers at the time weighed the positives against the negatives, and decided the earth could be spared more suffering if the continents were sunk," Helios said. "I'm not pretending to understand their exact reasoning. I'm not even pretending to agree with it. All I'm saying is that I'm sure they gave it serious thought."

Benjamin shook his head. "So here we are—twenty natural disasters later. Now what?"

Helios looked at Selene and Joey. "Now we try to rebuild and protect what we can. We maintain control of the government here in Atlantis. We strengthen our hold of the government in Lemuria. And then we send out emissaries. Joey stays here in Atlantis with Selene, and I'll keep control in Lemuria."

"And me?" Cory asked.

"Your place is with Benjamin now," Helios said. "It is imperative for the two of you to stay together."

"And do what?" Benjamin asked.

"For now, nothing," Helios said. "Whatever you do, don't leave the continent and go off trying to kill Caelus and Gaea yourselves." His eyes bore into Benjamin, and Benjamin felt his mind bock slipping away. "Just be patient," Helios continued. "We need to prepare, and once we're prepared, Caelus and Gaea will get what they deserve."

Benjamin knew enough to keep his mouth shut; he forced his mind block back in place. He'd stay in Atlantis for the time being, but he wasn't going to let the future get away from him. Caelus and Gaea had to die, and he was going to be the one to deliver their fatal blow.

They left the Ruling hall and headed out into the cold. Jack hovered in the air above Heidi's head and then rested on her hair until it sizzled. He flew off, taking his normal spot on Benjamin's shoulder.

Heidi brushed at her hair like she was trying to get any remnants of Jack out of it.

"You need to control that hair of yours," Jack said. "You could kill someone with it."

"You shouldn't sit on people's heads," Heidi said. She closed her eyes, and Benjamin felt her reaching out telepathically, trying to locate their friends. After a moment, she smiled.

"I found Iva and Andy at The Silver Touch." She sighed. "I can't wait to see Iva. After all that back in New Delphi—"

Benjamin tried to push the images they'd seen out of his mind. "I know."

"Why was New Delphi in the middle of a desert anyway?" Cory asked.

"New Delphi?" Jack said. "It got built near Las Vegas, sort of around the 'test-your-fortune' mentality. Like a new Fortune City."

"How is it that you know so much about the future world?" Cory asked.

Jack scowled. "Lulu skips around in time. She's addicted to it, I swear."

"Kind of like you and teleporting," Benjamin said.

"Speaking of which, do we have to walk?" Jack said. "Can't we just teleport?"

Both Morpheus and Mantis Midas were with Iva and Andy at The Silver Touch. And so was Walker Pan. And Magic Pan. Benjamin stopped dead in his tracks when they walked through the door.

Walker and Morpheus sat hunched over the chess board deep in thought, neither one looking up when they walked in. Benjamin was just about to ask what was going

 207

on when Iva saw him and rushed over. She hugged him first, which surprised Benjamin. Normally she would've hugged Heidi first. But then she hugged Heidi, and Andy walked over to join them.

"Dude, where have you been?" Andy asked, and one of those awkward moments passed when Benjamin felt like hugging Andy and was pretty sure Andy felt like hugging him, too. But needless to say they didn't. Instead Andy punched him on the shoulder. And Benjamin punched him back.

Benjamin looked over to Walker, and then back to Andy and Iva.

"What's going on?" he asked. "Why are they here?"

Andy looked over to where Benjamin's eyes directed him. "Oh, you mean Walker and Magic?" Andy asked.

Benjamin nodded.

"I think they're kind of on our side," Andy said. "It's a long story, but all the teleporter stuff and menu stuff was planned, and for the benefit of the whole government takeover thing."

"Making me eat liver helped them take over the Atlantis government?" Benjamin figured Andy had teleported one too many times and left some brains behind.

"That was sort of to build concern," Andy said. "Anyway, you can trust them. Helios does, and I guess I do too now. It took me a while, but I have to admit—they have some great espionage skills."

Benjamin made a mental note to still be careful around Magic and Walker. Andy's judgment might be skewed.

"So where have you been?" Andy asked.

Benjamin sighed and looked over at Heidi. "Talk about

a long story. I'll give you the short version, and we can save the long version for once we hook up with Gary." He looked around. "Where is Gary by the way?"

Iva rolled her eyes. "Where else? The Genetic Engineering Research Campus. He and Aurora have practically moved in there."

"Yeah," Andy said. "We only see them at bedtime, and I think that's only because they don't have anything to sleep on over there."

"The Genetic Engineering Research Campus?" Heidi said. "What's so interesting about it?"

"I wish I knew," Andy said. "No, scratch that. I don't really wish I knew."

Iva shot Andy a cool glance.

"What?" Andy asked. "Just because those two can't get enough on DNA doesn't mean the rest of us want to eat, breathe, and sleep it."

"It's not that bad, Andy," Iva said.

"It is that bad, Iva," Andy said. "But anyway, let's hear the story."

Benjamin still didn't feel comfortable going into too much detail around Magic and Walker. "Maybe we can go get something to eat," he suggested, "and I can tell you over lunch."

Andy shrugged. "Fine by me."

"Oh, wait," Benjamin said. "I just wanted to ask Morpheus one thing." He walked over to the chess board followed by his friends. He figured if there was anyone who might know the answer to his question, it would be Morpheus Midas. Or Mantis Midas for that matter.

Benjamin pulled the disk Phoebe had given him out of

his pocket and held it out flat in his palm.

Morpheus looked up front the chess board and sucked in his breath. "Whoa, what is that?"

Benjamin sighed. "That's what I was hoping you could tell me."

Morpheus reached out with his hand. "Do you mind if I hold it?"

Benjamin shook his head, though he actually did mind very much. Phoebe had given him this disk, and he didn't want to just hand it over. Right now, it was the only connection he actually had with her. Even though it was from ten years in the future.

Morpheus took the disk and studied it.

"Where did you get it?" Mantis asked, standing over Morpheus' shoulder.

Benjamin felt himself tense up and hoped nobody noticed. He didn't have to spell out the truth for everyone. "I got it in Egypt." Which was true. Phoebe had given it to him in Egypt. Just future Egypt. Was it even called Egypt in the future? Some name like Doom and Gloom seemed a better option.

"It doesn't look like any Egyptian coin I've ever seen," Morpheus said, handing the disk to Mantis.

"It looks too big to be a coin," Mantis said, taking the disk.

Benjamin's fingers itched as he watched it. He wanted to snatch it back and put it in his pocket. He never should have taken it out in the first place.

"And look at the strange engravings," Mantis said, turning the disk over and running his thumb on it. "They're similar to ancient Lemurian, but have some more modern

 210

elements to them."

"Do you mind if I take a look?" Walker asked, taking the disk from Mantis Midas. He studied it and held it to the point Benjamin thought Walker planned to keep it.

"Well?" Benjamin asked.

"I've seen something like this before," Walker said, handing the disk to Magic Pan.

Was everyone going to hold the disk? Benjamin started to think he should just put it on display and charge admission.

"What do you make of it, Magic?" Walker asked.

Magic smiled. "Your suspicions are dead-on, Dad."

"What suspicions?" Benjamin asked. He was starting to feel left out of a conversation which should very much include him.

"This is a life force disk," Walker replied, taking the disk back from Magic.

"I know that much," Benjamin said.

"What's a life force disk?" Heidi asked.

"An ancient kind of technology," Walker said, fingering the disk as he spoke.

Benjamin reached out and took it from Walker's hands.

Walker went on. "I haven't seen a life force disk in use since before Atlantis was sunk."

"You were around before Atlantis was sunk?" Heidi asked.

"I travel around quite a bit," Walker said. "But that's not important. What is important is where you got this. Egypt you said?"

Benjamin nodded. "That's right."

"Life force disks are one of the main reasons for the

sinking of Atlantis," Walker said.

"Why?" Heidi sat down on the edge of the chess board. Gary would have cringed if he'd seen her. Morpheus only grimaced but didn't ask her to move.

"Well, it was after the sinking of Lemuria. Kind of a peaceful time in world history," Walker said. "Lemuria set up the Ring of Fire to watch over the Atlantis rulers while the humans continued to advance. Thousands of years went by. And sure, humans advanced, but so did telegens. Which meant if telegens turned evil, humans wouldn't stand a chance."

"And telegens turned evil," Benjamin said.

Walker nodded. "The false gods and goddesses were born. Gaea and Caelus. You're familiar with them."

"Unfortunately," Benjamin said.

"They were power hungry, and they were smart which is a horrible combination," Walker said. "From the laboratories of Caelus came the life force disk. He slaved over its development for hundreds of years until it had been perfected. Innumerable humans died in its research and creation. But for Caelus, this was a glorious price to pay."

"He killed humans to invent the disk?" Iva's eyes were huge, and Benjamin noticed them flicker over to the disk in his hand. He felt like dropping it.

"That was the whole point of the disk," Walker said. "Don't you see? For each human Caelus killed while wearing the life force disk around his neck, the telenergetic force of the disk would be increased. And with it the life force of Caelus himself."

"You mean to tell me this disk got stronger and stronger each time a human died?" Andy asked.

Walker nodded. "And Caelus' life was extended."

"That explains quite a bit," Cory said. "It explains how Caelus and Gaea managed to live so long and remain so powerful."

"Right," Walker said. "Caelus shared his invention with all those craving power over humans. All the false god and goddesses willing to sacrifice humans for their own gain."

"Is that how human sacrifice started?" Heidi asked.

"In theory," Walker said. "Slaughter humans to increase the life and power of the telegens."

"No wonder humans feared their gods," Heidi said. "But some of the gods seem nice—like Apollo."

"True," Walker said. "Not all of them used human sacrifice. Some used the worship of the humans and the sacrificing of things like grain or iron to increase the telenergy in their life force disks."

"So if all these life force disks were floating around back then before the sinking, why are you so surprised to see this one here now?" Cory asked.

"Because when Atlantis was sunk deep into the ocean," Walker said, "all life force disks were destroyed." He looked over at the disk in Benjamin's hand. "Or so it was believed until I saw this disk here now. Did you tell Helios about this?"

Benjamin shouldn't have been surprised that Walker knew he'd already seen Helios, but he was. "No, I didn't think about it."

"A major oversight," Walker said. "Why don't you go over where and how you found this one more time?" He sighed. "And why don't you make it the truth this time."

Benjamin decided to throw caution to the wind and let

it all out. And let it all out he did. He and Heidi and Cory relayed everything. And when they finished, just as he knew they would, the questions began. But oddly enough, Iva sat silent. Benjamin didn't stop to think about it at the time. He should have probably noticed, but he didn't.

"You snagged this from the ruler of the future," Magic said.

Benjamin nodded.

"There may be hope for you yet," Magic said.

"Which brings up the question of how he got it in the first place," Walker said. "If in fact all of them were destroyed ten thousand years ago."

"They weren't all destroyed ten thousand years ago," Andy said.

"That is how history records it," Walker said.

"History is one thing," Andy said. "But history books can't be trusted any farther than they can be thrown. The question is—what really happened to the life force disks, and how many of them survived?"

"Could Caelus have traveled back in time to get his life force disk?" Cory suggested. "That way, he would have it in the future."

Walker felt his chin as he thought. "It's as good a theory as any."

"So what happens if we just destroy the disk right now?" Benjamin asked. "Will Caelus die?" For the first time, he felt hope. Hope that they might actually be able to destroy Gaea and Caelus.

But Walker shook his head. "Destroying a life force disk doesn't kill the telegen."

Benjamin's heart sank. It had seemed plausible. "But

if it's not tied to the life of the telegen, then how does it extend his life at all?"

Walker let out a humorless laugh. "Oh, it is tied to the life of the telegen," he said. "Just not in a destroy-the-disk-and-be-done-with-it kind of way. But the disks were powerful, and this one you have now is probably the most powerful one I've ever encountered. Hundreds of thousands of humans have been killed for its creation."

Benjamin looked at the disk and felt sick. The thought of humans being slaughtered by the thousands to create it made him want to throw it across the room. Or better yet, smash it under his feet. But Phoebe had risked her life, probably sealed her fate, to give him this thing—even if it was a monstrosity. Walker said destroying it couldn't kill Caelus, but Benjamin knew it had to have some power over the false god. Otherwise, why would Caelus have been so protective of it? He just had to figure out what.

CHAPTER 25

THINGS IN JARS

Andy and Iva led them to the Genetic Engineering Research Campus. They stopped in front of a sphere made of glass.

"Well, here we are," Andy said.

"This is it?" Benjamin asked.

Andy nodded.

"But it's a sphere," Benjamin said, stating the obvious.

"A big sphere," Heidi agreed.

"I can't tell you how awesome this place is," Jack said. He kept teleporting from Benjamin's shoulder to the door and back again.

Andy didn't move.

"So what are we waiting for?" Cory moved to the door and placed his palm on the pad. It didn't open.

"It's a retinal scan," Iva said.

Cory shrugged and placed his eyeball in front of the scanner. The light scanned it, and the door opened.

"We got you guys on the access list," Iva said, walking through the door.

Benjamin followed, but then turned when he realized Andy wasn't behind him. "Aren't you coming?"

Andy grimaced like he'd just taken a huge sip of Amoeba Juice. "No way. I've spent way too much time in there."

Iva sighed. "It's not that bad, Andy." She headed back, grabbed his hand, and dragged him through the door.

"It's horrible," Andy said. "All we've done for the last two weeks is watch Gary and Aurora compare test tubes. 'Oh, this one looks green,'" he mimicked. "'Oh, this one looks green and slimy.' 'Oh, and look at this one—it's green and slimy and chunky.'"

Benjamin laughed because…well…it sounded just like Gary and Aurora.

"But you have to come in this time," Iva said, still dragging Andy. "Benjamin and Heidi are back, and anyway, maybe Gary and Aurora have figured something out."

"I don't even know what they're trying to figure out in the first place," Andy said, shaking his head. But he followed Iva to the elevator where they went down to the floor labeled i20.

Gary dropped his test tube when Benjamin and Heidi walked through the door. It stopped mid-air, and Benjamin telekinetically settled it back in its tray.

"Oh, that was close," Gary said, grabbing the test tube again and brushing it off. "Where have you been?"

"Yeah, good question," Aurora said.

But Benjamin didn't answer right away. He was still looking around. "What is this place?"

"It's our own personal laboratory," Gary said.

"Yeah," Aurora added. "Selene pulled some strings and got us some space."

"To do what?" Benjamin asked. How many science experiments could any two people possibly do?

But Gary shook his head. "Just give me a few more hours. I'll tell you everything. I promise."

"See," Andy said. "I told you so. He's been saying that same thing for two weeks now."

"Which leads back to the original question," Gary said. "Where have you been for two weeks?"

"Well," Benjamin began. "After the shields came down, we accidentally ran into Kronos."

"I knew it!" Aurora said. "I knew Kronos had to be involved in this. I don't know why DOPOT doesn't just lock him up and throw away the key."

"How do you lock up a time traveler?" Andy asked.

"That's beside the point," Aurora said. "Let's hear what Kronos did this time."

Benjamin, Heidi, and Cory gave them the short version. The really short version. It was obvious from Gary's continued fiddling with the test tubes that he and Aurora had something else on their minds.

"Where's Jack?" Heidi looked around the room.

Andy shrugged. "Probably lost deep in GERC. He's been exploring for two weeks straight."

"GERC?" Cory asked.

Gary cleared his throat. "That's what Andy started calling this place."

"Genetic Engineering Research Campus is way too long," Andy said. "You'd have to be crazy to call it that."

"GERC is good," Heidi said. "Nice and short."

"Hey, it's great to catch up and all, but do you mind getting up?" Gary asked Benjamin. "You're sitting right on my notes."

Benjamin stood up and looked down at the thought cache he'd been sitting on. He picked it up and started to read it, but Gary, with telenergetic power Benjamin didn't even know he had, levitated it out of Benjamin's hands and across the room.

"I'll tell you everything in a couple hours," Gary said. "I promise."

"Fine," Benjamin said. "So what do we do until then?"

"I don't care," Gary said. "Just leave the lab."

If it had been anyone besides Gary, Benjamin might have been offended. But it was Gary. And Gary was all about science.

They headed out of the lab, leaving Gary and Aurora to their work.

"Let's look around," Benjamin said.

Andy shook his head. "Not me. I've done enough 'looking around' to last me a millennium." He'd hardly finished talking before he teleported away.

"Heidi and I need to catch up," Iva said. "We'll see you guys in a little while." And without even so much as a goodbye, the two girls teleported away, also, which left Benjamin and Cory outside the lab together.

"So what do you know about genetic engineering?" Cory said. "Because aside from the Cyclops, I never saw much of anything strange back in Troy."

Benjamin shrugged. "Not much. Who you really need to talk to is Jack."

And Jack materialized.

"Did someone call me?" Jack asked.

Benjamin laughed. "I knew you'd turn up. Cory wants a genetic engineering lesson."

Jack's golden eyes grew to the size of acorns. "Great! I found the perfect place."

They followed Jack as he wound a path even farther

underground.

"Are you leading us to Hell?" Benjamin asked as the halls seemed to spiral and loop back on themselves. How did anyone keep their sense of direction down here?

"It's just around the corner," Jack said. And he teleported them into a room the size of a large cafeteria. "This is the stuff they don't teach in Genetic Engineering 101."

"What are all these things?" Benjamin looked around. "Should we even be down here?"

"There aren't any 'no trespassing' signs," Jack said.

"Yeah, but there's also no door," Benjamin said.

"A technicality," Jack said. "If we can teleport in here, then we're allowed to be in here."

Cory walked to the nearest table and picked up a glass jar. "Doesn't this look an awful lot like a person?"

Benjamin walked over to see. It did look like a person. A small, bald person. "It kind of reminds me of a Nogical," he said.

Jack scowled. "It's not a Nogical." He squinted through the glass. "It's not even green."

Cory set the jar down and moved to pick up another one. This one's features were better defined, and small hair follicles grew from the skin. But the fingers were webbed. "How about this one?"

Jack got close to the jar. "The skin color is better, but the arms and legs look like flippers."

Benjamin turned and scanned the room. Table after table was covered in glass jars, each set apart and labeled with a serial number in ancient Lemurian.

"How old are these samples, Jack?" Benjamin asked.

Jack screwed up his face as he thought about it.

"Hmmm. Given that everything's in Ancient Lemurian, I'd say they're from before the sinking."

"Before Atlantis sunk into the ocean!" Benjamin said.

"Before Atlantis or Lemuria sunk into the ocean," Jack corrected.

"You're telling me these experiments are over twenty-five thousand years old?" Benjamin asked.

"At least," Jack said. "Keep in mind Atlantis was founded four-hundred thousand years ago."

"And genetic engineering went on back then?" Benjamin asked. He moved to another table and squatted down to look into a large jar, the size of a barrel. As he looked into the container, wide, lifeless eyes stared back at him. "Look at this." It was barely a whisper.

Cory and Jack came over to join him.

The figure in the container was as big as Benjamin himself. It sat in the gel; frozen; perfect.

"Jack?" Benjamin asked.

"Yep?"

"When did humans first appear on Earth?" Benjamin asked, and even as he asked it, he felt a sick, kind of hollow feeling in the pit of his stomach.

"Well, humanoid type people started appearing on Earth eight hundred thousand years ago at least," Jack said.

Benjamin shook his head. "No, not humanoid type people." He nodded his head in the direction of the barrel. "Humans in their present form."

"About two hundred thousand years ago," Jack said. "Probably about as old as this jar here."

Benjamin felt the truth as sure as he knew he had ten toes. "Jack?"

"Yep?"

"Do you think humans were genetically engineered?" Benjamin couldn't believe he was asking the question. He'd grown up with humans. Heck, he'd grown up thinking he was a human. Maybe a strange human, but still a human.

Jack looked around the room. "I don't really see how we could draw any other conclusion."

"So you're telling us that Atlantians genetically engineered humans two hundred thousand years ago and placed them on Earth?" Cory let out a low whistle.

Jack angled his head and scratched at some letters on the jar. "Yeah, I think that is what I'm telling you. And based on what we're seeing here, they took their own telegen DNA and started mutations and experiments."

"But why?" Cory asked.

"Why not?" Jack asked. "Why do scientists do anything?"

"Do you think humans were engineered to be slaves?" Benjamin asked.

"I don't know." Jack cocked his head. "But I think we should get Gary and Aurora down here."

As busy as Gary and Aurora were, when Benjamin contacted them telepathically and gave just a small teaser of where they were, they arrived via teleportation in about five seconds. Benjamin gave them a minute to get acclimated to the room.

"This place wasn't on the tour," Aurora said.

"And that surprises you why?" Jack said.

After a minute, Benjamin couldn't wait any longer. "Gary, humans are genetically engineered. Just like Nogicals."

"No," Jack said. "Not just like Nogicals. Nogicals were engineered to excel at everything telenergetic. Humans have no telenergetic skills whatsoever."

"Wait a second." Gary shook his head and took a huge breath. "Slow down. Humans? Genetically engineered. That's impossible. They evolved."

"Look around, Gary," Benjamin said. "These jars aren't lying. Telegens may have evolved, but humans didn't."

Gary didn't say a word. Instead he walked around the room, followed by Aurora. They studied each container, starting at the small hairless ones, and stopping at the full size human.

"Do you realize what this means?" Gary asked.

Benjamin nodded. "Humans were bred to be inferior. It was intentional."

Aurora threw up her hands in disgust. "Which makes all the research we've been doing for two weeks futile."

"What research?" Benjamin asked. "You never told us what you were doing."

Gary sighed. "It doesn't matter now. If this is really true."

"Why?" Cory asked. "What difference would it make?"

"We've been trying to find some telenergetic power in humans," Aurora explained.

"Right," Gary said. "We figured if humans were just on a slower evolutionary path than telegens, then they should still have telenergetic potential." He shook his head. "But if they were created specifically to not have any telenergetic powers, then it's all been useless."

Disappointment pounded through the Alliance bond, and Aurora must have sensed it also. She put her hand on

Gary's arm. "You know, we could still keep up the work."

Gary sank into himself. "What's the point?"

She shrugged. "I don't know. It just seemed like we were getting close. Maybe there's something we overlooked."

"I doubt it," Gary said. "I kept hoping we'd have an answer, and each day it seemed like we were getting closer and closer."

"Let's go back to the lab," Aurora said.

But Gary shook his head. "No, Not me. You go ahead and go if you want. I just want to be alone for a while."

Benjamin knew better than to say anything. Not that he would've known what to say anyway. They teleported out of the room and headed back to the main level, leaving Gary alone with the jars.

CHAPTER 26

AS IF DEALING WITH HUMANS WASN'T BAD ENOUGH

Gary wasn't the only one who needed time alone. What with time traveling to a bleak future, finding out his missing brother was really a sister, and learning humans had been genetically engineered, it was like his head would explode. So when Cory teleported away to take a shower, Benjamin found a fountain on the way back to the hotel and sat down. He closed his eyes and did his best to filter out the problems of the world, but they kept coming back, no matter what he tried. First he focused on the leaves, most of which had fallen to the ground. But the leaves didn't take his mind off Caelus and Gaea. Next he thought about the water, but it only made him think of Nathan. Then there was the fish, but Phoebe came to mind. He knew it was pointless.

"Mind if I join you?"

Benjamin opened his eyes and saw Ananya smiling down at him.

"I thought you were heading back to Xanadu," he said.

"That was this morning for you," Ananya said. "But for me, it has been four days."

"Four days!" Benjamin said. "You're kidding."

Ananya shook her head. "Remember what I told you

once before? Time does not flow the same in Xanadu as it does in other places on Earth. And for us at this time, that is not good news."

It didn't take a rocket scientist to figure out what she meant. "Caelus and Gaea?"

"Exactly," Ananya said. "In the half a day you've had here, they've had four full days to prepare."

"So at this rate—"

She cut him off. "No, the ratio is not always the same. Sometimes time flows faster, sometimes slower, and there are even times when it ebbs away at the same pace."

"How bad is it?" Benjamin asked. He didn't really want to know, but he knew he had to.

Ananya almost seemed to sink in on herself. "Far worse than I had suspected. They've taken complete control of the hidden city."

"Did they know you were there?" Benjamin asked.

"No," Ananya said. "My allies concealed me so I could observe without danger."

"Who? Apollo?" Benjamin asked, referring to when he'd actually first met Apollo in Xanadu.

"No, Apollo left Xanadu shortly after your visit," Ananya said. "Needless to say, your visit concerned us."

It had concerned Benjamin, but Apollo and Ananya had seemed unfazed. "Why?"

Ananya didn't speak for a while, and Benjamin didn't press her. He could tell she was deep in thought, though her mind was blocked like a steel trap. It was only after minutes had gone by that she finally opened her eyes and spoke.

"Benjamin," she said. "There is something I need to tell

 226

you. Something I probably should have told you before. But I'm not perfect, and my powers only reach so far." She put her head in her hands. "I just didn't think it was possible. I still can't believe it's possible."

"What?" he asked. "I don't have any idea what you're talking about."

She sighed and seemed to regain her composure. "It's about your test. The test you took to gain the second key of Shambhala."

It was the last thing Benjamin expected Ananya to bring up, and he hated that she'd brought it up. He'd hated the test. It was the worst thing he'd ever experienced in his life—even now—after everything that had happened. He'd put it as far back in his mind as he possibly could, but still it managed to resurface from time to time. Mostly when he was near his twin brothers, Derrick and Douglas, and his baby sister Becca.

"Do you remember what I'm talking about, Benjamin?" Ananya asked.

"Of course I remember," Benjamin snapped. "How could I forget something like that?"

"I'm sorry, Benjamin," she said. "But we need to talk about it. It's as hard for me to talk about as it is for you."

Benjamin laughed. "I doubt that. Your brothers didn't almost die. Your mother wasn't drowned in an underground cavern. You didn't have to pick and choose which lives to save."

"I'm sorry," she said again. "But we need to discuss it. It's important."

"You told me it was only a stupid test—something I dreamed up myself."

"I may have been wrong," Ananya said. "After you left, Apollo and I discussed it at great length and even went down the fountain ourselves. We came to the conclusion that there were greater powers at work during your test."

"I knew it!" Benjamin said. "I knew it even at the time. I'd never have dreamed up something that horrible myself. I couldn't possibly."

Ananya nodded. "After you left Xanadu and after we descended the fountain, Apollo and I detected a presence in Xanadu which I hadn't detected in thousands of years."

"Gaea," Benjamin almost whispered.

Ananya nodded. "Or Reva as she was known in Xanadu."

"Heidi and I felt it when we were leaving," Benjamin said. "On the way back to the Universal Travel Agent. We heard her howling in the wind, and Heidi said she'd never felt anything so evil in her life."

"We felt the same thing," Ananya said. "So we decided we needed to check the cell where Reva—Gaea—had been imprisoned. Nobody had been there in ages, but Reva shouldn't have been able to escape. When we got there, the cell was empty."

"How did she get out?" Benjamin asked.

"We think Nathan let her out," Ananya said. "And then she was free."

"Free to return to Atlantis and join Caelus in his plans to control the world," Benjamin said.

Ananya nodded. "You know the rest. But I need to apologize."

"For what?" Benjamin asked. As far as he could tell, Ananya didn't have anything to be sorry for.

"For not telling you sooner," Ananya said. "As soon as I thought the test was being controlled, I should have interceded. But I didn't. I let the test carry through, and luckily, nobody was hurt. I believe the only reason your family remained safe was because Gaea didn't want to alert anyone to her newly returned power."

"So my family really was in danger," Benjamin said with a sick feeling in his stomach. He thought of how helpless his brothers had been. He thought about his mother, under water behind the solid bars.

"Yes, they were," Ananya said. "And that is why I am sorry. I was blind. And after your test was complete, I should have told you my suspicions. But I didn't. I wanted to learn more—to be sure."

"Would it have made any difference?" Benjamin asked. "I doubt it would have changed the future. Though something needs to."

Ananya smiled at him. "If anyone can change the future we saw at the Necropolis, it is you. It's why the keys were entrusted to you in the first place. The Emerald Tablet chose wisely in its champion."

Talk about pressure. "What if I don't do anything differently? What if that future is the only one in store for us?"

"It's not, Benjamin," Ananya said. "You heard what Iva said to us. She'd seen other futures. She knew it was possible to change the world. It's why they wanted to kill her. Why Apollo was trying to protect her."

"I hope you're right," Benjamin said. "I hope Iva was right."

Once Ananya teleported away, Benjamin reached into his pockets and pulled out the two keys of Shambhala he still had, and his memories traveled ten years into the future when he, Cory, and Phoebe had been together in the dungeons of the Necropolis. The power of the keys hadn't been used, but Benjamin had felt it just the same. It had coursed through his body, and flowed through the air between Cory, Phoebe, and him. The air had been electric—at least that's how it had felt to Benjamin. The power had energized and strengthened him—made him feel whole. Benjamin knew it was no coincidence. The keys knew the triplets. They'd been there when the babies were born.

The fountain rippled, and Benjamin watched it, unable to think about anything else but the keys. And then he knew what had to be done: the first step to making anything different. Benjamin and Cory had to find Phoebe. They had to convince her to join their side, because deep down he knew that unless the three of them stayed together, the world would suffer its doom.

CHAPTER 27

AN ENGAGEMENT BENJAMIN WILL NEVER FORGET

When Benjamin got back to the hotel room, his friends were sitting around in the living room eating something that looked like sandwiches but needed a spoon. That is Andy, Iva, Heidi, and Cory sat around eating it.

"Where's Gary?" Benjamin asked, scooping one of the sandwich things onto his plate. "And Aurora?"

Andy rolled his eyes. "Where else?"

"Still at GERC?" Benjamin asked.

Andy nodded. "Does that really surprise you? Gary came back here for his toothbrush and left."

"Weird," Benjamin said. "I'd thought he gave up hope. But it's not what we really need to talk about."

"Which is what?" Andy asked.

"Which is finding our sister Phoebe," Cory said.

Benjamin turned to look at his brother.

"I can read your mind like a clay tablet, little brother," Cory said. "Plus, I came to the same conclusion."

"I thought she was working for Caelus and Gaea," Andy said.

"She is," Benjamin said. "At least she did before Caelus sold her off to Nathan. If we want her on our side, we need to act."

"Where is she?" Andy asked.

Benjamin looked to Cory, hoping that maybe Cory had some idea. But Cory shook his head. "I can't find her. I've been scanning the earth, but wherever she is, she's masked."

"We need to get her away from Nathan," Heidi said.

"Don't you think I know that?" Benjamin snapped without thinking.

Heidi's hair turned fiery red. She glared at Benjamin. "I'm not implying you don't."

Benjamin mentally slapped his forehead. Was he becoming a complete idiot around girls, just like Andy? "Sorry."

"How do we find her?" Andy turned to Iva. "Can you scan the earth and look for her DNA?"

"I think with both Cory and Benjamin here, I should be able to get through any masking." Iva grabbed their hands and closed her eyes. "Just give me a second."

And sure enough, in just under a second, images of the pyramid had planted themselves in Benjamin's mind.

"Egypt," Cory said.

"Nathan's probably in charge of starting the reconstruction," Benjamin said. And so Egypt it was. They had to get Phoebe.

Along with Andy, they teleported to the Sphinx. If luck finally decided to be on their side, Nathan wouldn't sense them coming. Then they'd be able to sneak up on Nathan, find Phoebe, and get out quick. They wound through the excavated buildings until they reached the line of three pyramids. Crouching low, they stopped next to the first one.

"Nathan's got to be in the big one," Andy said.

"Why?" Cory asked.

"That guy craves power," Andy said. "Given the choice of pyramids, he'd pick the big one every time."

But Cory stopped listening and put his hands to his head.

"What's wrong?" Andy asked.

"Do you feel her, too?" Benjamin asked Cory. Because now that he sensed Phoebe, her feelings seemed to explode in his head.

Cory nodded. "She's here."

"And scared," Benjamin said. "If I had to put a feeling to it."

"I'd be scared of Nathan too," Andy said. "That guy is downright disturbing."

"And he knows we're here," Benjamin said. "I can feel him in my mind."

"Coming to visit," Nathan's voice rang out in their heads. "We thought you'd never make it."

Benjamin's blood started to boil. Just hearing Nathan's thoughts infuriated him. He wanted nothing more than to tear our Nathan's throat. He took a step forward and felt Cory's hands encircle his shoulders.

"Not so fast, little brother," Cory said.

"I want to kill him," Benjamin said between gritted teeth.

"I know," Cory said. "And so do I. But now isn't the time."

"Are you coming to pay my bride and me a visit?" Nathan asked.

Benjamin tensed and felt Cory's grip tighten, but with great effort, he managed to keep his temper under control.

They walked to the front of the great pyramid and found the entrance restored. And magnificent. Curtains of silk hung from the entryway and the overwhelming scent of incense drifted from inside. It was an oasis in the middle of a desert of ruins.

"Humans didn't do this," Andy said, looking over the decadent opening.

Cory shook his head. "You're right. This is Nathan's work."

They stepped inside, pushing silk curtains out of their way, and entered another world altogether. It was like someone had taken the giant pyramid, gutted it, and created a palace inside.

"Won't you come join us?" Nathan's voice called out.

Benjamin looked to Cory who was poised like a cat ready to pounce. Cory nodded his head, and they walked forward, following a yellow carpet stretched out on the perfect, marble floor. It led them to an inner room, straight ahead.

"Do you like what I've done with the place?" Nathan asked.

Benjamin looked in and saw Nathan seated on a throne, atop ten steps. A few steps down and to the left was a second throne upon which Phoebe sat, held there with telekinetic bonds.

Nathan motioned around with his hand. "It may seem a little extravagant, but you should see what Caelus has in mind for Egypt in the future. It would blow your mind."

Benjamin gritted his teeth. He'd seen the future, and this was the seed of its beginning.

"Did you come for the wedding?" Nathan asked. "My

lovely Phoebe and I have just been finalizing the plans. Weddings you know. So many details. So we've decided to just skip all that and make it short and sweet."

"You better not have hurt her," Benjamin said, managing to lunge two steps forward before he was lifted off the ground and thrown back against the far wall. He hit the limestone like a ton of rocks.

Nathan laughed. "Such loyalty. A bit misplaced if I do say so myself. She may be your blood sister, but aside from the blood, she's nothing. She lied to you, deceived you, and pretty much used you for her own gain." He looked over at Phoebe, and her head snapped back as if she'd been delivered an invisible slap. "I'll find plenty of amusement in her, but I can't imagine what you would want with her."

Benjamin stood up and walked back to where Cory and Andy waited. He wanted nothing more than to unleash every bit of telenergetic power he had at Nathan, but knew that would be what Nathan was hoping for. He took a deep breath and struggled to calm himself.

"Just hand Phoebe over to us and we'll be on our way," Cory said.

"Just hand her over?" Nathan said. "But then who would I marry?" He put his finger to his mouth and pretended to be deep in thought. "Hmmm. There's always your friend Heidi I suppose. Or Iva."

Benjamin felt Andy tense next to him. Or maybe he just felt himself tense; he couldn't be sure. But whoever it was, Benjamin didn't trust himself to speak.

"I will repeat this one time and one time only," Cory said. "Give us Phoebe, and we will be going."

"And what will you do if I don't?" Nathan said.

"I'll kill you," Cory said.

Nathan threw back his head and laughed. "Kill me!" He laughed all the harder. "But don't you see. I am the one who is going to kill you."

Benjamin pushed images of his death out of his mind and reached his thoughts out for Phoebe, trying to shield his mind and hoping Cory's conversation would keep Nathan occupied. *"Can you hear me?"* he asked.

Her eyes flickered up, and she looked right at him. *"What are you doing here?"* she asked. *"Nathan is right. I lied to you and used you. Why are you here?"*

"We have you outnumbered," Cory said. "There are three of us and only one of you."

"But I was hoping the three of you would remain as guests for my wedding," Nathan said. "My lovely Phoebe has been waiting long enough. She is so anxious." Nathan looked over at Phoebe, and Benjamin tensed, hoping Nathan wouldn't detect their private conversation.

Luck was with Benjamin. Or arrogance. Nathan looked back to Cory.

"To save you," Benjamin said. *"We can argue about the details later."* Using his mind, he probed around the telekinetic bonds which held her. They were the same kind that had been used on him.

Given the situation they were in, Benjamin didn't even think twice about asking Andy for help. *"Andy, can you get rids of the bonds around Phoebe?"*

Andy didn't hesitate. He got to work immediately, and, before Benjamin knew it, he felt the first layer of telekinesis drop away from Phoebe's imprisonment. And for once he was happy Andy was so good at telekinesis.

Cory must've sensed what Benjamin and Andy were up to; he kept the conversation with Nathan going. "You can't kill us," Cory said. "I thought Caelus wanted us delivered alive."

Nathan snarled. "I'm well aware of our dear father's request. The fool. Doesn't he realize you're as much of a danger to him as you are to me?"

Benjamin felt the second layer of the telekinetic bonds drop away from Phoebe. Only one more layer to go. Where had Andy learned to do this?

"Why does he want us alive then?" Cory asked.

Nathan laughed with no humor. "To be made an example. He has some grand public execution planned. With a parade and a festival and everything. I do see his point. He wants to execute you as the anti-government conspirators that you are, but he's wrong." Nathan slammed his fist down. "We should do away with all of you now."

Benjamin's mind flew to the public execution Iva had talked about. The purges. Caelus and Gaea had purged the world of those they considered enemies to the state, and Benjamin, Cory, and Andy had been at the top of the list. His stomach twisted as he thought about it. Walking into this pyramid may have been what started the whole thing. They might be captured here and taken to Caelus.

"*Hurry, Andy.*" Benjamin knew they didn't have any time to waste. No matter what, they could not let themselves be taken prisoner here by Nathan. Benjamin knew it as sure as he knew Cory was his brother.

"*I'm working as fast as I can,*" Andy said.

Benjamin felt the final bond break away. Phoebe visibly loosened her muscles; the bonds had been holding her

 237

tight. But she didn't get up off the chair. Her hands moved behind her back, and he sensed a telenergetic release coming from her. But then it was gone.

"I really can't believe we're blood related," Cory said to Nathan. "I've gone over it time and time again in my head. There must be some kind of mistake."

"I'll tell you the mistake," Nathan said. "That tramp who called herself your mother. She gave birth to nothing but three abominations. If she hadn't died in childbirth, I'd have killed her myself."

Benjamin couldn't help himself. He severed every single chandelier from the ceiling and flung them at Nathan.

Nathan stopped them in midair and looked at Benjamin. "Is that the best you can do?" The chandeliers dropped to the floor, shattering glass everywhere, but leaving Nathan untouched.

Cory put his hand on Benjamin's arm. "Not now, little brother. He can pay for that comment later."

"Oh how touching," Nathan said. "Loyalty for your mother. Let me tell you something about loyalty. The only person worth being loyal to is oneself. Nobody else is deserving."

"You know nothing about loyalty," Benjamin said. "Or love."

"Love!" Nathan said. "Speaking of love, we must get on with the ceremony." Nathan looked over at Phoebe and again her head snapped back from an invisible slap.

But this time she looked back at him and smiled.

"Getting excited for our wedding?" he asked her.

"Of course," she said. "But what about these three?" She motioned to Benjamin, Cory, and Andy. "Shouldn't we confine them first so they don't ruin everything?"

Benjamin felt his face start burning; he couldn't believe what he was hearing. Phoebe had used him again. This time to get out of her bonds.

Nathan smiled. "Now that is the bride-to-be that I know."

And before Benjamin could do or say anything else, telekinetic bonds wrapped around the three of them, cinching them together. He struggled but couldn't move.

"Good job, Benjamin," Andy said. "We got her out, and this is the thanks we get."

Benjamin didn't know what to say. He felt like nothing short of a total idiot. They should have waited until after they'd killed Nathan to free Phoebe—and only then if she'd been cooperative. He should have been smarter, and he knew it. She'd been raised around Caelus and Nathan her whole life.

"I thought we could trust her," Benjamin said.

"Yeah, well you thought wrong," Andy said.

Nathan walked over to Phoebe and smiled. "Dear Phoebe, I'll release you once we are married."

Nathan didn't know she was already free.

Benjamin opened his mouth to say something but stopped when Cory thought, "*Shut up!*"

Nathan leaned over the throne where Phoebe still sat, imprisoned as far as Nathan knew. He grabbed her and jammed his mouth on hers, kissing her so hard, Benjamin cringed as he watched. And if he hadn't known better, he would have sworn Phoebe was actually kissing him back.

And then Nathan fell to the floor. Dead. Benjamin was sure of it since the bonds around the three of them fell apart as soon as Nathan hit the ground.

And Phoebe fell to the ground beside him.

CHAPTER 28

THE WEDDING IS OFF

Benjamin didn't stop to think. He rushed over to Phoebe, sure she was dead. But when he reached her and squatted down, he realized she was sobbing. Without thinking, he put his arms around her and pulled her close.

"He's horrible," she cried. "I can't stand him. He's a monster."

"He's dead now," Benjamin said. "He was a monster, and now he's dead. It's going to be okay."

"What happened?" Andy walked over to join them.

"I killed him," Phoebe said. "I killed him like I've wanted to do for fifteen years. I hate him." Her tear-streaked eyes looked over to the body of Nathan Nyx, which lay on the ground, and she shuddered.

"But how did you kill him?" Andy asked.

"I teleported blood burrows into his heart," Phoebe said. "It's an old family secret. Our assassins use them all the time."

"Nice family," Andy said. "But a pretty handy trick; I have to admit."

Cory walked over and prodded Nathan's body with his foot.

"He's dead," Phoebe said. "It's foolproof."

"Where did you get the blood burrows?" Benjamin asked. "Not that I even know what they are. I can't believe

Nathan would have let you just carry them around."

Phoebe shrugged, wiping her eyes. "After you guys got rid of those telekinetic bonds around me, I was able to teleport them here from Atlantis."

"It's a good thing you had some handy," Andy said.

"I didn't," Phoebe replied. "I got them from Nathan's rooms. He's been collecting all sorts of killing implements these last few months." Her face darkened. "I never knew why until you told me about his death quest."

Benjamin let out what kind of sounded like a laugh. "Well, I for one am glad that's over. At least that's one less person I have to worry about killing me." He noticed Phoebe looked away when he spoke.

"Phoebe," he said. "Caelus wants to kill me."

She looked back at him. "I know."

"He's going to try to kill all of us," Benjamin continued. "You, too."

Phoebe's mouth dropped open, and she glared at him. "My father is not going to kill me. He may not have any use for me now that the shields are down, but he would never kill me."

"Wouldn't he?" Benjamin asked.

"Of course not," Phoebe said.

"Think about it, Phoebe," Benjamin said. "The only reason he was going to let you live was because Nathan wanted to marry you."

Phoebe looked over at Nathan's body, staring at it long and hard before looking away.

"Gaea will want you dead for sure now," Benjamin continued. "Not only are you—and me and Cory for that matter—a sign of Caelus' infidelity, you've also just killed

 242

Nathan—her true son."

Benjamin couldn't have missed the panicked look that moved onto Phoebe's face if he tried. It was like she hadn't thought about the consequences of killing Nathan Nyx. Benjamin was right thought; Gaea was going to be peeved big time.

Cory moved closer. "It's okay, Phoebe. You can come with us. We can protect you."

Phoebe pulled away, walking down the steps from the thrones. "I don't need your protection. I am plenty capable of protecting myself."

"I'm sure you are," Cory said. "But since we don't want to run into Caelus and Gaea just yet, and you don't want to run into Gaea at all, it only makes sense for us to stick together."

Phoebe opened her mouth to reply, but nothing came out. She closed her mouth, trying to think of something else to say, but apparently found no valid arguments. Benjamin watched as she started to speak and stopped, each time wondering what she'd been planning on saying. Even with the triplet bond, the mind block she put up was impenetrable.

Finally she put her hands on her hips and spoke. "Fine. I'll come with you guys, but only because it makes sense right now. When I'm ready to leave, I'm leaving, and nobody is going to stop me."

CHAPTER 29

California Almost Falls off the Map

They teleported back to Atlantis as fast as they could. Not only would Iva and Heidi be climbing the walls waiting, Benjamin wanted to get Phoebe away from here before she changed her mind. Who knew what she'd been through the last couple weeks? Life with Nathan had to be worse than death. They teleported back to the hotel, and found Heidi and Iva outside by the pond. Just as Benjamin turned to the water, he saw a large tail disappear under the surface.

"What's that?" he asked.

Heidi cocked her head and looked at him. He felt like walking over and kissing her, but decided against it. There were just so many people around.

"Some kind of Loch Ness Monster thing," she said.

"Genetically engineered?" Cory asked.

"Without Gary here to confirm it, no one will ever know," Iva said.

Andy walked over to Iva and gave her a huge hug and a more than embarrassing kiss. Benjamin's face flushed as he looked away. He felt even more stupid now, unsure how he should have greeted Heidi. So he just stood there in place.

"Looks like you guys brought someone back," Heidi

said, walking over to Phoebe. "I'm Heidi Dylan. And you must be Benjamin and Cory's sister."

"I'm Phoebe." Her mouth twitched like she was trying to smile but couldn't quite let herself.

"It's nice to finally meet you," Iva said. "We've been looking for you for a long time."

Phoebe let a smile escape this time, even if it was tinged with sarcasm. "That's funny, because I've been looking for Benjamin and Cory most of my life, too."

"Then why was it so hard for us to find you?" Iva asked. "We scanned the earth for your DNA more times than I even want to count."

"DNA masking," Phoebe said as if that explained everything. But seeing the blank expressions on everyone's faces, she continued. "The shields could genetically filter out key DNA elements from being transmitted. It's an old family secret."

"Once again," Andy said. "More of a conversation for Gary." He looked around. "Don't tell me he's still at GERC."

"GERC!" Phoebe said. "You don't mean—"

Andy nodded. "The genetic place. I can't stand to say the name."

"What's he doing there?" Phoebe asked. "Nobody's supposed to go near GERC without proper clearance."

"According to the old government," Andy said. "The new government issued Gary and Aurora security passes. And that's where they've been ever since."

"No, you don't get it," Phoebe said as her eyes opened wide. "They keep all sorts of dangerous mutations there. Your friends could be in serious danger."

"Phoebe," Benjamin said. "We've been there ourselves.

 245

There aren't any dangerous mutations. But I know why people were told to stay away from GERC."

"Because they could get killed," Phoebe said. "That's why."

Benjamin shook his head. "No. It's because of a secret Atlantis has been hiding there for two hundred thousand years."

Phoebe whirled on him. "What secret?"

"The secret that humans are genetically engineered," Benjamin said.

Phoebe laughed. "That's ridiculous. They were not."

Cory nodded his head. "I saw it, too. It's all right there in a hidden lab. Humans are just telegens bred with no telenergetic powers."

"But that's just plain wrong," Phoebe said. "Humans will someday evolve to be like us, and that's why until then, they need our guidance so they learn to properly use their powers."

Benjamin couldn't stop from rolling his eyes. "You are so brainwashed. Humans don't need guidance. They need to be left alone."

"Left alone," Phoebe said. "Look at history. Before Atlantis stepped in to help humans, the world was in chaos. It was out of the kindness and mercy of Atlantis that humans were ever able to break out of their warring patterns and actually begin to lead civilized lives."

"False gods and goddesses from Atlantis caused all the problems in the first place," Andy said.

"If that's the case, then why is the human world in such chaos now?" Phoebe asked. "After thousands of years without Atlantian involvement."

"Because there has been involvement from Atlantis," Andy said. "You know as well as I do that the shield didn't hold everyone in. Atlantis brewed discord on Earth for ages."

"That's just not true," Phoebe said.

"Don't even try to lie," Andy said. "Humans would be way better off if Atlantis had never been involved with them in the first place."

"Well, technically, that's not really true," Heidi said. "If Atlantis had never been involved in the first place, humans wouldn't even exist. Right?"

Andy opened his mouth to reply, but shut it. Benjamin almost busted out laughing. Heidi was absolutely right. Since humans had been genetically engineered, Earth wouldn't even have them if it weren't for Atlantis. Heck— there might have still been Neanderthals roaming the earth.

"Why don't we drop the subject," Cory suggested. "It's probably time to make a few more introductions."

"I don't know why we have to go," Phoebe said as they walked the distance to the Ruling Hall. "I know what the place is like. I grew up there."

"You need to meet Joey and Selene," Benjamin said.

"Right," Cory said. "And isn't there anything you need to get?"

"Yeah," Benjamin said. "Like a toothbrush or favorite killing implement?"

Phoebe ignored the intended joke. "Maybe." But from the way she avoided the subject, Benjamin didn't push it.

They stopped in the throne room first, and if Benjamin

hadn't known better, he would have sworn Joey Duncan was stressed out. He had his hair, which normally was pulled back in a pony-tail, hanging into his face, and he stood over a huge table staring downward.

"Are you staying out of trouble?" Cory asked as they walked in.

Joey and Selene looked up from the table; Joey's usual smile was missing, and Selene had circles under her eyes the size of galaxies. Even Lulu kept her standard sarcastic comments tucked away.

"Hardly," Joey said. "Look at this." He motioned for them to come over to the table.

Benjamin walked over with Cory and Phoebe trailing behind. On the table, a large map had been spread out, and Benjamin realized it was a geodine of sorts—animated and constantly changing and shifting. The coasts of California were lit up, blinking red.

"What's wrong with California?" Benjamin asked.

Joey leaned back, and pushed his hair behind his ears. "It's on earthquake alert. We've been trying to find a way to stop it all morning, but frankly, we've run of ideas."

"Have you telekinetically strengthened the surface of the ground?" Cory asked. "Just a small increase in strength could make a big difference."

Selene sighed. "It was the first thing we tried. It actually made things worse. The earthquake will hit two hours earlier now."

"Can you evacuate everyone there?" Benjamin asked. "Otherwise, won't lots of people die?"

Joey shook his head. "Even if we'd started first thing this morning, those kinds of massive teleportations would take days to orchestrate." He took a deep breath. "No, teleportation is out."

"Why don't you just visit the plate-tectonics room and level out the plates from underneath?" Phoebe suggested.

Benjamin turned to look at her. He'd almost forgotten she'd come along. He'd been so caught up in what Joey and Selene were saying.

"The what?" Joey asked.

"The plate-tectonics room," Phoebe repeated. "It's what we always did when we wanted to control the plates under the surface of the earth."

"Who are you?" Joey asked, but then shook his head. "Actually, I don't want to know right now. All I care about is getting this California thing under control before the next catastrophe strikes. Can you lead the way to this plate-tectonics room?"

"Sure. Follow me," Phoebe said.

After an hour in the plate-tectonics room, California was safe—at least from the impending earthquake.

"Who did you say you were?" Joey asked as they walked back up the steps leading to the throne room.

"This is Phoebe," Benjamin said. "She's our sister."

Joey raised an eyebrow first at Benjamin and then at Cory. "Well, I can see who got the good looks in the family."

Benjamin was about to open his mouth with a sarcastic response when he heard Phoebe laugh. Needless to say, Benjamin held the sarcastic response at bay.

"Well, good looks or not," Joey said, "I, for one, am sure glad you showed up when you did. The last thing telegens need going against them is another earthquake. So

 249

you've used that room before to stop them?"

Phoebe's smile vanished.

"What?" Joey asked.

She shook her head and bit her lip, and for a second, Benjamin thought for sure she was going to cry. Girls were such emotional roller coasters.

"No," she finally said. "I've never used it before myself. But I saw my father use it plenty of times."

"Same thing," Joey said.

"No, not really," Phoebe said. "Every time I saw my father use it, he was actually causing an earthquake with it—not preventing one."

"Causing an ear—" Joey began, but shut up as soon as Cory elbowed him sharply in the side.

"He always said it was for the good of humans," Phoebe said. "And I never had any reason to doubt him. But why would someone want to cause an earthquake? Didn't you say lots of humans would've died if we hadn't stopped that?"

Selene nodded. "Thousands."

"How could that be a good thing?" Phoebe asked, turning to Benjamin and Cory. "Why would he have said that?"

"Because that's what he wanted you to believe, Phoebe," Benjamin said. "It's what we've been trying to tell you. Atlantis has been causing problems for humans for thousands of years."

Phoebe shook her head. "There must be some kind of misunderstanding. There has to be. It's the only explanation."

Benjamin didn't reply. He didn't think he really needed to say anything else. The plate-tectonics room had spoken for itself.

Phoebe let Benjamin and Cory go with her to her rooms. At first, Benjamin thought she didn't want them to come along. Actually, he was pretty sure of it. Even though she acted like there wasn't anything there she wanted to take, he could tell she was lying. Apparently, she wasn't used to the triplet bond yet.

Benjamin wasn't sure what he'd expected her rooms to look like, but he knew it wasn't what he saw when the door slid open. His mouth fell open as he looked around.

"What?" Phoebe said.

Benjamin shook his head. "I just thought it would be more...oh, I don't know...more simple."

Phoebe cocked her head. "Why would you think that? Caelus and Gaea are the rulers—I mean were the rulers—of Atlantis after all."

"But just look at this place." Benjamin walked over and picked up a pillow off a chaise lounge. "This pillow has diamonds sewn into the fabric."

Phoebe shrugged. "I like diamonds."

"On your pillows?" Benjamin asked.

She walked over and grabbed the pillow from him. "Why shouldn't I have diamonds on my pillows? Why should I even have to move out of here?"

Benjamin looked at her and then looked over to Cory. "I don't know," he said. "That's a good question. Couldn't Phoebe just keep living here? Heck, couldn't we all just move in here for a while; it's big enough." He spun around. "This place is great."

Cory laughed. "It is a step up from the hotel."

"That's putting it mildly," Benjamin said.

"I don't think we should talk about living arrangements until everything's resolved," Cory said.

"Resolved?" Phoebe said. "What needs to be resolved?"

Cory stared at her like she'd just asked why the moon goes around the earth. "Caelus and Gaea are still out there," he said. "And they intend to kill us. All of us."

"Including you," Benjamin added. "You killed Nathan. Remember?"

Phoebe's eyes flashed. "Of course I remember. It's not like I've killed so many people I'd have forgotten."

"Have you killed anyone before?" Benjamin said which seemed like a strange question to have to ask.

"Well, no," Phoebe said. "Our family assassins always took care of that." She shuddered. "I'm just glad Nathan's dead."

Benjamin laughed. "Yeah, it was either going to be him or me."

He stopped laughing when he noticed Phoebe hadn't joined in. Instead she kept looking at Cory and him and then looking around the room.

"What?" Benjamin asked.

"Do you think you guys could go wait in the other room?" Phoebe asked. "There are a few things I need to pick up, and I'd rather do it in private."

"Which room?" Benjamin asked, looking around at the five connecting doors. "Should we go through the one with the emerald curtains or the sapphire trim?"

"Ha ha," Phoebe said. "Very funny." She pointed to the doorway trimmed in blue stones. "Just go wait in there. I won't be long."

Benjamin and Cory headed through the sapphire doorway, but Benjamin made sure to keep the telepathic

connection he'd formed with Phoebe open. He didn't think she was even aware of it—at least he hoped she wasn't.

As soon as the door slid shut, he sensed her moving.

"What do you think she's doing?" Cory asked, and as he said it, Benjamin felt Cory's telepathic bond also. Apparently, he'd had the same idea as Benjamin.

"Looking for something," Benjamin said.

They didn't say anything else as they eavesdropped telepathically on Phoebe.

From the main room, she watched the door shut and then moved into one of the other rooms, sliding the door closed behind her.

With practiced precision, she walked over to a holographic projector on the wall and pushed her hand through it. It evaporated and a keypad appeared, hovering in the air. Benjamin felt Phoebe's mind as she keyed in a sequence, and a hidden door flipped open.

Benjamin wasn't sure what he'd expected to be in the secret compartment. Maybe some sort of weapon. Maybe something she could use to escape. But the first thing she pulled out was an engraving tool etched with the three heart pattern. She must've used it to seal all the letters and clues she'd left. As she pulled it out, she almost caressed it. It struck Benjamin as an odd thing to do, but he just chalked it up to her being a girl.

After placing it in a small bag, she again reached into the compartment. When Benjamin saw the disk she pulled out, he gasped aloud, and then covered his mouth as fast as he could, afraid he'd given himself and Cory away.

The disk was as large as a golf ball and as blue as the ocean. And it reminded Benjamin exactly of the life force

 253

disk she'd stolen from Caelus in the future. Phoebe removed it from the compartment and held it in her palm, cradling it.

"Caelus gave it to her," Benjamin said.

Cory nodded. "I know. I feel it too."

Phoebe sat there looking at the disk for nearly two full minutes. After a while, Benjamin figured she'd forgotten where she was, and that somehow the life force disk had hypnotized her. But finally, she stood back up and replaced it in the compartment, before resealing the door and regenerating the holographic projector.

"She's leaving it," Cory said.

Benjamin nodded. He couldn't figure out why Phoebe was leaving the disk. Her mind had been too chaotic. That or she'd detected their telepathic bond and was deflecting their eavesdropping.

"Did you get everything you needed?" Benjamin asked when the sapphire door slid open.

Phoebe nodded. "Yep. I got everything." And she didn't meet his gaze.

CHAPTER 30

Benjamin has a
Horrible Nightmare

Benjamin fell asleep that night mulling over all the problems in the world—which all seemed to be on his shoulders. And he didn't have a clue what to do about any of them. Or when to do it. And that's when he had the dream. At least he'd thought it was a dream at first. But only too soon, he realized it was more like an out of body experience, with his body still in bed but his mind too far away. Not to mention he was awake.

He stood in Delphi, near the Navel of the World. And Iva sat on the dais. But instead of a line of people extending back from the oracle, Benjamin was the only other person there.

"You've changed the path already, Benjamin," Iva said.

This was the real Iva talking, but something about her looked different—yet familiar. And then it hit him. This was Iva—but it was Iva from the future. From New Delphi ten years from now. The Iva he'd seen when he'd time traveled.

"Which path?" he asked.

"The future," she replied. "Nathan is gone, and Phoebe is with you. The future you saw can't be."

Benjamin shook his head. "It could still be pretty close," he said. "Just without Phoebe and Nathan at the

 255

Necropolis. Killing Nathan hasn't changed anything."

"But you have Phoebe on your side now," Iva said.

"Do I?" Benjamin asked. "Has she really come around?"

Iva gazed deep into his eyes. "You would know better than anyone. What does your heart tell you, Benjamin?"

Benjamin thought about it. If Phoebe had to choose between him and Caelus, what would she do? Would she pick the father she'd known her entire life? Or would she pick her newly found brothers who stood against everything she'd ever known?

"I don't know," he said. "I need more time with her. We all need more time with her."

Iva shook her head. "Time is the one thing you don't have."

And that's when Benjamin saw the alarm in her face.

"What?" he asked. "What happened? Did Caelus and Gaea leave Xanadu?"

Iva didn't answer. At least not at first. But her face spoke volumes. And panic rose into Benjamin's throat.

"Tell me what's going on," he demanded.

Iva rose from the dais and started walking away from the Navel of the World. "Come with me, Benjamin," she said. "I can reach back in time and show you a glimpse."

With his mind, Benjamin followed her down the path. And the world shifted around them.

They still walked on a path, but not the one in Delphi they'd been on seconds before. He'd been on this path before, but it took him a minute before he could place it.

"We're in Xanadu," he said.

"Not wholly," Iva replied. "But be cautious. Someone may be watching."

Benjamin followed her up the sloping hill. "Why are we here, Iva?" he asked.

Iva pointed up to the crystal dome on the top of the hill. The dome inside the walled city of Xanadu. "There's something you need to see up there."

Benjamin followed her in silence, and with only another couple steps, they'd arrived at the top of the hill. The fact that it only took a fraction of the time it should didn't even register on Benjamin. He sent his thoughts out to the dome, searching.

"Not in the dome," Iva said when she felt Benjamin's thoughts. "Over there." She motioned with her head to the fountain. "But we can't go any closer. It's not safe."

"Then how will I know what we're looking for?" Benjamin asked.

"Try reaching out with your mind again," Iva said. "But prepare yourself."

Benjamin's heart pounded as he sent out his telepathic tendrils. And then he felt his heart stop. And his face drain. And his hands start shaking.

"I'm sorry, Benjamin," Iva said.

"They have Derrick and Douglas," Benjamin said. "And even Becca."

"I know," Iva said. "And you needed to know."

"I swear if they so much as hurt a hair on their heads, I'll skin them alive," Benjamin said. His heart had started beating again, but his shaking continued. Caelus and Gaea had kidnapped Derrick, Douglas, and Becca. Did his parents know yet? Why hadn't they told him? Why hadn't Iva told him sooner?

"How did you find out?" Benjamin demanded. "Why

didn't you tell me sooner?"

"Time doesn't work that way," Iva said. "You know that."

"But it might be too late," Benjamin asked.

Iva shook her head. "It's not too late. Even in the future where I am now, I've seen alternatives—alternatives that frighten Caelus and Gaea. I told you the clock had sped up, and now you know why. Caelus and Gaea have set a trap for you, and you have to trip it. There is no other choice. Your time has come."

Benjamin didn't know what to say. He wanted to jump out of the mind link and slit Caelus and Gaeas' throats right now. But that wasn't possible—at least Benjamin didn't think it was. So he did what he could do. He started planning his attack.

CHAPTER 31

THE TROJAN HORSE

Benjamin woke Cory, Andy, and Gary, and ran out into the sitting room. Iva was tying her bathrobe when she stepped through the door. He glared at her.

"What?" Iva asked. "What did I do?"

Benjamin didn't look at her. "Here's a message to give yourself in the future. 'Don't wait so long to tell me.'"

Iva looked at him like he'd spoken in ancient Lemurian. "I don't know what you're talking about," she said.

"And let's hope you never do." He shook his head. "It doesn't matter. All that matters is that we go now."

Heidi, Aurora, and Phoebe walked out, and about that time, Cory, Andy, and Gary joined them.

"Go where?" Andy asked.

"We're going to Xanadu now," Benjamin said. "They've kidnapped Derrick, Douglas, and Becca."

"Who's kidnapped them?" Phoebe asked.

Benjamin whipped his head in her direction. "Your precious father, that's who."

Phoebe bit her lip and looked down. "He wouldn't hurt them."

"Of course he would, Phoebe!" Benjamin said. "When are you going to wake up and smell the ambrosia? Our father is evil. He's bad. He wants to control the world. And he'll kill anyone he needs to do it."

Jack teleported into the room. "So how are you getting there?"

"I don't care," Benjamin said. "All I care about is going now."

"We can teleport," Andy said.

"We don't know where Xanadu is," Heidi said.

"You guys have been there, right?" Andy asked.

Benjamin and Heidi nodded.

"So isn't that good enough?" Andy said.

Benjamin felt his frustration start to get the better of him. His mind felt like it was spinning out of control. "No. I tried going back. Last summer. But it didn't work out. I couldn't seem to get the destination right, and I just kept ending up at my starting point."

"Why don't we use the Universal Travel Agent?" Andy asked. "Wouldn't that be easiest?"

"It's Helios's travel agent," Heidi said. "Last time we were there, he actually caught us using it."

"And I'm not telling Helios about this trip," Benjamin said. "He'll try to stop me from going. He'll say we're not ready. I can't let that happen."

"So we just don't let him know what we're doing," Andy said. "That shouldn't be too hard."

"You're forgetting this is Helios we're dealing with," Jack said. "Not much gets past him."

"This will if we provide a distraction," Andy said.

"What kind of distraction?" Gary asked.

Andy turned to him. "It's a good thing you asked, because I think you and Aurora are exactly the ones we need to do it."

"So go over this one more time," Gary said.

Andy sighed and put his head into his hands. "We've already gone over it like twenty times."

"It's only been three," Gary said. "I just want to make sure I have everything right."

"I don't know what you're worrying about, Gary," Heidi said. "This is right up your alley."

Andy nodded. "Heidi's right. This is the lab we're talking about. Genetic engineering. Just take Helios to the GERC lab—the secret one. And show him the humans. Then you can go into the explanation of what we suspect."

"And how much detail should I go into?" Gary asked. "Do I talk about the DNA splicing hypothesis Aurora and I came up with earlier today?"

"Yes," Andy said. "You talk about anything. DNA splicing. And dicing. I don't care. Just keep him occupied long enough for the six of us—," he looked over at Jack, "and Jack—to get to the Lemurian map library."

"You're assuming the travel agent will be online," Heidi said. "What if it's not?"

Benjamin faced steeled over. "If it's not, then we'll make it come online."

But the Universal Travel Agent was online, and worked perfectly. They transported in pairs except Jack who went with Benjamin and Heidi. They moved through the vortex as before and ended up on the sandy beach.

"How do we get into the city?" Heidi asked. "I don't think Caelus and Gaea will let us walk right in."

"I'm taking suggestions," Benjamin said.

"Teleport?" Jack suggested.

"No," Andy said. "Too obvious. They'd kill us as soon

as we appeared."

"They aren't going to kill us," Phoebe said with no conviction in her voice.

Benjamin didn't waste his energy responding. He'd had just about as much of her defense of Caelus as he could take. She'd obviously blocked out the fact the Caelus had handed her over to Nathan for fun.

"Can we sneak in?" Andy asked.

Heidi shook her head. "No, the defenses around the city are too intricate. I can feel the telepathic barriers from here."

"You know if everything you saw was from someone in the future, then maybe they didn't really kidnap your brothers and sister," Phoebe said.

Benjamin didn't look at her. Again, he didn't feel like arguing about it.

"I have an idea," Cory said. "But we'll need to work out the details."

"Let's hear it," Andy said. "It's gotta be better than anything else we have right now."

"Well, remember what you guys told me about the Spartans?" Cory said.

"We told you something about the Spartans?" Andy asked.

Cory nodded. "Yeah. The part about Odysseus. And how the Spartans won the war against Troy?"

Andy slapped his forehead with his hand. "The Trojan Horse. Of course."

"Right," Cory said. "You called it the Trojan Horse. You said the Spartans snuck into Troy inside a giant horse. Couldn't we do something similar now? Create

 262

some deception to sneak inside the Xanadu city walls."

"I love it!" Andy said. "Our very own Trojan Horse. It's perfect."

"Sure," Jack said. "Perfect. Now the only thing we need is the horse."

They retreated to some caves to brainstorm, and even then it took way too long to figure out the plan. Benjamin was ready to tear his ears off. He looked over to where Phoebe sat under a tree outside the cave. She'd been out there the whole time. At first he'd thought about complaining she'd give them away, but he decided against it. If Caelus and Gaea had been aware of their presence, they'd all be dead by now.

"It has to be something moveable," Cory said. "Something that can get through the city walls."

"If you each could transmute yourselves into Nogicals, you'd be small enough to sneak through one of the holes in the wall," Jack said.

Andy raised his eyebrow. "Yeah, I don't think I was in science the day Mr. Hermes talked about telegen transmutation."

"A perfect idea blown because you skipped class," Jack said, sitting back on a rock.

"What about one of those boats?" Cory asked.

"What about them?" Andy said.

"We could use one to float down the river, directly to the city wall," Cory said. "They're supply boats; the city programming would automatically let it in."

"No they wouldn't," Andy said. "They'd know we were on board."

"Not if we masked our DNA telepathically," Cory said.

"That had to be the way Odysseus did it. Otherwise the Trojans would have known for sure."

Andy didn't respond right away. He actually seemed to be thinking the idea over. "Okay, so you're saying we snag one of those boats, hop inside, mask our life signatures—however we do that—and then wait for the city operating system to let us through the walls."

Cory nodded. "That pretty much sums it up."

Andy clapped his hands together and stood up. "Great. Telepathic DNA. Trojan Boat. It actually sounds like we have a plan."

They crept around to the north side of Xanadu and found cover near the river bank. Phoebe kept her distance, and Benjamin felt like with each passing hour, the wall between them grew higher. Why did she have to be so pigheaded? Cory and Andy seemed to have everything under control with stealing the boat, so Benjamin figured maybe the time had come to talk with her. Really talk with her.

She'd walked farther away than normal, but he found her sitting under a tree watching a small brook. The water jumped around on the rocks, and Phoebe stared, hypnotized.

"Mind if I join you?" he asked, not waiting for an answer as he sat down next to her.

"I was enjoying being alone," she said.

"You need to get over it, Phoebe," Benjamin said. "You need to stop feeling sorry for yourself and get on with your life."

"Life!" she said. "What life? Everything I've ever known is gone. You're trying to tell me the people I've known forever are actually ruthless killers trying to rule the world.

 264

Am I just supposed to accept that? Say 'Oh, okay, thanks for the information,' and move on?"

Benjamin nodded. "It's the truth. You need to accept it."

Phoebe shook her head. "I don't believe it's true. I don't want it to be true. My dad isn't as brutal as you seem to think."

Benjamin didn't reply, at least not immediately. He'd been toying with something but had no idea if Phoebe would be willing to do it. But he had to try something. He knew if he didn't somehow convince her of the truth, she could—and would—ruin everything. She'd give them away in her efforts to prove her—their—father's good intentions.

"Would you be willing to join minds with me?" he asked, not wasting any more time thinking about it.

He felt the block slam into place around her mind as she sat up straight.

"Why?" she asked.

"There's something I want to show you," he said, "and the best way would be by joining minds."

"You can just tell me," Phoebe said.

But Benjamin shook his head. "You need to see this firsthand, and I can't think of any other way."

Phoebe sat in silence, again staring at the water on the rocks. For a minute, he thought she wasn't going to answer, and then he was sure she was going to say no. He'd just have to find a way to convince her.

Phoebe turned to him. "Fine. I've got nothing to hide." And her mind block went down.

Benjamin smiled. "Neither do I."

Thinking about joining minds with Phoebe didn't seem the least bit romantic. She was his sister, and he knew it would be an entirely different experience than it had been with Heidi and Iva. Which turned out to be a huge understatement. He saw most of Phoebe's life—at least he felt the emotions of it. Her life had been nothing like his. He'd grown up among humans, thinking he was a human. Maybe a very strange human, but still a human. She, on the other hand, had grown up believing humans were inferior and learning why they needed to be controlled. He wasn't the least bit surprised to find out that Phoebe had never actually met a real live human.

After the initial phase of getting to know each other's minds, Benjamin didn't waste time. He went right to the visit he'd taken to the future with Cory, Heidi, and Ananya. He tried not to leave anything out, showing Phoebe everything he could.

He showed her the people of the future—their fear, their hatred. He showed her the priestesses being led into the Necropolis for sacrifice. He went back to the throne room of the Necropolis. He felt her shock when she saw herself, seated on a throne next to Nathan. But he didn't care. She had to see what the world would be. She had to see what kind of people Caelus and Gaea really were.

Benjamin felt her mind wilting and caving. He knew the raw emotions of what he was showing her would far surpass any idyllic images she had of their father. And he was right. It wasn't long after they'd been taken captive in the Necropolis that she broke off the mind meld.

"That's enough," she said, and tears streamed down her face.

He leaned over and held her, not trying to stop her tears, not worrying about anything. And he knew he'd won. Phoebe would no longer be a threat.

"I didn't want to believe you," she cried. "I knew you were right, but I didn't want to believe you."

He pulled back from her and looked her right in the eye. "Phoebe, I want you to remember one very important thing."

She wiped her eyes. "What?"

"You are not alone," Benjamin said. "And you never will be again. Do you understand?" He reached into his pocket and pulled out the Xanadu key—Phoebe's key. Without giving any explanation, he placed it into her hand and closed her fingers around it.

She looked at him before slowly nodding. "I know. I can feel it. The bond I have with you and with Cory. It's so different than anything I've felt in the past."

"It's the triplet bond," he said. "It runs deep."

She shook her head. "No, it's more than that. It's love. The love of our mother for us when she died giving birth to us. The love we feel for each other. I didn't want to love you and Cory. I tried everything I could to deny it. But it's there. I can't stop it."

"I feel it to," Benjamin said. "And you're right. It'd be impossible to miss."

Phoebe reached into her bag and pulled out the three heart engraving tool she'd taken from Atlantis. She held it out for him.

"You see this?" she said.

Benjamin nodded and took it from her. "You took it from your rooms in Atlantis."

She nodded, not even asking how he knew. "It belonged to our mother."

Benjamin felt himself suck in air and stop breathing. "Our birth mother?"

Phoebe nodded. "Caelus never knew where I got it, but when I was only about five years old, someone delivered it to me with a note. The note told me it had belonged to my mother." She looked at the heart pattern. "I don't know why I never told Caelus where I got it, but now I know he'd probably have taken it away."

"He never loved our mother," Benjamin said.

"I know," Phoebe replied. "I know that now. He never talked about her, and I never asked. There was some kind of unspoken barrier there that I never understood."

Benjamin remembered something else. "There was something you didn't take when you were in Atlantis," he said. "You thought about it, but put it back."

Phoebe nodded but said nothing.

"Why didn't you take it?"

Phoebe sighed and threw a rock in the water. The rippled spread across the whole width of the brook. "It was a gift from Caelus," she finally said. "But I didn't want it when he gave it to me, and I sure as heck don't want it now."

"What was it?" Benjamin asked even though he knew the answer.

"A life force disk," Phoebe whispered. "He gave it to me for my birthday last year. I knew what it was when I got it, and I knew it wasn't an ordinary one—you know, that any normal type of sacrifices will fill up with telenergy."

"You needed human sacrifices," Benjamin said, and Phoebe nodded.

"Caelus told me it could be filled just from humans getting old and dying," Phoebe said, "but I still didn't want any part of that. It seemed wrong. But I guess the promise of immortality made me hold onto it." She looked him right in the eye. "How do you know about life force disks anyway?"

They hadn't gotten that far in the mind joining. They hadn't made it to the part where Phoebe had helped them escape the Necropolis. Benjamin reached into his pocket and pulled out the disk.

Phoebe gasped and covered her mouth. "Where did you get that? It belongs to Caelus."

Benjamin nodded. "I know. Apollo told me after you gave it to me."

Phoebe's eyes were as wide as the disk. "I never gave that to you. Caelus would kill anyone who took that away from him."

"You gave it to me in the future," Benjamin said. "And I think that we can safely assume that if Caelus found out you took it, he had you executed." Benjamin held it out for her, but she shrank back, crossing her hands in front of her chest.

"Don't get it near me," she said. "I can't believe you have it. Caelus is going to kill you—us—when he finds out."

Benjamin actually laughed. "Caelus is going to kill us anyway." He put the life force disk back in his pocket, and Phoebe visibly relaxed. Not that he blamed her. He didn't much like the idea of walking around with a bunch of human sacrifices in his pocket either.

"*Benjamin.*"

Benjamin looked in the direction of his friends, even though the voice had come telepathically. It was just a natural reaction.

 269

"*Gary?*" he asked.

"*Good,*" Gary said. "*There you are. There's something we need to talk about right away.*"

It didn't take Benjamin's being a genius for him to realize Gary was excited about something. He could almost envision Gary bouncing off the walls.

"*Okay,*" Benjamin said. "*When and where?*"

"*Aurora and I are coming on the travel agent now. Which means that we should be able to join you guys in approximately twelve minutes.*"

Benjamin smiled, even as he signed off telepathically with Gary. He stood up and helped Phoebe to her feet. If Gary and Aurora were about to come join them, then he'd better at least warn his friends so they didn't transmute them into toads upon arrival.

CHAPTER 32

GARY SAVES THE WORLD

"Are you sure no one saw you?" Heidi asked once Gary and Aurora appeared.

"There's no time to worry about that," Gary said. "Aurora and I discovered something no one alive could possibly fathom."

Benjamin looked from Gary to Aurora. She flipped back her blue dreadlocks and nodded.

Gary looked around. "Where are Andy and Cory? They should hear this too."

"They're stealing a boat," Jack said. "Some half-baked scheme to get into the city."

"A boat?" Gary shook his head. "Well, we can't wait on them." He paced back and forth under the trees.

Finally, Iva stood up and walked over to him. "Gary."

"What?" he asked, still pacing.

She put her hands on his arms. "Calm down. Sit down. Take your time and tell us what you found."

Gary sat down, but stood back up. "I haven't recorded anything yet. Do you understand?"

Benjamin nodded.

"No, you don't understand," Gary said. "What that means is that there are absolutely no records of what I'm about to tell you. Not back at GERC. Not in Lemuria. Nowhere."

 271

"Does it matter?" Phoebe asked.

"Of course it matters," Gary said.

"Why? What's the big deal?" Phoebe asked.

Gary puffed out his breath. "The big deal is that if something happens to Aurora and me, no one will ever know what we've discovered."

"Then maybe you should just tell us already," Benjamin said. "Spit it out."

"Yeah, because I'm getting sick from all the spinning thoughts in your brain," Jack said.

Gary sat down and put his hands on his legs. Benjamin noticed Gary's hands were actually shaking. Whatever Gary was about to say—and Aurora had it telepathically blocked—must have been important. Gary was never this worried. Smart. Focused. That would be Gary. Nervous about a scientific discovery—not Gary.

"Humans are not without telenergetic skills," Gary blurted out.

"But I thought they were," Benjamin said.

Gary shook his head. "All the scientific data we discovered in the lab led us to believe exactly that. With all the facts in front of us, there was just no other logical conclusion to draw." He looked to Aurora. "That is until we stumbled upon a unique splice in the DNA strain. Actually, Aurora stumbled upon it." Gary looked down when he said this. It probably took a lot for Gary to admit someone had found something scientifically important before him.

"Okay, so the DNA was spliced," Benjamin said. "So what?"

"Well, we didn't understand the splice at first," Gary said. "It wasn't in any of the normal telenergetic areas

 272

we're familiar with."

"Not telepathy?" Heidi asked.

Gary shook his head.

"What about telegnosis?" Iva asked.

"Or telekinesis," Benjamin said.

"No, no, no," Gary said. "It was none of those. In fact that's why we missed it for so long. We hadn't been looking in the right place, and even with the splice, the gene was dormant."

"Meaning what?" Heidi asked.

"Meaning that even once we figured out what it was, it wasn't an active skill," Aurora said.

"So let me get this straight," Benjamin said. "Humans have some worthless telenergetic skill that isn't even active. So they can't use it?"

Aurora and Gary looked at each other.

"Yeah," Aurora said. "I guess that pretty much sums it up."

Benjamin threw up his hands. "And that's what's so important? That's why you guys risked coming here to tell us that?"

Gary raised an eyebrow and looked at Benjamin. "You still don't know what skill it is."

"Who cares?" Benjamin asked. "It doesn't matter."

Jack whistled low under his breath. "Oh, I get it now. And trust me, it matters."

"What is it?" Iva asked.

Gary nodded. "Telejamming."

Benjamin turned and looked at Gary and felt his stomach clench, whether in surprise or anticipation he couldn't be sure.

"Did you say telejamming?" he asked.

"Yep, telejamming," Aurora said.

"Humans have a dormant ability for telejamming so strong it could easily overcome every single telegen strength added up—even with the weakest human paired against the strongest telegen," Gary said. He nodded his head toward Jack. "Even against Nogicals."

Benjamin looked at Jack who nodded. He sat back down and tried to stop his voice from quavering. "So you're telling me that if this gene wasn't dormant, then telegens would have absolutely no control over humans."

"That pretty much sums it up," Gary said.

"How does a genetic splice become non-dormant?" he asked, almost dreading the scientific answer he knew would follow.

Gary smiled and sat back down across from Benjamin. "Funny you should ask," he said. "Aurora and I actually have a theory on that."

It took a few minutes for the words to sink in, and even then, Benjamin still processed the information over and over in his mind.

"What the earth needs is a burst of telenergetic power super strong, and directed to just the purpose of igniting the dormant splice," Gary had said.

A super strong burst of telenergetic power. Something tried to creep to the front of Benjamin's mind, but didn't quite make it there.

"So how could that happen?" Heidi asked. "What could cause such force?"

Gary shook his head. "That's pretty much where our

research stopped. We figured out what was required, but that's when Aurora suggested we come here and tell you guys about it."

Telenergetic power. Benjamin thought and thought. He was missing something. What could cause telenergetic power?

"What about a telemagnifier?" Iva asked, holding her Ammolite pendant. "Couldn't a telemagnifier cause the desired effect?"

"Not on the level we need," Aurora said. "We did some preliminary calculations, and pretty much found that even the strongest telemagnifiers in the ruling hall wouldn't change more than a couple human's genes."

"So we just do it a few at a time," Heidi said.

"Do you realize how many humans there are on Earth?" Jack asked.

"A lot," Heidi said.

Gary let out an exasperated breath. "Anyway, I just thought you guys should know."

Benjamin couldn't shake it. The telenergetic power thing. And then the pieces came together.

They came together for Phoebe too. "The keys," she said. "They'd have the power needed."

"It's what the Emerald Tablet had in mind all along," Benjamin said. He felt the excitement building up inside him and could hardly control himself. He stood up and started pacing. "The Emerald Tablet knew the keys needed to be found—not only to bring down the shields, but to release the dormant gene of the humans."

"It makes perfect sense," Heidi said.

Benjamin nodded. "I knew the shields were meant to

be brought down, even when part of me fought against it. I knew it was wrong to keep all of Atlantis imprisoned. But humans needed a way to contend." He ran over and hugged Gary. "Gary, you are a genius. With the research the two of you have done, we're going to save the world."

It was then that Cory and Andy walked in. "Who's going to save the world?" Andy asked.

"We are," Benjamin said. "Well, actually the keys of Shambhala are. With the help of Cory, Phoebe, and me."

CHAPTER 33

BENJAMIN SAVES
THE WORLD

Even with the excitement of Gary's discovery, Benjamin still had a hard time focusing on what they needed to do. Releasing the telejamming power of humans might save the human race from enslavement by Caelus and Gaea, but it didn't save Derrick, Douglas, and Becca. And the more he thought about it, the worse it seemed.

"We should kill Caelus and Gaea first," Benjamin said.

"No," Cory said. "If we're going to do this, we need to do it now. We can't risk one of us dying."

Phoebe nodded. "Cory's right. There are three keys and there are three of us."

"But Caelus and Gaea might hurt my brothers and sister," Benjamin said. "I can't take that risk."

Cory looked at Benjamin and sighed. "I see how you feel, but Phoebe's right. It has to be the three of us. No one else will do. If one of us gets killed while attacking Caelus and Gaea, then life for humans is over."

"And if we use the keys first, then life for my brothers and sister could be over," Benjamin said. "We have to save them first."

"*Benjamin,*" Phoebe said telepathically. "*Look inside your mind. You know what the right answer is. I can see you do. No one is arguing the risk you'd be taking, but it's a*

risk that has to be taken."

Benjamin looked at her and forced the hint of tears from his eyes. He was not going to cry. This was not the time to turn into some kind of stupid softie. He firmed his mind and looked back at all his friends, not just Phoebe.

"Then the timing has to be perfect," he said at last. "We need the boat ready to go. We release the power of the keys, but I want to go as soon as it's done."

Cory nodded. "Good plan. Caelus and Gaea will be so distracted from the telenergetic release, they may not even notice the boat."

"Perfect," Benjamin said. "Let's do this then."

Gary didn't just tell them where the DNA splice was; he gave them a sample of the DNA before the modification and a sample of the DNA after the modification.

"It's simple," he'd said. "Just change this," he handed the first sample over, "to this," he handed the second sample over.

Benjamin looked down at the two Petri dishes. "They look the same."

"That's because you're not looking close enough," Gary said. "You need to delve into the DNA and extract the differences. Once you do that, the mutation is elementary."

Benjamin laughed. "That's pretty much what I was thinking. If by some miracle I can extract mutations from DNA strains, then I can do anything."

"Just be careful, okay?" Heidi said. "And get on the boat the second you're done." And before Benjamin realized it, Heidi had leaned over and was kissing him. He kissed her back, even as he felt his face flush with embarrassment. Everyone watched. But, actually, when he thought about

 278

it, he didn't care. Let them watch. He'd watched Andy and Iva kiss enough times that he probably owed them a few.

Finally, Cory cleared his throat. "It's getting late."

Benjamin pulled away from Heidi. "Yeah, I know. And I'm ready." He laughed. "At least as ready as I'll ever be."

Phoebe looked over at Benjamin as they waited for everyone to leave the cave, and he smiled back at her. He could feel how nervous she was. Or maybe it was just his own nerves pushing through. Regardless, it seemed like of the three of them, only Cory was calm. Like he saved the world every day.

Once the cave had cleared out, Cory turned to them. "I've been thinking some about how we should do this."

But Phoebe immediately shook her head. "Then you need to stop."

Benjamin and Cory looked at her like she was crazy.

"These keys are a part of us," she said. "I can feel it deep down." She held her key in her right hand and pressed it to her heart. "This key wants to help us. Don't you feel it?"

Cory looked at Benjamin and shrugged. They reached into their pockets and each pulled out their respective key. As soon as all three had been exposed to each other, the glowing and thrumming started.

"See," Phoebe said. "Don't you feel it?"

Benjamin held his key close to his heart as Phoebe had done. And he felt something ignite within him. "Yes!"

Cory raised an eyebrow and looked at the two of them. Then he put the key to his heart, and his eyes lit up to match the glowing key.

"Good," Phoebe said, and none of them spoke another word.

 279

They stood in a triangle, and the three keys blazed. Light sprang out from each key and formed a laser light triangle in the center of them. Benjamin felt the direct connection between himself and Cory and Phoebe grow, until before he knew it, he could hardly distinguish his own thoughts from those of his brother and sister.

He'd never felt closer to anyone in his life. Not Derrick or Douglas or Becca. Not Heidi. Not Mr. Burton when they'd shared the power of the keys. It was as through the three of them had become a single entity—a single telegen with the power of the world within their fingertips.

The warmth of the keys filled him, and for a moment, he forgot their true purpose. All he wanted to do was bask in the glory of the telenergy. He knew that with it, he could do anything. Would do anything. He could rule the world, and for an instant, that was all he wanted to do. He could defeat the strongest of foes, and suddenly, battle was all Benjamin could think of. And he could prove once and for all who the most powerful telegen really was. Nobody would ever be able to compete against him. Nobody would ever dare try. And as far as telekinesis went? Andy was nothing in comparison to what Benjamin could be. What Benjamin was. He was unstoppable. He could move mountains. And bridges. He alone could move all the Moai on Easter Island. He could move the world.

Benjamin's head swam with the joy of it. The dreams he knew were within his reach. And then he looked down at the DNA samples on the ground. Right where he'd placed them. And he remembered.

There was a reason they were using the keys now. And it wasn't to rule the world. It was to save the world and the humans living there. And it was up to Phoebe, Cory, and himself to do it.

Benjamin tore his eyes off the Petri dishes and looked over to Phoebe. Her eyes had glazed over, and he pushed his thoughts to the forefront of her mind. Her head snapped over to him and she glared, narrowing her eyes. But then her face softened, and together they looked to Cory.

Cory who always seemed to be the sensible one.

Cory who always seemed to be the rational one.

The mature one.

The grown-up one.

Cory was in a different world. Benjamin felt into Cory's mind and saw the battle against Achilles, the mightiest warrior of all time. It didn't take Benjamin long to realize that the competition between Andy and himself was nothing compared to the competition Cory had apparently felt with Achilles. Even as Benjamin thought this, he felt Cory flinch and look over.

"I am the greatest warrior of all time," Cory said. "I have always been and will be in the future. No one will ever stand in my way." But as he spoke, he didn't meet Benjamin's gaze. Cory's glassy eyes focused beyond Benjamin. Beyond Phoebe.

Panic rose inside Benjamin. The telenergy within him from the keys was building, and Benjamin knew they'd need to use the keys soon to change the DNA.

"The time for battle is over, Cory," he said. "We have work to do."

Cory laughed. "Don't you see it's not important? Don't you see what we can really do with our power? We can rule the world."

Benjamin held his key firmly, willing it to help him. "No, we need to save the world. Not rule it."

"We can save it by ruling it," Cory said. "Don't you see?"

Benjamin opened his mouth to reply, but it was Phoebe who spoke. "No, Cory. I know how you feel. Look into my thoughts. You can see it. You know that even more than you, I want to rule the world. It's what I was raised for my whole life. It's what I would do best. But it's wrong."

"No," Cory said. "It's not wrong. It can't be wrong."

"Look into yourself," Phoebe said. "Look deep. Deeper than Achilles. Deeper than the Trojan War. Deeper than all the battle training you had. You are destined for more than that. Those things mean nothing. And you know it."

Benjamin felt Cory's mind as it churned. The battle raging within him caused Benjamin to pull back—just a little. He knew keeping the connection between the three of them and the keys was the only hope for their success. And so he watched. And waited as Cory struggled.

The battle in Cory's mind ebbed and flowed. And finally relented. Relief flooded through Benjamin as Cory's face smoothed over. Relief combined with a fair amount of disappointment. His own dreams of ruling the world were vanishing along with Cory's. He'd known it was wrong, but he couldn't help how he'd felt. If Cory hadn't been able to pull himself back, Benjamin knew he and Phoebe would have eventually succumbed.

But they hadn't, and Cory had recovered. And the three of them focused all their energy on the DNA samples on the floor.

Genetic engineering knowledge obviously wasn't a

requirement, because as soon as the power of the keys focused on the DNA samples, telenergy sprang from the three keys of Shambhala and exploded all over the earth. It left the small cave in Xanadu, shooting out from their hands where they held the keys. And Benjamin felt it doing its work. He felt the humans changing. He felt them all in his mind.

Benjamin had no idea how long it took, but when the light vanished from the cave, he looked down at his hands.

"My key is gone," he said, quickly looking over at Phoebe and Cory.

"So is mine," Phoebe said. "Used as it was meant to be used and now gone."

"Where did they go?" Benjamin asked, but knew, even as he asked it, that she wouldn't have an answer. They might never know the answer.

Benjamin looked to Cory, watching his brother sink to the ground and put his head in his hands.

"I almost ruined everything," Cory moaned.

"No, little brother," Benjamin said. "We almost ruined everything."

Phoebe nodded and sat down beside Cory. "Benjamin's right. It was all of our minds working together. I wanted it every bit as much as you. It manifested itself in you, but it was all of us as sure as it was one of us."

"It would have been the end," Cory said. "The end of everything we've worked so hard for."

"But it wasn't," Phoebe said, putting her hand on Cory's arm. "The keys tested us and we passed. That's all that matters."

"And now they're gone," Benjamin said. "And we

need to go." Now that the initial task at hand was complete, thoughts of Derrick, Douglas, and Becca flooded Benjamin's mind. He knew Caelus and Gaea would find out what they had done with the keys. Find out that their hopes of ruling humans as before would be gone. And once they found out, there would be no telling what they would do. And Benjamin didn't want his little brothers and sister to suffer their wrath. He only hoped he wasn't too late.

CHAPTER 34

TROUBLE IN PARADISE

They tried not to move as the boat floated down the river. The darkness smothered them the closer they got to the city walls. The boat floated until they'd reached the gate, and then, as they'd hoped, automatic systems unlocked the barriers, the gates opened, and their Trojan boat floated inside the city of Xanadu.

As soon as the gates slid closed behind them, Cory levitated off the boat onto the bank and telekinetically pulled it to shore. Benjamin waited until everyone else had gotten off safely before levitating off himself.

As the boat slipped away, back into the darkness, Ananya rushed up to join them.

"The world shook," she said.

Benjamin reached out and felt the strength of the telejamming gene increasing with each passing minute. Humans were going to be all right.

"We altered humans so they could telejam," Benjamin said.

"Extremely strong telejamming," Aurora added.

Ananya nodded. "I felt as much. The gods are not going to be happy. I'm afraid with that single move, you've made yourselves some pretty serious enemies."

Benjamin shrugged. "It had to be done. It's what the Emerald Tablet had in mind all along."

Ananya eyed him. "Can you be sure, Benjamin Holt?"

He opened his mouth to reply, surprised that of all people, Ananya would question him on this, but she held up her hand.

"I'm not saying I disagree with what you have done," she said. "I only want you to know the consequences of your actions."

"All we care about now is getting rid of Caelus and Gaea," Cory said.

"And saving my brothers and sister," Benjamin added.

"I know," Ananya said. "Just know that even after Caelus and Gaea are gone, there will be others. Many others."

But Benjamin didn't care, and he knew Ananya could tell. And he didn't care about that either. He didn't have time to waste thinking about his growing list of enemies.

"Where are they?" he asked.

"Under the fountain," Ananya said. "Where you found them last time."

Benjamin didn't stop to think. He started moving and then ran toward the fountain where he'd found the second key of Shambhala before. Where he'd had his test. Where he'd saved Derrick and Douglas before. But them he remembered his mom. He hadn't saved her in the test. She'd drowned—or would have if it hadn't been a test—during the search for the second key.

"Wait, Benjamin," Heidi called, but Benjamin didn't slow, and even when he reached the cascading fountain, that didn't stop him either. He moved his hand in front of it the way he'd seen Ananya do a year and a half before, and the water stopped.

Benjamin started down the wet, circular staircase. He knew he had to be careful of his footing; it wouldn't help anyone if he fell to his own death. But the slowness drove him crazy, so he counted the steps down to keep himself from going nuts.

At five hundred, he'd reached the bottom and found the path marked by the flowing water. And as before, the water already pooled around his ankles.

Relief washed through Benjamin when he came to the cavern wall and there wasn't a cell carved into it. But the shelves set high on the wall were the same, and on each one stood a twin. They had telekinetic restraints surrounding them; Benjamin felt the energy. And this was no test. Benjamin knew it as sure as he knew he would destroy Caelus and Gaea.

"We've been expecting you, Benjamin Holt."

Benjamin turned to see Gaea standing up on a ledge holding Becca in her arms. Becca—who was only two and a half years old.

"Let her go," Benjamin called above the sound of the blood pounding in his ears. He lashed his telenergy out as forcefully as he could in an attempt to teleport Becca out of Gaea's arms. But the room had been telejammed. Sealed off completely.

"Benji," Becca called, and stretched out her tiny little arms.

"Let her go now and ruin all the fun we could have?" Gaea asked. She laughed and turned to her left. "I'm afraid my dear husband Caelus would be ever so angry if I did that."

"Benjamin, I can't get loose," Derrick called. "Get me down!"

Benjamin dared to take his eyes off Gaea and Caelus and look up to the shelves. Calm. He had to remain calm.

 287

They wanted him to get angry. They wanted him to act first and think later. But he'd had enough of that. He wasn't going to give them the satisfaction.

Benjamin laughed at Gaea and Caelus, who'd moved next to his wife. Benjamin forced out the laughter even though on the inside all he wanted to do was lunge for them and pull their guts out through their throats. "Don't you see you've already lost?" he called. "Can't you feel it?"

He saw the doubt flicker across Gaea's face even as she masked it. She knew something had happened. But from her doubt, Benjamin gathered she didn't know what.

"Lost?" she called. "Nothing is lost. The world is ours. We shall rule it side by side, and our first act will be to execute you and your friends."

"And what about me?"

Benjamin turned at the sound of Phoebe's voice. She walked into the underground cavern with Cory at her side.

"Would you execute me?" she asked.

Gaea grinned in reply. "I have waited for longer than I care to think to see you dead. To see all three of you dead. All you are is a constant reminder of my husband's continual infidelity."

Caelus looked out at Phoebe, and Benjamin saw their eyes lock.

"Would you kill me, father?" Phoebe asked.

Caelus put up his hands palms up. "I'm afraid my hands are tied on the matter. You signed your own death sentence when you killed Nathan. He was my son, too, after all."

"It doesn't change anything," Benjamin called. "Even killing us won't help. You'll have no power. You can't control the humans."

Gaea stopped smiling and looked Benjamin in the eye. Benjamin saw her grip on Becca tighten, though Becca squirmed and whined.

"*Be quiet, little Becca*," he willed her telepathically. "*Everything will be okay.*" With the telejammers in place around the cavern, he didn't know if she heard his telepathic thoughts, but he had to say something.

"What do you mean, we can't control the humans?" Caelus asked.

"He's lying to us, dear husband," Gaea said, turning to him. "He's trying to deceive us."

"There's nothing deceptive about it," Cory called. "Humans are no longer within your control. In fact it's now you who should be worrying about them."

"Liars!" Gaea called. "All of you."

"Benji," Douglas called. "The water's getting higher!"

Benjamin had forgotten about the water which had been steadily rising since he'd reached the cavern. If he could just distract Gaea and Caelus for a while longer, he figured maybe there'd be some way to stop it. Maybe.

"*Stay calm*," Benjamin sent out telepathic thoughts to the twins.

"But that's the funniest thing," Benjamin said. "We're not lying. Humans can now telejam better than the strongest telegen."

"That's not true," Gaea said. "How would you know such a thing?"

"Because we altered their DNA to give them the ability," Benjamin said.

"He's not lying, father," Phoebe said, and inwardly, Benjamin cringed at her reversion to calling him father.

 289

He only could hope she'd remain steadfast in her position against him.

"You altered human DNA?" Caelus asked.

"Not for every human," Gaea stated. "It's simply not possible."

"But it is possible," Benjamin said. "With the three keys of Shambhala. We altered the DNA of every human on the face of the earth."

And with that comment, events started into motion. Gaea flew into a rage and threw Becca down from the ledge. Benjamin, having somewhat suspected this, caught her in midair, and using the power of the teleportation surger he'd slipped from his pocket into his hand, he teleported her away from the cavern.

And while Gaea looked down to where Becca should have landed, Benjamin didn't hesitate. The telekinetic bonds dissolved around the twins, and, again using the teleportation surger to break through the telejamming shields, he teleported both of them at the same time out of the cavern. Inside, he sagged with relief. By distracting Caelus and Gaea, and by preparing for their reaction, he'd managed to teleport all three of his siblings back to the safety of Lemuria. Far away.

Lightning flew from Gaea's fingertips as she pointed her hands at Benjamin, Cory, and Phoebe. Together, they diverted the lightning, though Benjamin wasn't sure if the three of them would be enough to fight the combined powers of Caelus and Gaea for long. And then Benjamin remembered his next trick.

He pulled the life force disk from his pocket and held it out in front of him. Caelus' life force disk.

Gaea and Caelus both froze, and the lightning stopped.

"Where did you get that?" Caelus spat out. He reached to his neck, to the chain which hung around it, and pulled out his own disk. The one from the present.

"It doesn't matter," Benjamin said. "All that matters is that I have it. And if you destroy us, then you destroy it too."

"I don't care," Gaea said, and threw another ambush of lightning at them. Benjamin hadn't expected that, and it caught him square in the chest. He fell backward to the floor, landing in the water, but still managed to hold onto the disk.

"Stop!" Caelus commanded Gaea. "You'll destroy me!"

She whipped around to face him. "I don't care, you fool. Don't you see that? I don't care. These three will ruin everything. The plans of my lifetime. And I'm not going to risk that. Not for you. Not for anyone."

Caelus' mouth dropped open. "You'd kill me. Me! How dare you?"

He reached out and placed his huge hands around her throat. Apparently, Benjamin wasn't the only one with that sentiment.

"Get out of my way!" Gaea tried to scream, but with her throat being crushed, it came out pretty garbled.

"No!" Caelus said, increasing the pressure of his hands.

Benjamin could feel the energy rising in the room. But the lightning had stopped, and with Phoebe's help, he managed to pull himself up to his feet.

"What do we do now?" he whispered to Cory and Phoebe.

"I honestly don't know," Cory said. "If we try to destroy him now, then we'll still have Gaea to contend with."

  291

"We need to destroy Gaea," Phoebe said. "We need to help Caelus destroy Gaea."

Benjamin looked back over to Caelus and Gaea. They were locked into combat, and sparks flew around them, surrounding them in a blue haze.

"Reach your power out to Gaea," Phoebe said. "I know we don't have the keys anymore, but we're still bonded through a triplet link."

Cory nodded. "Phoebe's right. We are more powerful then I think we know."

Benjamin stretched out his telenergy and felt Cory and Phoebe do the same. He directed everything toward Gaea. And it hit her. She turned to look as the telenergetic pulse hit her square in the chest. And Caelus grinned.

"You would kill me?" Caelus snarled at Gaea. "Who will die now?"

Benjamin sent out another pulse, and Gaea, again, shook as it hit her. The sparks subsided as she seemed to consider her situation.

"Not me," she said, but she'd hardly gotten the words out when a storm of sparks erupted and she crumbled to the floor. Dead. Every bit of energy flowing from her banished.

Caelus stared at Gaea curled up on her stomach on the floor. "She would have killed me," he said, and turned to them. "But the plan must continue, and the three of you must die."

"Then you'll have to find us," Benjamin said. He reached out and grabbed a hand of each of his siblings.

"Teleport now," Benjamin said to Cory and Phoebe, and engaged the power of the teleportation surger.

CHAPTER 35

GHOST CURSES FROM THE FUTURE

Benjamin had to assume Cory and Phoebe knew where they were going. He'd put an image of the place in his mind. They had to get Caelus away from the protection of Xanadu. And so they teleported away from the underground cavern.

When they arrived on the grounds of the future Necropolis, the place was empty. It didn't take Caelus long to track them—which Benjamin had hoped he would, and when he appeared only a few yards away, Benjamin was ready. Caelus lunged at them with everything he had. And Caelus still had a death grip on his life force disk.

Benjamin held the life force disk from the future high in the air. Needless to say, Caelus stopped immediately.

"Don't you wonder where I got it?" Benjamin asked.

Caelus swallowed hard and clenched his own present day disk all the tighter.

"It's a fake," Caelus said.

Benjamin shook his head. "No, not a fake."

"Then it's a copy," Caelus said. "A cheap copy."

Phoebe laughed. "You know that's not true, Father. You can feel its power. And the funniest thing about it is that you're wondering why it's so much stronger than the one you have in your hand."

Caelus looked down at his disk, turning it over in his hand, contemplating what she'd said. But his confusion evaporated. "Give it to me now," he ordered them.

"No way," Benjamin said. "Like I'd really just hand this over."

"You may not, but my daughter will," Caelus said. He turned his attention to Phoebe. "Get the disk and bring it to me, Phoebe."

But Phoebe shook her head. "I'm not going to do that. You don't have any power over me. All you ever did was lie to me."

"Lie to you!" Caelus said. "It's these two who are lying to you. Now bring me the disk."

Phoebe grabbed the disk from Benjamin's hands before he could stop her. "I'd destroy it before I'd ever hand it over," she said.

Anger flickered in Caelus' eyes, but he tried to replace it with love for Phoebe. "No you wouldn't because you still love me and want me to love you. And I will love you, daughter, if only you do this one small thing for me. Bring me the disk."

Benjamin felt the power of the two disks in the air. The life forces of the dead humans used to fuel them crackled around them, and Benjamin realized that many of the humans had died on this very spot. Ten years in the future maybe, but here at the Necropolis. He felt their spirits reach up from the ground to grab at the disk. He would have sworn he actually felt their ghosts. Like the ghosts at the Crags. They wanted their lives back. They wanted their spirits back from the futuristic disk. And he felt their hatred for Caelus. And he got an idea.

"Go ahead, Phoebe," Benjamin said.

She looked at him like he'd lost half his brain. And maybe he had, but he had to go with his instincts.

"What?" she said.

"I said go ahead," he said. "Go ahead and give Caelus the life force disk." The ghosts screamed louder in his mind.

Phoebe looked from him to Cory. Cory must've felt it too. "Benjamin's right, Phoebe. Give him the disk."

Phoebe's hands shook as she held the disk, even as her knuckles whitened from clenching it so hard.

"But—" she began, then stopped, and her face drained of color. Had she felt the ghosts too? She must've. Benjamin's head was about to explode from their cries for revenge.

Phoebe moved forward and got within a few feet of Caelus.

"That's right," Caelus said. "Just give me my disk and all this will be over."

Benjamin felt the energy from the ghosts growing. They were gaining power with every second that went by. Drawing it from the disk. He heard them begin to howl. Their voices grew, and joined together. And Benjamin was sure he saw sparks in the air.

But Phoebe didn't reach out and hand the disk to Caelus. She threw it at him and jumped backward for cover. Caelus caught the disk in midair with the same hand that held the other disk. And that's when the world exploded with light.

The ghosts reach up from the ground when the disk was freed from Phoebe's grasp. And even as Caelus caught it, they too caught it. And as their souls exploded from the confines of the disks, the light erupted, and the disks dropped to the ground.

"What have you done?" Caelus fell to the sand to pick up the disks. "They're ruined. My life force disks. Ruined. What have you done?"

"Nothing, father," Phoebe said. "We did nothing."

"It was the ghosts," Benjamin said. "You can't control that much power. You should have known that, but you didn't. It was bound to control you in the end."

Caelus sobbed on the ground, pawing at the lifeless disks, before standing up and lunging at the three of them.

Benjamin released a final burst of telenergetic power and felt Phoebe and Cory do the same. He wasn't sure whose reached Caelus first, or if it even mattered. Caelus fell to the ground, and Benjamin knew he was dead. Not-a-chance-of-coming-back dead.

"After this long, without the disks, he was powerless," Cory said, walking over and moving the body with his foot.

"And without Caelus and Gaea, the world is safe," Benjamin said.

CHAPTER 36

IN CASE LIFE WOULD EVER BE NORMAL AGAIN

It took Benjamin a while before he was ready to head back. He walked away from Cory and Phoebe, and sat down near the Temple of Thoth. Not in the temple. The last thing he needed at a time like this was some haphazard visit from the god of time. The last thing he needed was a visit from any false god or goddess. He'd had enough of those to last a lifetime.

Benjamin put his head in his hands and thought. He went through everything in his mind, hoping he hadn't forgotten anything. Caelus, his biological father, was dead. Gaea, Caelus' wife, was dead. Nathan was dead. Humans couldn't be controlled by telegens. Atlantis was free. What else was there?

He went over it time and time again, but came up with nothing. They'd covered all the bases. They'd saved the world. And now, for the first time in like forever, Benjamin thought about leading a normal life. Sure, it was only the last two years when things had really heated up, but his whole life before then had been nothing but hiding his exceptional telegen brain power from the humans. Now, nothing had to be hidden anymore. He could live free. He could live in Lemuria. Or Atlantis. Or anywhere.

Even with all the possibilities, Benjamin knew he wanted to return to Lemuria. His family was there—not that he wanted to live with them all the time. School was way too much fun. Benjamin smiled as he thought about it. School being too much fun. It was like a paradox. But the best friends he'd ever had in his life were at school. Andy. Gary, Iva. And Heidi.

He pushed an image of Heidi over and over in his mind. Were they together now? Were they an official couple? Benjamin had a hard time admitting it even to himself, but he'd wanted that for like forever. And now, Heidi seemed within his grasp. Sure, she hadn't told Josh they were through, but that was just a formality at this point, wasn't it?

"So are we ready to go, little brother?" Cory asked.

Benjamin smiled. Truthfully, he liked when Cory called him little brother. He was just happy to have Cory as his brother. And Phoebe as his sister.

"Sure," Benjamin said. "Where to?"

"Let's head back to Xanadu," Phoebe said. "The others should still be there."

"I know how to get there now," Benjamin said.

"Yeah, me, too," Cory said. And whether it was because of what they'd just been through or the triplet bond or something else, the location to teleport to Xanadu was clear in their minds.

Xanadu was a flurry of activity. Ananya had regained control. Andy, Gary, Iva, and Aurora were helping her pull everything back together. And Jack was overseeing the whole operation. Benjamin wasn't even surprised to see

 298

Apollo by Ananya's side. And if Apollo was upset about the whole human telejamming thing, he wasn't letting on.

"Did you guys miss us?" Benjamin asked.

Heidi laughed. "Yeah, we were starting to wonder if you needed some help, but it looks like you got everything under control."

"Completely under control," Ananya said. "*You did a good job, Benjamin,*" she added telepathically, and went back to work.

Benjamin smiled and pitched in where he could. Part of him wanted to curl into a ball and relax for the next month, but the rest of him wanted to leap back into life full force. Which is what he did.

They used the Universal Travel Agent to get back to Lemuria, and when they exited into the Map Library, Helios and Selene Deimos stood there waiting.

"Now wasn't it silly of me to think they might need our help," Helios said to Selene when Benjamin walked into the room.

"Entirely silly," Selene replied. "It seems the triplets were more than capable of everything The Emerald Tablet charged them with."

"We would have been happy for some help," Benjamin said.

"Wouldn't that have defeated the whole purpose?" Helios asked.

Benjamin shrugged. Maybe it would have. Probably it would have. But still—he would have been thrilled to have the Deimos twins by his side in the fight against Caelus and Gaea.

"So what now?" Benjamin asked. He thought about Cory and Phoebe. And Heidi.

"What do you want to do, Benjamin?" Selene asked.

"I want to be near my family," he said. "And my friends."

Selene laughed. "So you want the best of both worlds."

"Yeah, that pretty much sums it up," Benjamin said. Was that too much to ask for?

"I'm too old for school," Cory said. "But Joey mentioned something about needing help in Atlantis. I thought I might take him up on that."

"Atlantis could use plenty of help," Helios said.

Cory smiled. "Sounds kind of challenging. And kind of perfect."

Benjamin could imagine Joey and Cory in Atlantis right now, poking fun at King Helios. Helios shot him a quick look, and he wiped the thought from his head.

"What about me?" Phoebe asked.

"What do you want to do?" Selene asked.

Benjamin held his breath. He wanted Phoebe to stay near him. He'd been afraid this whole time that she'd want to return to Atlantis.

Phoebe looked at Benjamin and then looked back to the ground. "I'm ready for a change."

"You could stay in Lemuria," Benjamin said. And he sent some happy thoughts through the triplet bond for good measure.

"You'd just be a regular student," Helios said. "No more royal treatment. No more servants catering to your every wish. It may be a boring life."

Phoebe smiled. "It sounds like just the kind of change I need."

By the time they got back to school, they'd worked everything out. And Benjamin and Heidi held hands. She'd initiated it, and Benjamin had grabbed hers right back. He wasn't totally clueless.

"Now what?" Andy said as they all walked into the main atrium.

Gary raised an eyebrow. "What else? We head to our dorm rooms and get ready for classes. Tomorrow is a school day after all, and if our schedules are still the same, that means I have an early lecture on bio-mutations of algae species."

Andy yawned. "You've got to be kidding me, Gary. I'm not going to classes tomorrow."

Gary's jaw dropped. "But you have to. You can't skip."

"Want to watch me?" Andy said.

"Not a chance," Benjamin said. "I'm sleeping in, too." And he figured maybe if he were lucky he'd have all happy dreams about the future ahead of him. He hoped it was filled with a whole bunch of nothing. No Emerald Tablet. No Navel of the World. No Necropolis. Nothing. Just a nice normal life, at least for a while.

ACKNOWLEDGEMENTS

To Riley for always believing in me.

To Zachary for reading my books and telling me you love them.

To Lola for giving me a fresh perspective on everything in the world.

To my critique buddies, both online and local—you guys are the best!

To the awesome Austin writing community...could I have picked a better city to live?

To my Texas Sweethearts, Jessica and Jo—I feel like I've found my writing soul mates!

To all my in-person friends—life would be awfully lonely without you guys.

To all my online friends—you guys put the love in blogging, Facebook, and Twitter.

To Madeline for some awesome editing.

To my parents and sister for teaching me to be independent.

To my extended family and friends for the multitudes of support.

And in case I missed you, consider yourself thanked. Because I truly am thankful!